Border City Blues _____

PROSPECT AVENUE

Michael Januska

DUNDURN
TORONTO

Cover image: Het Leven, Spaarnestad Photo
Printer: Webcom

Library and Archives Canada Cataloguing in Publication

Januska, Michael, author
        Prospect Avenue / Michael Januska.

(Border City blues)
Issued in print and electronic formats.
ISBN 978-1-4597-3594-1 (softcover).--ISBN 978-1-4597-3595-8 (PDF).--
ISBN 978-1-4597-3596-5 (EPUB)

        I. Title.
PS8619.A6784P76 2018   C813'.6   C2018-900978-0
                                                C2018-900979-9

1   2   3   4   5   22   21   20   19   18

We acknowledge the support of the **Canada Council for the Arts**, which last year invested $153 million to bring the arts to Canadians throughout the country, and the **Ontario Arts Council** for our publishing program. We also acknowledge the financial support of the **Government of Ontario**, through the **Ontario Book Publishing Tax Credit** and the **Ontario Media Development Corporation**, and the **Government of Canada**.

Nous remercions le **Conseil des arts du Canada** de son soutien. L'an dernier, le Conseil a investi 153 millions de dollars pour mettre de l'art dans la vie des Canadiennes et des Canadiens de tout le pays.

Care has been taken to trace the ownership of copyright material used in this book. The author and the publisher welcome any information enabling them to rectify any references or credits in subsequent editions.

— *J. Kirk Howard, President*

The publisher is not responsible for websites or their content unless they are owned by the publisher.

Printed and bound in Canada.

VISIT US AT

 dundurn.com | @dundurnpress | dundurnpress | dundurnpress

Dundurn
3 Church Street, Suite 500
Toronto, Ontario, Canada
M5E 1M2

For Charlotte

He can get anything from a thousand dollars up for each one he lands. That's about the how of it. He runs the guns over for Chang, and brings his own stuff — coolies and no doubt some opium — back, getting his big profit on the return trip.

— Dashiell Hammett, *Corkscrew*

If what you say is positive truth,
O Death, where is thy sting?
I don't care now 'bout the pearly gates,
Or to hear those angels sing;
With booze and women down below,
Mister Devil and I will just put on a show.

— Montrose J. Moses, *O Death, Where Is Thy Sting?*

I do not like vaudeville, but what can I do? It likes me.

— Anna Held

ACT ONE

Chapter 1

IN THE SOUP

Thursday, August 2, 1923

The roadster was bouncing like a mattress at the Honeymoon Motel. McCloskey stole a quick glance at the passenger wedged between him and Shorty and saw an expressionless face lit by the dim glow of the dashboard light. While it may have been a hot, humid night, his rescue was shivering like they had just pulled him out of purgatory, and smelled of standing water and mouldering grass.

McCloskey had to shout over the roar of six gung-ho cylinders. "Hey, kid … you all right?"

Nothing but dead eyes staring straight ahead at the open road. McCloskey was starting to think this one spoke neither the King's nor anyone else's English; either that or he was being shy with it. He was also thinking he had seen eyes like this somewhere before: sinking in muddy trenches. With one hand on the wheel, McCloskey fixed his own eyes back on the tarmac. He had to be careful; there were no streetlights in these parts and at this hour it was mostly drunks ricocheting their cars off roadhouses and the few cops still silly enough to be tailing them. McCloskey just kept dodging. His mind went back to a conversation he had overheard in a barbershop the other day, a discussion about the current pace and trend of things. He was also reflecting on how it seemed to keep falling upon him to pull the bodies out of the mire. Like when he pulled his near-dead brother out of a foxhole in France.

Another member of the crew, Mud Thomson, had been with them on this particular rendezvous, a trip meant to forge a new business relationship. McCloskey saw it as another opportunity for Shorty to shine, but Mud had a certain edge to him, and McCloskey wanted to make sure it stayed sharp. Between the roadhouse and the shore he had told Mud in a few select words to be inconspicuous tonight. Mud had simply nodded and took to the road.

McCloskey and Shorty were heading to Oriental House, the place before Chappell's. It wasn't far, just a skip down the road. McCloskey was counting on someone there knowing the lingo. The joint snuck up fast, so he started with the clutch and the gears until he smelled the metal burn.

He hung a sharp right into the parking lot. Shorty and what's-his-name reached for anything that might keep them from spilling out the door and onto the narrow boulevard. The roadster held together and stirred up some dust before grinding to a halt near the entrance. There were only two other vehicles making shadows under the floodlights, their drivers probably settling their tabs right about now.

Shorty climbed out first. "Jack, he got my shirt wet ... my trousers, too."

"Send me the bill."

Apart from the shivering, the celestial still wasn't moving. With a combination of gestures and loud talk — "C'mon ... let's inside ... there" — McCloskey got him walking.

Like Chappell's, it was a big old house built with good intentions, but now found itself standing on the wrong side of town, refashioned into an eatery and illicit drinking establishment. They made their entrance, trying to keep it low-key, but their looks and demeanor probably screamed a little too loudly.

In the foyer was a lectern that must have graced a church in its previous life. An eagle was emblazoned on the front, holding a sign in its beak that said NO RESERVATIONS. McCloskey made his inquiries with the man standing behind it, a certain Frank Rymes he read to be the proprietor. Rymes looked them up and down.

"No," he said, answering McCloskey's opening question. "We ain't got no Chinamen here."

"What do you mean you don't got any Chinese? Isn't this place called Oriental House?"

"We're working an Oriental theme here, mister. Check the decor; we got bamboo." Rymes gestured towards the curtain that led to the dining room, a doorway to the Mysterious East.

McCloskey walked over to the bamboo curtain and parted it with two hands. There was a waiter addressing the floor with a broom and turning chairs over onto tables. McCloskey dropped the curtain and returned to the lectern.

"Let's see the menu."

Rymes gave him a card.

"You got noodles?"

"Of course we got noodles. It was our dinner special."

"Okay then," said McCloskey, scanning the card, "we'll take some chicken lo mein to go. I think my friend here could use a hot meal."

"I think he could use a towel. What, you drag him out of the river?"

Shorty said, "As a matter of fact —"

"Just make the noodles. Hey wait — you serving?"

Rymes stopped and turned. "Nah, us and Chappell are in agreement."

McCloskey grabbed both sides of the lectern. He was thinking there might be an opportunity here. "This agreement sounds to me like it might be a bit one-sided."

Rymes shuffled and blushed. "They pay me a small stipend to stay dry," he said, "and in exchange I keep out of trouble."

"Ah," said McCloskey. He'd get a couple of the boys to come back later and lean on Chappell, maybe swing some lumber ... but a soft pine. They'd save the oak for the next visit, the next conversation.

"Be right back," said Rymes.

While Rymes and an unseen Reggie put together a takeout package, the trio wore the glaze off the tile in the foyer and tried to relax. McCloskey pulled out his pocket watch, examined its dead hands, shook it, and then held it to his ear.

Gotta get this thing fixed.

Shorty was tapping the side of the fish tank and managed to scare a goldfish that looked big enough to be an appetizer. The stranger stood there, silent, dripping and shivering, his arms wrapped around his shoulders in a feeble effort to warm up.

Rymes came out with the goods: three little white cartons. McCloskey popped one open and his partners gathered around him.

"This?" he said. "What's this?"

"It's what you asked for."

"These noodles … it looks like spaghetti."

"Trust me, the locals don't know the difference."

McCloskey handed the carton back. "No, no they wouldn't, especially not after you've dazzled them with the decor. C'mon, boys."

Shorty hesitated, did a double take between McCloskey and Rymes, then grabbed the celestial's elbow and led him back out to the roadster. "Where to?" he asked.

"Downtown," said McCloskey.

"Now?"

"Yeah," said McCloskey. "Now."

"You know," said Shorty, stopping suddenly, "you got that thing again."

McCloskey stopped. "What thing?"

Shorty let go of the Chinese so that his hands could do some of the talking. "That thing you get when you get going on something and I'm not sure exactly where you're going with it."

"When I *get going on something*?"

"Yeah," said Shorty.

"Shorty."

"What?"

"Maybe not in front of company."

"Jesus, Jack."

The soggy stranger stood still, observing, listening.

"Get in, everybody," said McCloskey. "Let's go."

They got situated and he pushed the engine into gear, letting the roadster's rear wheels kick gravel at the cars parked behind him, speckling their varnish. He turned onto the Drive.

McCloskey was going to take this up with Chung Hong. Hong was high up in the Chinese community. He owned Oriental

Dry Goods, a barbershop, a piece of a diner on Wyandotte, and was partners with one of his brothers in a laundry. Thursdays were his weekly poker game, so he'd be sitting in the back of his dry goods place with a few of his fellow countrymen, stone-faced, holding a fan of dog-eared playing cards. No food and no booze; just cards, cigarettes, and a few dirty looks.

McCloskey cruised slowly across the Avenue so as not to draw any attention and then took a right onto Goyeau. He pulled into the first alley on the left. Stray bits of light fell on ashcans, crates, and greasy cobblestone. He navigated a parking spot without disturbing too much of the refuse. Even garbage had a reputation to uphold.

The three disembarked, again, and McCloskey found Hong's door. It's never difficult to find, what with the green-and-yellow dragon crawling up the brick and across the lintel, looking down upon all who came to call. McCloskey gave the door a few quick raps. A tiny slot opened, exhaling hot, sticky tobacco smoke, and a voice wrapped around a foreign tongue.

McCloskey leaned his elbow against the jamb. "English."

"To know the road ahead …"

"Ask those coming back."

The slot closed and the door creaked opened. McCloskey stepped forward, but the scene made Shorty and the stranger pause.

A red paper lantern hung over a round table where four men were seated, looking like they had just finished a hand. One of the men was Detective Morrison. Morrison could tilt the Earth's axis with his girth and swagger. McCloskey managed not to look surprised at seeing him there. He then noticed a figure standing in the shadows, stripped down to his shirtsleeves, holding a cigarette, and with one arm folded across his chest. He stepped forward into the light and, leaning over the table, butted the heel of his cigarette into an ashtray with a bronze snake coiled around it.

"To what do we owe the pleasure, Mr. McCloskey?"

McCloskey gave a short bow. "Chung Hong."

Morrison stood up and reached for his hat.

"I hope you're not leaving on my account," said McCloskey.

"See you next week?" asked Hong.

Morrison nodded and the burly gatekeeper grunted something mild and unlatched the door.

"Did you see the look on his face?" asked Hong.

"Like he's never been caught with his pants down."

"Pants down?"

"Something we used to say in the trenches."

"Ah. You know him?"

"Our paths cross occasionally," said McCloskey. "We try to keep out of each other's way."

Hong sat down and exchanged words with two of the other card players, younger men, perhaps his sons or nephews, who then got up and moved through the dark and into the store. McCloskey heard them ascending the stairs. An older gentleman — a brother or a business partner — remained seated. McCloskey was still trying to figure out the cast on Hong's playbill. It seemed the players kept changing.

"Sit down," said Hong, "and introduce me to your friend."

Shorty and the stranger each pulled up a chair.

"I don't know his name," said McCloskey.

"He doesn't speak English?"

McCloskey glanced over at the stranger. "I'm not sure. He said a few words when we pulled him out of the river."

"Where?" asked Hong.

"Prospect Avenue," said Shorty, "right behind the Westwood."

Hong nodded, eyes closed, and then looked over at the elder seated next to him. The old man had a few words to add. There was some more discussion and nodding before McCloskey could jump back in.

"I thought he might relax a bit if he got to talk to one of his own people," he said. "Can we start with his name?"

Hong asked the young man.

"Lee Quan, or Quan Lee," said Hong, "depending on your affiliation. He knows some English, but he doesn't like his accent."

"Okay," said McCloskey, "so what's his story? Is he in some kind of trouble?"

Hong strung some queries together, at the same time condensing and translating the answers. "Canton … a long boat ride, and then … odd jobs … labour … kitchens."

McCloskey identified a few cities through Quan's accent: Vancouver, Calgary … "Moosejaw?" he asked.

"Yeah, Moosejaw … and then Montreal … Toronto. After that, he didn't know where he was."

"But he kept moving. Why?"

Quan and Hong were having their own conversation now, and then Hong picked up the translation once more.

"No, he's not in trouble … nothing serious … the other fellow, the one who must have drowned … he did not know him … he was paired with him in Toronto … by the people handling their passage here." Hong paused and turned to face McCloskey. "Jack, there might be two others on the farm."

"The farm?"

"Where the boat came from."

McCloskey glanced over at Shorty and then turned back to Hong. "Ask if he knows whereabouts. Ojibway? LaSalle? Amherstburg?"

Hong didn't even bother asking. "Jack," he said, "the kid has no idea where he is. All he knows is he's at the border." Hong said a few more words to Quan and then brought the other gentlemen into their conversation. Hong then turned to McCloskey and, lowering his voice, said, "Jack, these smugglers, they take their money and, rather than get caught on the river with foreigners like Quan, just spill them over the first chance they get. Those guys could have been in a drawstring sack, maybe a canvas mail bag."

"Jesus," said Shorty.

"Are we fools to ask if he's even got papers?" said McCloskey.

Hong knew what the answer would be, but he asked Quan anyway. "No," came the reply, "they were stolen in Toronto." The two exchanged a few more words and then Hong turned back to McCloskey. "His father came here first, and earned the money to cover the tax on Quan. His father is still in Vancouver, but too ill to travel. Quan was legal, now he is like a ghost."

Quan spoke.

"What did he say?"

"He says he heard he could make himself lost in America."

McCloskey leaned forward and folded his hands on the table. "Or make himself the Border Cities' newest resident. Chung, do you think you could —"

"Jack, I can't. Now's not a good time. You know I've taken people in before, but —"

"You've got no work for the kid? C'mon, Chung."

Hong had more words with Quan, and then said, "He wasn't just washing dishes. He says he can cook; that's what he was doing in Montreal and Toronto."

"Okay, so what about your kitchen on Wyandotte?"

"And who in my family should I let go to make room for him?" Hong had a notion. "Jack, what about your club?"

Back in April, when McCloskey was looking for ways of diversifying his interests, he took out a lease on a space in the Auditorium Building. It had been doubling as a rehearsal studio by day and a dance hall by night. He thought he could turn it into a dinner club. He expanded the kitchen and handed the entertainment reins over to Pearl Shipley, a local girl who had made it to vaudeville and eventually Hollywood before one scandal too many sent her running back home. There was a rotation of guest acts, but the regular entertainment was provided by a troupe dubbed the Windsor Follies, a chorus line of six girls who could also carry a tune, all schooled by Pearl. The place was doing all right, but something was missing, and that something was a proper menu. *A mix of East and West to set it apart from all the other joints*, thought McCloskey.

"You're not worried about the competition?"

"Different clientele." Hong smiled.

While Quan was trying to catch a word or two, Shorty was trying to catch McCloskey's drift. "Jack —"

"I wouldn't entirely do away with the roadhouse food," added Hong.

"No, a new Chinese-Canadian menu," said McCloskey, his wheels turning, thinking out loud, "and hey, you can help with the kitchen and tableware."

Hong leaned back and folded his hands behind his head. "I don't come cheap."

"Nothing but the best." McCloskey paused, and then, leaning closer to Hong said, "Pardon my forwardness — and this stays within these walls — but I gotta ask. Are you getting cozy with Morrison?"

Hong smiled. "I'm letting him think he's getting cozy with me."

"I thought it might be something like that. And your friend here?"

"Let's call him my counsel."

"All right, let's call him that," said McCloskey, scratching his chin again. "Know any English tutors?"

"Jack, you are asking and asking."

"Hey, I pay my debts."

"That's my problem with you." Hong paused for a moment, thinking. Or maybe it was just hesitation. "My niece, at the laundry, she's good. Both of you meet me there tomorrow morning at ten. Quan can have his first lesson. That much I can do. You putting him up for the night?" Hong was obviously heading off what he thought would be the next request.

McCloskey looked over at Quan. "Until we find something."

"We? Anything else?" asked Hong.

"Yeah, you got anything to eat?"

Hong chuckled. "Go see Ping at the Cadillac. You know how he likes to cater to you night owls."

"Jack," said Shorty, "can't we hit a grill somewhere instead?"

"I'm hungry," said McCloskey. "Let's grab a quick bite downtown and then you can hit the sack."

Quan said something to Hong; Hong nodded and the young man rose from the table. It was his turn to speak.

"What is it?" said McCloskey.

"He wants to know your name."

"Oh … tell him he can call me Jack, and this piece of work here is Shorty. There, we're all friends now."

Quan pointed at McCloskey and said, "*Jie-ke*." And then he tried "Shorty." It wasn't pretty.

"We'll work on that," said McCloskey.

The three headed for the door. Hong stopped them, and with his hand on McCloskey's shoulder said, "Jack, let's try to keep the kid out of trouble."

McCloskey knew what Hong was talking about.

"Yeah," he said, "let's."

Chapter 2

DESCENT

They called it an elevator, but it was really nothing more than an oversized birdcage dangling from rickety chains, moving up and down through a corroding framework, servicing one of the near-forgotten mines as old and deep as the river. Occasionally there was a little too much metal on metal, and that's when the sparks would fly. Detective Campbell lifted a hand, fingers splayed against the tiny flashes so as not to miss too much of the show and noting how the colour of the sparks could change.

The mechanics of it all *clink clink clinked* along like weights in a great clock, then stopped and started again, stopped and started again.

"Sorry, sirs" said the operator, gripping the controls, "it isn't exactly a straight drop." He was looking up through the top of the cage, rubbing his chin with the back of his other hand. "Not like it used to be, no it isn't."

"What do you mean, *not like it used to be?*"

"The ground can shift," he said, turning for a moment to meet Campbell's gaze.

"Of its own accord?" asked Dr. Laforet.

"Oh, we help it along sometimes," said the operator, turning back to the controls. "We give it the business, gentlemen, that we do." His playful tone implied he was only teasing.

And one day, thought Campbell, *there will be a sinkhole the size of this town to prove it.*

They passed through more layers and rock strata, falling noisily, disconcertingly. They stretched their jaws as their ears popped.

Clink, clink, clink.

The doctor hooked a finger underneath his collar and gave it a gentle tug. "Are we almost there?"

"Wait for it," said the operator, grinning wide.

The detective looked at the doctor before turning to the operator. "Wait for what?"

"It's coming up ... look this way." He was pointing to Campbell's left.

They dropped past a black *X* painted on the wall. If they had blinked they would have missed it.

"There," said the operator, "we're halfway."

Laforet gripped his doctor's bag a little tighter and shifted his attention to his brogues, watching their shine grow duller and the tiny holes fill with grit.

Campbell studied first the operator's gnarled hands and then the creases in his face. The creases were slowly being filled with fine dust, either putting years on or taking them off.

Pancake makeup.

The detective returned his gaze to the walls of the shaft, observing the scrapes, gouges, and what appeared to be fingernail or claw marks. He tried not to let his imagination run away with him.

"Eyes left, and when you see two *X*s, bend your knees."

"Sorry," said Campbell, "what was that?"

"That's when you bend your knees," repeated the operator. "We're about to hit bottom." He then shook his head and mumbled something at the floor, possibly a prayer, with a faint smile on his lips.

"What was that?" said Campbell.

"*Ye shall go no further.*"

The detective felt he was at the mercy of something slightly less than divine. He watched Laforet set down his bag, bend his knees, and brace himself.

It was sage advice from the operator; the cage hit the floor with some purpose and Campbell, bending only slightly so he could measure the impact, had to steady himself against the cage to keep from falling over. Thick dust rose, not in a cloud, but rather like a froth around their ankles.

"In those last few feet, she kind of lets go. Did you notice?"

Campbell and Laforet looked at each other.

"We get some sags and buckles in the framework down here and things can get a bit loosey-goosey." The operator wrestled the door open — wrestled because he was correct, there were no more right angles to be had.

"He's mad," Laforet whispered, picking up his bag and waiting for Campbell to straighten his hat. The pair followed the operator through a scissor gate.

"I'll be waiting right here," said the operator.

Campbell turned and nodded, wondering if he should have tipped the man.

Someone was waiting to greet them. He was trim, upright, clean-shaven, and outfitted in what Campbell couldn't decide was a suit or some sort of protective gear. A lantern hung from a hook at the end of his left arm. The man extended the right, still punctuated with a hand.

"The name's Bridgewater, security detail. Would you be Detective Campbell?"

Campbell gently took the hand. "I would, and this would be Dr. Laforet."

"Follow me, gentlemen."

Bridgewater swung his lantern here and there, pointing at empty spaces he called galleries, explaining their history as if he was leading a group through the ancient catacombs. It didn't exactly sound scripted, more like his own running commentary as he roamed the place.

The detective pointed his flashlight in every other corner, trying to get the full picture. Used to the hot and humid aboveground, his senses were now trying to come to grips with the cold and dry. He could see colour returning to Laforet's cheeks and thought that maybe a little small talk might help get his blood flowing better.

"So how long have you worked here, Bridgewater?"

"Since Van Horne," he replied over his shoulder, not breaking his stride.

"Cornelius Van Horne?"

"This was all his idea … and word is we're taking the operation full scale downriver. But you didn't hear that from me."

"Did you ever meet him?" asked Laforet, drawn in now.

"No," said Bridgewater.

"Oh."

So much for the small talk.

They passed large vehicles and heavy machinery that could have only been assembled in these depths, rather than transported whole. They looked like nothing that Campbell had ever seen before: mechanized subterranean creatures designed for pulling apart the insides of the Earth. And then there was the space: pillars, aisles, a transept ...

"How do they ever know what time of day it is down here?" asked Laforet.

"There's no watching the clock," replied Campbell.

"Or staring out the window."

"Over here," said Bridgewater, waving his lantern, his incandescent appendage.

Campbell looked over at Laforet, who was back to looking like he was just waiting for the river to come crashing through the walls at any moment. Some people didn't like heights, while others weren't particularly fond of depths.

"Are you all right?" asked the detective.

"There's something wrong about this," said Laforet.

"I'm sure we don't even know the half of it."

"This section hasn't been worked for quite some time," said Bridgewater, continuing his lonely tour guide blather.

"A sprawling space," remarked Campbell, "or so it seems. Am I right? And all opened? No partitions, no —"

"They don't hang doors down here," said Bridgewater. "There haven't been any doors invented that can keep out what the river has to offer up."

Campbell noticed Laforet suddenly looking a little pale again.

"Oh — this is it," said Bridgewater, "this is the place." He stepped back. "You first, detective; you be the fresh eyes."

As he turned the corner, Campbell watched his shadow wrap around a salt pillar and then dissolve into darker recesses.

Campbell waved his flashlight about slowly, and lo and behold, there he was, curled in the fetal position in a shallow, waist-level bowl of a space. Campbell's mind got to work.

Bridgewater approached, as did Laforet, both casting more light on the subject.

"Any idea how long he could have been here?" asked Campbell.

"Hard to tell. I think the cold, the dry, and the salt would have preserved him well. I've read some cases."

"Maybe his clothes can tell us something," said Campbell, prodding away with his fountain pen.

"Have fashions changed that much among these men?" muttered Laforet. "And they could be hand-me-downs."

"True," said Campbell, standing back. "But doesn't this remind you of something?"

Laforet raised his own flashlight and panned the area slowly. "No, should it?"

"Those saints, preserved and stuffed into niches in holy sites, or cathedrals." Campbell was indulging his imagination, starting to think that it might be some necessary ingredient to solve the case.

"Is there a patron saint of salt?"

"Of salt miners," said Campbell. "Kinga of Poland."

Laforet gave Campbell a sideways glance.

"For my confirmation I received from one of my aunts her book of saints, canonized and beatified. Kinga was beatified. A wedding ring ..."

"Mm." Laforet was unpacking his camera. "Bridgewater, can you possibly get your hands on some lights, preferably on stands?"

"Way ahead of you, doctor." Bridgewater disappeared into the darkness with his lantern and returned pushing, with some difficulty, a flatbed cart. On it was a folded piece of canvas and a couple of battery-powered lights with stands. "I thought these things might come in handy," said Bridgewater, and he proceeded to set the stage.

Campbell wanted to get right to work on his initial observations. He removed the man's hat. It was something like a pith helmet but not quite. "So far no obvious indications of a blow or such."

"But the discolouration, the contortion —"

"An uncommon kind of decomposition, for sure." Realizing it could be just as easy to get lost in his thoughts as it was in these galleries, Campbell straightened up and said, "I suppose it might simply be a matter of checking the missing persons files."

"How does one usually come to be missing?" asked Laforet.

"When one has lost oneself," said Campbell, gently moving his hands over the victim, "and the newspapers and the mail starts to pile up."

"Go on."

"And then there are the cases where one chooses to go missing." Campbell stepped back and took in the entire scene. "Someone took great care here."

"But why?" asked Laforet.

The lights were growing hot.

"I haven't a clue," said Campbell.

Laforet stared at the body and stroked his beard for a moment before getting to work. He pulled the collapsible monopod out of his bag, mounted the camera, and started taking pictures. The light wasn't ideal, but he managed to maintain a steady hand.

"Now look …" Campbell continued, leaning over the body again, "he was tucked in … the folds in his clothes … in his trousers behind his knees … and behind his elbows."

Laforet handed his camera apparatus to Bridgewater and stepped closer.

"What do you want to do?" asked Campbell.

"My first choice," said the doctor, "would be to start the examination right here."

"And your second?"

"To take him up, as is," he said, looking over at the flatbed, "cradled in that canvas."

Campbell took another look at the surroundings. "Consider where we are, what it took for us to get here. Bridgewater, is there any other way to get to this part of the mines besides that elevator?"

"Those passages are sealed up tight, filled in as it were."

"Are you sure of that?

"That's part of my rounds. I visited both of them tonight, and they were still closed up, tight and dry."

"And the operator who brought us down, would he be the only one allowed … capable of using the lift?"

"Many of us have been instructed on how to use it, for safety reasons."

"Why not seal it off all together?"

"I'm sure the company has its reasons."

"How often do you make these rounds?"

Bridgewater cleared his throat. "That may have been a bit misleading, sir. This area isn't normally my purview."

"What do you mean?" said Campbell.

"Normally —"

"How often?"

"Every other day we'd send someone down the elevator shaft with a flashlight. He'd look to make sure there wasn't any water, and then he'd come back up and report. A week or so ago they asked me to do a more thorough inspection. I was given a map, and on every shift, I was to take a section and give it the once-over. I know what you're asking, and this is the first time I've ever laid eyes on this …"

"We'll call it a chamber," said Campbell. "Let's get down to it."

Bridgewater moved the cart closer and then unfolded the small stretch of canvas.

Campbell was looking closer again. "How old do you think he was?"

"Difficult to tell. The hair …" Laforet carefully pulled the leather-like lips back with his pencil, splitting them, "… his teeth; midtwenties …?" The doctor opened his bag, found his shears, and gently cut up the length of the exposed coat sleeve and then the shirtsleeve. He set the shears down on the canvas and went for his magnifying glass, focusing on the victim's upper arm. The flesh was splotchy yellow, white, purple, and black, but he could still make out some ink.

"Ninety-nine," he said and straightened up. "Ninety-nine what?"

Campbell took his own glass out of his coat pocket. "The Essex Scottish Regiment," he said. "This body has been here at least since the war. When you examine it, you might find the injury that sent this man home. Now we have something. You don't recognize this man, Bridgewater?"

"No, but …"

"But what?"

"They come and go. Some learn quick it's not for them."

"I'll need the name of your supervisor. We'll be starting here, looking for names of anyone who may have failed to show up for work, pick up his pay packet, that sort of thing. I'll check with missing persons."

"Yes, sir."

Campbell stepped away, pacing again.

"What is it?" asked Laforet.

"I'm not quite sure," said the detective. He was examining the jagged ceiling. "But I think that's it for now."

"Take his legs then," said Laforet, "and lift him — gently — on three. Bridgewater, you lift his back and I'll lift his head and shoulders. Ready … one, two —"

They lifted and set the body onto the flatbed, split boards set on rusty wheels.

"There's no blood," said Campbell, examining the now-vacant niche.

"No, no there isn't," said Laforet.

"Look at this poor soul," said Campbell. "What do you see?"

"I see all of the people he trusted with his life."

"Is that always the way you see them?"

"Yes," said Laforet quietly, reflectively, "yes it is." He carefully gathered the canvas closer around the body.

"Bridgewater," said Campbell, "can I ask you — and this is off the record — you do have accidents down here, don't you?"

"This, sir," he said, pointing at the flatbed cart, "is our ambulance."

"I see."

Campbell and Laforet together had to grip the bar handle of the cart, because one of the wheels was a little wobbly and they were pushing an off-kilter weight. Bridgewater lit the way. He greeted the operator, who had been waiting patiently. The detective and the doctor squeezed into the cage and the three of them arranged themselves around the cart. The chain started again, taking up the slack at first and then lifting the cage off the ground.

They made their slow, jerky ascent. When the cage door opened, Laforet set his bag on a corner of the cart so that he and Campbell could push it out of the elevator and toward the nearest unoccupied loading platform. They were approached by a supervisor, still shouting orders over his shoulder at a few workers who appeared to have misjudged the gap between the back of a truck and a platform, and were trying to figure out how to move the vehicle without either crushing or letting drop sacks of what was presumably salt. Campbell had to shout louder than the supervisor.

"Excuse me, I say, excuse me," he said, still manoeuvring the cart alongside Laforet.

The supervisor, attention shifting back and forth, now fixed his eyes on Campbell. He looked not a little miffed, perhaps tired of juggling his priorities.

"Detective Campbell of the Windsor police. Can you or someone call Janisse for an ambulance and tell them to get here right away? And have someone stand on the street and wave them in, otherwise they'll never find us."

Without a word, the supervisor marched off, giving the workers a moment to regroup and catch their breath.

Campbell was debating opening the canvas and resuming his examination of the body, but stopped himself. He knew what fresh, humid air might do to a cadaver.

"We need to get him to my lab as soon as possible," said the doctor.

"May I follow?"

"Not this time."

"Shall I drop by tomorrow morning?"

"I'm sorry; I have a full day. I'm putting him on ice," said Laforet. "I have a practice, you know. I'm not at the beck and call of the Windsor Police Department."

"I know, but ... I thought —"

"Come by the house."

"Your house?" said Campbell.

"My house, Saturday morning. Make it eleven; I have to go to the markets and my butcher gets very impatient with me if I'm not there before a certain hour."

ACT TWO

Chapter 3

ALLEY CATS

Friday, August 3

"Whoop," said Jefferson, smacking Linc's shoulder, "we're done here."

Linc was bent over the engine of a parked car, relieving it of its spark plugs, when Jefferson, acting as lookout, spotted a blue uniform down the alley. The badge was a couple blocks away but he had a pair of legs on him — of the running variety.

"Hold on — I almost got it."

"No time — c'mon."

"Got it." Linc straightened up, brandishing a spark plug like it was a holy relic. Then he spotted the cop — "Where'd he come from?" — and his smile quickly faded.

"The cop shop, where else? C'mon, Linc — run, run like hell."

Linc and Jefferson had reputations in this quarter as petty thieves who also liked to steal cars, take them for joy rides, and leave them on other people's front lawns. The boys — and they were boys, fresh out of the Technical School where they met in one of the machine shops — had been thrown into the deal when McCloskey bought Border Cities Wrecking and Salvage. They came highly recommended. But before they were signed up, McCloskey thought it was only fair to brief them on the new business model. The two had gone into a huddle that was just for show; they didn't have to think twice. The work sounded exciting, and also highly lucrative.

Right now they were zigzagging through a maze of alleyways lined with picket fences occasionally broken by parking spaces and make-do garages. They tipped ashcans, broken furniture, and anything else they came across into the path of the fleet-footed cop. Linc fell behind at one point and in a split second had to leap over a busted, mouldy old dollhouse that Jefferson had just tilted over. They couldn't go leading the uniform to the salvage yard; McCloskey would have their heads. As serious as all this was, they grinned like it was just a tickle. This was their style.

Linc, all huffing and puffing, could feel a stitch in his side, but he pushed on and caught up with his partner in crime. He glanced back and could see the cop gaining on them.

"Why don't we … split up?"

"Because we … got nowhere … else to hide," wheezed Jefferson.

They were almost there when the neighbourhood rag-and-bone man crossed the alley with his horse and wagon and spotted the boys, stopping cold.

"Damn," said Jefferson.

"Over?"

Jefferson hesitated, gave it a think, and said, "Under."

"Okie."

The scavenger watched with one eye closed. Jefferson went under the wagon while Linc went under the horse. The mare was still fidgeting, and one hoof grazed Linc's belly. The boys came out the other side with only minor scrapes. They got to their feet and over the moustachioed man's curses, Jefferson panted, "Under the *cart* ... the cart's what I meant. That animal ... could have kicked your head off."

"He's still running," said Linc, ignoring Jefferson and spying the cop. "Did this guy medal in Antwerp?"

"I don't know," said Jefferson, "but let's keep on; he's getting too close."

"Don't move," Linc hollered at the collector with his hands around his mouth.

An eight-foot-high wooden fence separated the salvage yard from the alley. It was crowned with coils of barbed wire like it was the field marshal's headquarters. It was more like the field marshal's supply depot. The fence had been modified recently so that if someone shouldered three of the vertical boards hard enough and in the right place, a latch would pop and the fence turned into a gate.

The boys were beyond huffing and puffing and were now wheezing like thirsty radiators. Stealing more glances behind them, they made sure the cop wasn't on their heels.

"Wha'd Gorski say? ... On the right ... or left?"

"Left," said Jefferson.

"Sure?"

"Yeah … I got it."

Jefferson poured it on and went shoulder first, full on into the three boards on the far left, bounced off them, and landed flat on his back in the weeds and gravel. It was like running into a brick wall. Linc saw that, didn't slow down, and ran straight into the three boards on the right. The latch released. He regained his balance, eased open the gate, and helped Jefferson to his feet. The two slipped in and slammed the gate behind them.

Inside, Jefferson stopped and bent, his hands cupping his knees, trying to catch his breath without vomiting. Linc peeked through a strategically placed hole in the fence. "I think we shook him," he said, before turning to his friend. "So it's the boards on the right … right?"

"Yeah, remember that."

"Me? I should remember that?"

Jefferson wiped his forehead on the inside of his sleeve. He didn't need the jabs. "C'mon, let's check in."

The yard was a small fortified compound in the middle of a growing working-class neighbourhood. McCloskey thought the little clapboard houses would serve as a nice buffer. The L-shaped building — a small office fronting Mercer Street and a workshop trailing behind — had a secret basement where the crates were packed, crates containing a mix of auto parts and contraband liquor destined for service garages scattered across Detroit. There was no evidence of this lower level outside or inside the building. It was accessed through the floor where the office joined the workshop. Ropes and pulleys hanging from the rafters now handled the booze from below as well as the engines and transmissions from the yard.

The yard was the slaughterhouse. Rows of waist-high, open-ended bins with slanted corrugated metal roofs lined the perimeter, and in the middle of it all were usually two or three cars in various stages of disassembly. Glass shards and unidentifiable bits of automobile were scattered on the ground. The rust-coloured dirt smelled of motor oil and gasoline. The boys traipsed through and entered the workshop, kicking their shoes against the door jamb before entering, as if it made a difference. The workshop was only slightly cleaner than the yard.

Shorty, Gorski, and Mud were sitting around the long workbench, sharing sections from the *Border Cities Star* over coffees.

"Boys," said Shorty, "take a load off."

"In a minute," said Linc.

"We need to walk this off first."

"Don't tell me — a dine and dash?" guessed Gorski.

"Was it worth it?" asked Shorty.

Linc reached in his jacket pocket, pulled out half a dozen spark plugs and set them on the workbench.

"What's this?"

"That's the take."

"That's it?" said Shorty. "The take from what?"

"Gee," said Gorski, "pearl diving, were you?"

"Old habits die hard," said Jefferson. "Linc can't pass a car without stripping it of its plugs." He looked over at his friend. "The thrill of the game, right?"

"Yeah, something like that," said Linc, sensing the opinion in the room was still that he and Jefferson were, as they overheard McCloskey recently say, *punching below their weight.*

"Boys," said Shorty, "when are you going to start thinking a little bigger? These are high school pranks. Hey … were you two running from a cop?"

Linc and Jefferson exchanged looks.

"No," said Jefferson. "It was a dine and dash, just like you said."

"Yeah? How close did he get?" said Shorty.

"Three blocks," said Linc.

"How close did he get?" repeated Shorty.

"We checked when we got inside the gate and we didn't see him."

"Honest," insisted Linc.

Gorski gave Shorty a look that said, *I told you these guys wouldn't be worth it.*

Mud sat tight and ran his fingertips along the edge of the workbench, not saying anything, just listening.

"Jack here?" asked Jefferson.

Linc looked at Jefferson.

Shorty was thinking, *You're asking because you want to see him or because you want to avoid being seen by him?* The rest of them were thinking the same thing. They had each one of them been down that same road at some point with McCloskey, so, without discussion, they somehow agreed to drop it.

"No," said Shorty, returning to the sports pages. "He had some business to take care of. Meanwhile, we're waiting on a few things."

"Jack adopted himself a pet Chinaman," said Gorski.

"What?" said Jefferson.

"Last night Jack and Shorty pulled a Chinaman out of the river," said Gorski. "Jack's probably training him to go on the papers as we speak."

"Enough of that," said Mud.

"The Chinese, Quan Lee is his name, and one of his compatriots got dumped in the river," said Shorty. "As the story goes, they paid someone to smuggle them across the border. Quan Lee made it back to shore. The other one's probably still floating downriver, or washed up on Fighting Island."

"Shit," said Linc.

"So is Quan in the gang now?" asked Jefferson, worried that his already small piece of the pie just got that much smaller.

"No," said Shorty. "Jack's going to have him fry noodles at

the club. He's not our problem. And if you need to talk to Jack, he said he'd be back around noon."

Jefferson grabbed the discarded front section of the *Star* on the workbench. "Harding's dead?"

No one better to change the subject than a dead president.

"You should try to keep up on current events," said Mud.

"He had a heart attack," said Shorty, "or something like that. Coolidge is going to get sworn in."

"Man alive," said Linc.

"Not so much," said Jefferson, still reading. "We're getting out the black crepe?"

"Means nothing to us," said Gorski.

"It depends," said Shorty. "Events like this, you're either distracted from drink or you drink to distraction. It'll probably all even out."

"Back to this Quan guy," said Jefferson, "does he know about us, I mean all about us?"

"No," said Shorty, pivoting on his heel. "I don't know. What's it matter?"

"The gang sure is getting colourful," said Gorski.

"I told you, he's not in the gang."

"Whatever you say," said Gorski. He raised the paper and leaned back in his chair.

"So do we have any crates ready?" asked Linc, hoping a little work might settle things down to the normal amount of tension.

"We're supposed to pick up some from Hong's. You two can go fetch them, along with some straw from the creamery. When you get back, you can stencil the crates and start packing. Mud's got the parts set to go."

"What are we moving?" asked Jefferson.

"Seventy-three steering wheels," said Shorty. "Makes your handful of spark plugs pale by comparison."

"Seventy-three steering wheels?" said Linc. "Where are we … how did we get seventy-three steering wheels?"

"This guy was collecting them," explained Gorski. "He kicked a few weeks ago and his wife has been cleaning house."

"Who collects steering wheels?" Jefferson asked.

"Why do people collect anything?" replied Shorty.

"So where are they going?" asked Linc.

"To another collector," said Gorski.

"Okay," said Jefferson, "what else?"

"This other guy is also collecting gin," said Shorty. "Fellas, this is easy money. We're just the brokers here."

"And where'd we get the gin?" asked Jefferson.

"From the widow. After the husband died she took the oath," said Shorty.

"I'm confused."

"Why do I get the feeling there's more to this story?" said Linc.

"You don't want to know," said Shorty.

Linc and Jefferson headed out to what was referred to as the "company car," a beat-up old Ford TT stake-bed truck. Actually, it looked like pieces from a bunch of other trucks put together. They called her Betsy and they kept her parked perpendicular to the entrance of the yard as kind of a "do not enter" sign. Border City Creamery was just around the corner so that would be the boys' first stop. When they climbed in, Linc was behind the wheel. Jefferson reached in his jacket pocket for his cigarettes.

"Hey, I told you I'm not comfortable with you smoking in this thing."

"You seriously think if I light up in this car it's going to blow us to smithereens?"

"Can't you just do this one thing for me?"

Linc was always saying that.

"All right." Jefferson pocketed his cigarettes and let Linc

negotiate the reverse, turn, and the roll out of the yard onto Mercer Street, smoke-free.

They were quiet for a moment before Linc said, "What did Gorski mean when he said, *The gang sure is getting colourful?*"

"Just ignore him," said Jefferson. "I told you, if you're going to listen to anyone, listen to Mud."

"I know, I know. But Mud doesn't say much."

"All the more reason to listen."

Chapter 4

THE PURGE

Detective Morrison was sitting at his desk at police headquarters, skimming the morning edition of the *Star*, which waited for him on his desk each morning. He read it to stay on top of things, more the reason if he might happen to be the one creating the news. He had to know what message the readership — including the police department — was getting, what their opinions were, and how they were reacting to things. He had to try to decipher it all, and then form a plan of action before finishing his first coffee of the day.

It was a grimy, unnamed street urchin who had recently started delivering copies of the first edition to the detectives, with *Compliments of the Star* scrawled along the margin of the fold. Morrison pictured the kid squatting, sitting on the flatbed of the loading truck with his legs tucked under him, grammar primer on his knees for a writing surface, his tongue sticking out of the corner of his mouth, and a type-written note that had been handed to him by a boss only two years his senior. After the war, kids learned the ropes from other kids.

The detective always started at The Third Page. That's where the news of arrests, petty crimes, court reports, and general misbehaviour landed. He wouldn't even take his hat and coat off before settling like a rumpled landslide into his chair, with the column opened and his coffee parked within reach, where his mug had tattooed a ring on his desk.

POLICE MAKE RAID ARREST TWO CHINESE

Cocaine and Opium Paraphernalia Are Found
Authorities Say Determined Effort to Be Made to Ban Narcotics

In an effort to purge the Border Cities of the evil of the drug traffic, local and federal police are working together to entirely eradicate traffic in narcotics. Last night a raiding party, composed of Sergeants Byng, Pereau, Acting Sergeant Richmond and Constables O'Dell and Hawkeswood, raided the premises of Lo Ying, 117 Sandwich Street East, and arrested Lo and another Chinese, Lo Wing.

The police state that a considerable quantity of cocaine was found on Lo Ying, while an opium pipe, opium lamp, and all the paraphernalia of the opium addict was found in the possession of Lo Wing, together with a considerable quantity of opium.

This makes the second arrest in a week, a considerable quantity of drugs being seized when Yong Poy was arrested last week by a detachment of RCMP officers. The police state a determined effort will be made to stop the traffic of the peddlers, and also those who are bringing drugs into Windsor to smuggle them into the United States.

An unwelcome phone call in the middle of the night had informed Morrison of the raid. He had had a feeling something was brewing.

There were scant details and no names mentioned, but he recognized the voice at the other end and caught its drift. It was Hawkeswood. Morrison knew that the constable enjoyed this sort of thing — the risk, the secrets, and the games that could be played. Morrison was also aware that someone like Hawkeswood could be dangerous; luckily he knew how to make a constable dangerous only to himself.

Hawkeswood claimed he didn't know the raid was "going to bolt," as he put it, until he was tapped to be part of the team just minutes before. That also gave Morrison some concern — it meant that either the Mounties were holding their cards that close or that, though needed, Hawkeswood was beginning to look suspicious to certain members of this already tightly wound force and might be expendable.

But Morrison had to set all that aside for the moment. Right now he wanted to know what *Star* subscribers were reading about.

And he would have to give this morning's edition as close a read as he did every morning, line by line, word by word, to make sure there was nothing buried in code. He licked his already ink-stained thumb and turned the page, blackening the tip of his tongue, and shifted his attention to Border Briefs.

Break and enter ... vagrancy ... drunkenness ... speeding ... causing bodily harm ...

He turned next to the classifieds to look for any other possible messages. His communicants rotated their categories weekly. Last week it was automobiles, the week before that it was real estate. This week it was supposed to be livestock. He skimmed the ads.

Airedales for sale ... a bull terrier ... foxes. "Three live red foxes. Three months old; two males, one female." People buy dead foxes? ... Wait, who buys foxes? ... Barred rocks ... what the hell is a barred rock?

He felt he needed a new codebook because these people already seemed to be speaking another language.

Nothing here.

Morrison didn't like *nothing*. What he liked was information, even the wrong information — the lies, the boasts, the shilling for a buck. All of it told him something, if not directly then at least it would help him draw a picture. Never *nothing*. To him, *nothing* always meant that something wasn't right.

Regardless, last night's raid meant he had to check in with his contacts. They had to be careful, lest they got caught in the net of this so-called purge. He didn't want them, but he needed them. He also needed the cops that, unbeknownst to them, were being used by him to run interference. He couldn't cut them loose, not easily at least, and not without creating bigger problems or increasing risk. There was already enough of that. He had to keep these so-called law enforcement officers held in position, looking in other directions while he went about his business.

For now, he was like a hotel operator working two switchboards, one carrying the facts and the other carrying disinformation. This was his currency, his stock and trade. He just had to make sure the wires never got crossed. It wasn't easy. He trusted no one and he never put anything to paper. He carried it all around in his head. But there were fissures forming.

He lifted himself out of his chair, folded the newspaper, and tucked it in his coat pocket. It was time to get to work. He made his way down the hall, nodding at the staff and constables he passed, and then made his way down the stairs and into the lobby, letting others weave their way around him.

"Will you be back today, detective?" said the staff sergeant.

"After lunch. I have to pay some visits."

"Something tells me they're not expecting you."

"You know, with this bunch, no matter how many times I drop by, they always seem surprised to see me."

The staff sergeant grinned. "Not too bright."

"No," said Morrison, "not too bright, but just a little dangerous."

"To the city?"

"No, to each other." He paused. "Yeah, the city. Maybe we got a few too many live wires walking around."

He headed out the door and down the steps, passing a few constables on the way. He briefly considered tracking down Hawkeswood, but then thought it might be wise to avoid being seen with him for a day or two, not unless they were in a group where no one would think twice.

His first conversation would instead be with a lab coat at one of Lanspeary's locations. While the man didn't handle prescriptions, he seemed to know a thing or two about morphine. He sweat like an addict and his conversations were often a word game ending in funny syllables, a sort of gibberish that only Morrison seemed to be able to understand. Morrison never wanted to defeat him in this game; he only wanted to keep the druggist talking, and talking in the right direction.

Has to be someone's *nephew.*

Chapter 5

ENGLISH LESSONS

Chung Hong's brother Woo's laundry was on the south side of London Street, between Connaught Lunch and the shoeshine. The family lived upstairs. Woo had two sons and a daughter, Li-Ling. She worked at the laundry during the day and did some English tutoring in the evening. Woo made an exception this morning and temporarily relieved her of her laundry duties so that she could give Quan Lee his first formal lesson. Up until now, all Quan knew of the language was what he had picked up off the street or from countrymen who had managed to cross the divide. The lesson was chaperoned by Li-Ling's mother, Qingzhao. While the lesson took place, McCloskey, Chung Hong, and Woo talked business — business and Quan Lee — in the back garden.

"I'm settled on offering him a position at the club, in the kitchen," said McCloskey.

"And he will take it," said Woo. He was enjoying his first cigarette of the day. The garden was the only place his wife would let him smoke.

Hong nodded in agreement.

"Done," said McCloskey. It was obvious there would be no further discussion. "Last night, Chung, I brought up living quarters. I can put him up for maybe one or two more nights, but —"

Hong smiled. "But your girlfriend doesn't approve of the arrangement."

McCloskey bristled. "My girlfriend?"

"C'mon, Jack," said Hong. "It's your worst-kept secret." He chuckled, his cigarette dangling from his lower lip.

"It's not —"

"There's a spare room with a bed above Allies," said Hong.

"The diner?"

"Far from the action, if you know what I mean, but still on the streetcar line. Clean, quiet. Good people there."

Allies Lunch was the diner that Chung Hong held an interest in. It was on the north side of Wyandotte, between Gladstone and the Walkerville Theatre. It was a Border Cities oddity: built on the dividing line between Windsor and Walkerville, theatre goers could attend the same show in separate Border Cities. Between the local residents during the day and nightly theatre crowds, the diner was doing a solid business.

"But it's not a free ride," said Hong. "He's got a job now; he pays rent."

"Of course," said McCloskey.

"Good timing," said Hong. "My partner just lost a son."

"I'm sorry to hear that."

"He eloped with one of the waitresses." Hong closed his eyes and shook his head. "Not Chinese."

"*Laowai*," muttered Woo.

"What was that?" asked McCloskey.

"Nothing," said Hong.

McCloskey leaned back in his chair and looked around the yard. "This is nice." There was a vegetable garden that ran in an "L" along the south and west side, catching the sun. Onions, carrots, celery, a few other leafy things, some of which McCloskey couldn't identify, and a few plum trees inside the angle, presumably for making wine.

"You should start a family, Jack," said Hong. "I'm not saying you should quit. We are businessmen; it is in our blood, that much we have in common. And as long as there is ground to be broken … we will always be working. But you should think about a family, too."

Woo chuckled again.

"You need balance," said Hong, "harmony."

"I don't know anything about starting a family," said McCloskey, "and I sure as hell don't know anything about settling down."

"Maybe that's something Quan can teach you," said Woo.

McCloskey looked at him.

"You never know from whom you might learn a valuable lesson, or be shown a new path," said Hong.

It sounded to McCloskey like Hong was quoting from scripture, or whatever it was the Chinese quoted from.

"Who said that?"

"My delivery boy."

Quan, Li-Ling, and Qingzhao were making their way into the garden.

"Lesson over?" asked Woo.

"For today," said Li-Ling.

"And the next lesson?" asked McCloskey.

"Tomorrow," said Li-Ling, "Quan needs work."

Woo looked at his wife. She closed her eyes and nodded slowly. This didn't escape McCloskey.

"I'll pay for it," he said.

Woo rubbed his chin. "Half hour."

"An hour," said McCloskey, "and when he starts really picking it up, we take it down to a half hour."

"To start, no more than one week at one hour a day."

McCloskey glanced at the fruit trees, paused to think, but only for the split second he knew that Woo would permit.

"All right, one week at one hour a day, and then half an hour a day." He could smell the fruit mingling with the herbs.

"Same rate," said Woo.

McCloskey looked over at Hong.

"Same rate," said McCloskey. "What about results?"

"You test him," said Woo. "You will see results."

McCloskey faced Quan. "Quan, you're working for me now ... understand?"

Those words were already part of Quan's vocabulary. He nodded and said, "Yes."

"And as far as room and board goes," said McCloskey, turning to Hong and giving him his cue.

Hong nodded and addressed Quan in his own language. Li-Ling was listening carefully and she translated for McCloskey.

"Make sure Quan is here by ten tomorrow morning," said Woo. "Later, one of my sons will take him to Allies, get him a key, and introduce him to everyone. He will learn the route and get his bearings. We will see if he can find his way back to your club. And then you might want to get him to a tailor."

"Okay. I also might want to get him some papers."

"We will work on that. For the time being, a tailored suit will be his papers."

"I can't speak for him, Chung. I hope you understand."

"I understand. Right now I will speak for him."

McCloskey stood and gave a short bow, which was closer to a nod. "Thank you, both. I think I'd like to take him over to the club. May I use your phone to gather my troops?"

"Li-Ling will show you."

Li-Ling entered the house first, followed by Qingzhao and then McCloskey. Qingzhao directed McCloskey to the phone. He rang up the club.

"Claude? … Jack … Yeah, I'm bringing someone by and I'm putting him to work in the kitchen … No … No, nothing like that … Just hold on until we get there … Yeah, we're on our way." McCloskey hung up the phone, thanked Qingzhao and Li-Ling, turned to Quan and said, "Okay, let's go."

"Let's go?"

"Yeah, let's go to the club."

Chapter 6

ON BENDED KNEE,
NO LESS

"Jack, where've you been?"

McCloskey let out a sigh of relief and took his hand out of the inside of his jacket. "Jesus, Maudie." She had been banging on his door as if she was none other than the provincial licence inspector. But no, it was Vera Maude, a young bohemian, sometimes-librarian and now oftentimes bookseller, a woman with whom he — as they say in the magazines — had been slowly but steadily becoming entangled. Fierce, attractive, and bewildering, he had been trying to hold her at bay ... but he had always been drawn toward complications, hers in particular. McCloskey thought it might be time to invest in a peephole.

"Well?"

"Out, I was out," he said. Thinking back on Hong's words, McCloskey added, "I got businesses to run, remember?" He was trying to remember the names of some of his newer, smaller front operations but for some reason was drawing a blank. He tended to leave those details to his accountant.

Vera Maude folded her arms across her chest and leaned against the doorframe. "In the morning? Business in the morning? Since when? Or did Thursday night somehow spill into Friday morning? And you —"

"Last night ended right on time," said McCloskey.

"And you never answer your phone."

"I answer it when I'm expecting a call. Is this about something besides my work schedule?" He knew he had to defuse this, whatever it was, before he could get on with his day.

She unfolded her arms and started to relax a little. "Yeah, something besides."

"Then c'mon in."

Vera Maude ducked under his arm and wiggled into the room. McCloskey checked the hallway before closing the door.

"Sorry, I didn't know you had company."

"Oh — Maudie, this is Quan; Quan, this is Maudie."

"Really? A house boy, Jack?" She threw her purse on the loveseat and straightened her headscarf in the mirror that hung outside the bedroom.

"No, I'm helping Quan find his feet here. He's new in town. Do you want a coffee?"

"Sure."

McCloskey disappeared into the kitchen and left Vera Maude and Quan standing in the middle of the room, staring and smiling at each other. Quan was wearing an ill-fitting suit that had been offered to him by Hong's brother. It had been thirty days unclaimed at the laundry, so it was up for grabs, and Quan could have it fitted tomorrow.

"So, Quan, what line of work are you in?"

Silence.

"Jack?" said Maudie.

"What?" Jack shouted from the kitchen.

"Does Quan speak English?"

"He had his first real lesson today."

A pause. "Do you need any help in there?"

McCloskey emerged with two mugs and handed one to Vera Maude.

"Course not."

"Really? Whenever you get to work on something in the kitchen it sounds like a chandelier just fell from the ceiling."

The two sat in separate chairs and Quan followed their cue, sitting between them on the loveseat next to Vera Maude's purse. He clutched the cup of tea that McCloskey had poured him earlier.

"Okay, so what's up?"

Vera Maude took a second to remember. "Oh — you won't believe it! It's Uncle Fred."

"Is he all right?"

Vera Maude's Uncle Fred wasn't getting any younger and he had the occasional bad spell, usually attributed to his chronic indigestion. McCloskey had met him a few times and they got along just fine. He did, however, keep noticing the old man tended to look a little sideways at him, and he didn't always put it down to gas. He always wondered how much Uncle Fred knew about him, and about him and Vera Maude.

"It's serious."

"What is it?"

"Get this: he proposed to Mrs. Cattanach."

"Well … that's swell." McCloskey shifted to the edge of his seat, and then noticed Vera Maude's reaction. "Isn't it?"

"She accepted."

"Good news." He was still trying to get a read on Vera Maude, wishing he had a program to follow the performance.

"Of course it's good news," she said, "and they'll be wonderful for each other, but …" She looked around as if the chorus might be hanging over her shoulders.

"But what?"

"Don't you think they're a bit old for this? I mean a bit past …"

"They weren't planning on starting a family … were they?"

"Jack!"

"Well, I don't know." McCloskey was a bit surprised to hear this coming from a person who was usually so much more open-minded. He suspected there might be something more to it. He blindly veered into, "So they want to get married; what's age got to do with it? Do they love each other? Are they a good match?" He had no idea what he was getting himself into and he was regretting it already. Right now he was just wishing Vera Maude would get up and walk around the room some more — he'd feel much better about everything if he could just watch her move around in her new skirt — new to him, at least. Sometimes he just wanted to let himself be distracted.

"Well, yes," said Vera Maude, "on all counts."

"I've seen them together and I'd have to agree." McCloskey glanced over at Quan, sitting there like he was watching a tennis match, and then McCloskey wondered if they had anything like tennis in China. "I think it's fine."

"Oh, and another thing," said Vera Maude, "they're planning to kick me out. Can you believe it?"

McCloskey leaned back in his chair. He was going to try and let that one drift for now. All he could think right now was, *Let's get a grip; I got guns pointed at me before I button my suspenders in the morning.*

"So when's the wedding?" he said.

"Labour Day weekend … stop staring at my ankles! It isn't like you've never seen them before."

"Actually, I was looking at the tan line around your ankles from the straps on your shoes — wait, why the rush? Are you sure she's not —"

"Jack! Stop it with that." She paused and took a sip from her mug and Quan followed suit. "Actually … I asked him the same thing."

"If she was with child?"

Vera Maude rolled her eyes. "No, I asked, *Why the hurry?*"

"And what did he say?"

Vera Maude did her best Uncle Fred imitation. "*What? Wait until next June? We're ancient by anyone's measure. One of us might be dead by Christmas.*"

"Would make a hell of a funeral."

"Jack, I need a place."

Is that what this is really about?

"I'm not boarding at some old spinster's doily palace again," she said, "or rooming with some fool shop girl."

"But you're —"

Vera Maude almost spat. "Don't say it! Don't say it! I'm a bookseller!"

Actually, McCloskey wasn't sure what he was going to say. Quan grabbed the arm of the loveseat, waiting for the next volley.

"All right, you're relocating," said McCloskey. "What've you got in mind?"

Vera Maude paused. Even though Quan barely understood a word, he was obviously in suspense.

"Maudie, you can't be thinking —"

"What?" She sat up. "You think … no … that's not what I was thinking."

McCloskey was wishing for that theatre program again. "Okay, so what were you thinking?"

"I don't know. What were you thinking?"

Quan's neck must have been getting sore.

"I like the location and the building," said Vera Maude. "I could walk to work from here. A place anywhere in here would be nice. I don't care if it's on the Dougall or Chatham side, first or second floor. Is there anything you can do?"

"You mean apart from throwing someone out onto the street?"

"No, no, I don't want you to do that." She had to be careful what she wished for around McCloskey. They had been out for a stroll on the Avenue one evening last month and she said she had a hankering for a float. They were approaching the Andros Brothers' Confectionary. McCloskey walked in, peeled some bills off the roll he always kept in his pocket, and whispered something in the ear of one of the brothers. He had the place evacuated while the other brother played soda jerk.

"There's more, Jack."

McCloskey put his mug on the floor and cupped the sides of his face in his hands. "What?"

"They want me to plan the wedding."

He looked up. "You?"

"What? You don't think I could do it?"

"No … I mean why not Dorothy or Jennie?"

"You know they're not living in the city. And you know we're not all that close. Oh, they'll come to the wedding, all right." She paused and looked around the room. Olive drab walls and mismatched furniture. "Jack …"

"What?"

"I don't know anything about planning a wedding."

"It's a church wedding?"

"Yes, it's a church wedding."

"Where?"

"St. Andrew's." She glanced toward the window. "Of course I should be flattered … but …"

"But what?"

"Jack … I haven't set foot in a church since the funeral back in February, and before that I can't even remember."

"Don't worry about it. Maybe start with a conversation with Mrs. Cattanach." He paused. "You know, she really does like you, Maudie."

"And here I thought she was trying to get back at me for something."

Yes, this was a good start. He was wishing right now he could finish something, and not have it be by accident.

"Maudie, can we talk about this later? I gotta take Quan to the club to meet with some of the staff. It's Friday so most of them, Pearl included, should be there." He thought for a moment. "They better be there. Anyway, I got some ideas and I want to make sure everyone's on board with them."

"Oh," said Vera Maude, "speaking of ideas for the club, you still need to talk to that sketch writer I was telling you about, the one who works at the store."

McCloskey had been putting that off, but now that he was looking to make some serious changes at the club, it might be the right time to meet with this guy and hear what he had to say for himself.

"What was his name again?"

"Bernie, Bernie Lipinski. He's working tomorrow if you want to drop by. Maybe you two could go for a coffee."

"All right. I just might do that," he said, still talking himself into it. "And then you can do something for me."

"What?"

"Take Quan here to get a library card."

Quan perked up again.

"No, Jack, no." Vera Maude hadn't set foot in the library since she abandoned that ship last summer.

"Yes, Maudie, yes."

"They hate me there."

"No they don't. You don't know that. Do you want me to go with you?"

"No! No," she said, her palms held out like a traffic cop at Ferry Hill.

"This afternoon," said McCloskey.

"I thought you were taking him to the club."

"I am."

"What? Did you think all I had to do was buy him one? He's going to have to fill out a form."

"Forms?"

"Yeah, forms."

McCloskey didn't like the sound of that. He had to think this through. "All right, then. I'll bring him to the front steps of the library in one hour. You'll be there?"

"Yeah," she said, "with bells on."

He watched her walk out.

Chapter 7

GRACE HOSPITAL
WRECKING AND SALVAGE

"We thought you might be interested," said the constable.

Campbell tilted his flashlight in the direction of the voice. He was making his way down a section of alleyway east off Ferry Street, just a shade this side of the Drive.

"Is that you, Bickerstaff?"

"Yes, sir."

The detective pivoted the light. "And Dr. Laforet."

"Damn the telephone."

"Yes," said Campbell, "damn the telephone. Is that a smoking jacket?"

It was indeed a smoking jacket: maroon and black brocade with quilted lapels.

"They caught me at a bad time."

"I'll reserve comment. What do we have here?"

The two steered the detective's attention toward the wooden crate they were standing over. The container was about two feet tall and just as wide, with Chinese characters painted on the sides. An address label for Hong's Oriental Dry Goods was stuck on front.

"Not a body," surmised Campbell.

"Not as much," said Laforet.

"Okay. What's in it?"

"Well, it's not rice," said Bickerstaff, and he raised the lid.

"Heavens," said Campbell.

"To Betsy."

The crate appeared to contain three human arms loosely packed in straw.

"Here," said Campbell, "point your flashlights in here."

The doctor and the constable did just that, trying to avoid casting too many shadows.

"Clean cuts."

"Yes," said Laforet. "Either they sat very still for it or —"

"Or they were already dead?"

"Isn't this the worst thing you've ever seen?" asked Bickerstaff, still coming to grips with the crate's contents.

"No," said Laforet. He didn't elaborate.

"Left arms," said Campbell.

"Right on all counts."

Campbell gently lifted one of them by the wrist, examining it with his magnifying glass while the other two continued to cast some light.

"There's something else, sir," said Bickerstaff. "Have a look at this." Bickerstaff was pointing his light on the side of the crate, where stenciled over the red Chinese markings was BORDER CITIES WRECKING AND SALVAGE.

"You just happened to come across the crate, Bickerstaff? You weren't responding to a telephone call?"

"I've been getting into the routine of walking this particular stretch; it's lately become known as a drop-off point for illegal liquor —" he cleared his throat "— and for other sordid activities."

Campbell was now pointing his flashlight beam up and down the alley, and up and down the backs of the buildings. He checked a few of the nearest doors. The Murray Building was on the south side, and to the north was the Imperial Hotel. The rear entrances were all locked.

"Does this location mean anything to you?" said Laforet.

"No," said Campbell.

"Something a constable was meant to stumble across perhaps."

"Yes, perhaps," said Campbell.

"How long could the crate have been sitting here do you think?"

Campbell examined the crate more closely. "There was a light shower late in the afternoon, wasn't there?"

"Yes," said Laforet. "About four o'clock, as I recall."

"The crate is dry." He looked at the ground in the immediate area. "Not much puddling, but look, look at this bit of mud splatter, just a little on the corner here. Dry, but not bone dry, not cracked." Campbell stood up. "Still room enough in the alleyway to let an auto pass." He kneeled down again. "And no chaffing or splintering noticeable at the bottom of the crate, so it wasn't dragged. More like it was deposited here by someone in a vehicle, around sundown."

"But they could have dropped it anywhere," said Laforet. "Why here?"

"Back to your conjecture of it being meant to be found. But by whom?"

Campbell pulled his notepad out of his coat pocket.

"I'd like to get to this right away," said Laforet.

"Of course," said Campbell, writing. "I assume you have your car."

"Just around the corner."

"Bickerstaff, would you help the doctor get this to Grace?"

"Certainly, sir."

"Shall I drop by in the morning?" asked Campbell.

"Nine-ish," said Laforet.

Campbell set his hat on Laforet's desk and headed straight for the crate. It was on a table at the end of the long room, the cool end.

"The front of the hospital looks like a used car lot."

"These automobiles are becoming contagious."

"Contagious? I was going to ask if they were being handed out in the maternity ward as part of a welcome package."

Laforet looked a little more than preoccupied.

"Did I come at a bad time?" asked Campbell.

"No." Laforet was standing between the crate and another table with a sheet covering half of it, something — or things — underneath. Laforet gently pulled the sheet back. "Male; no distinguishing markings; each no more than a few days apart."

"Between the time they were severed?" said Campbell.

"Yes."

"Give me your thoughts on the cuts."

"Not crude, but not quite surgical either; a skilled hand. In all three cases, the ulna and radius appear intact, along with the complete elbow joint."

"The same instrument used on each one?"

"Yes."

"A butcher, maybe."

"The thought had crossed my mind," said Laforet. "Definitely someone experienced with this sort of thing."

"Post-mortem?"

Laforet wiped his hands clean and took a deep breath.

"No. So, not murders."

"Mutilations. But what if they bled to death afterward?" said Campbell. "How long would a wound like that take to heal?"

"With care, and barring any complications, wounds begin healing right away, but a victim wouldn't be out of the danger zone for a few days. No one has checked into the hospitals recently with a wound like this. It would be a couple of weeks to completely heal, again, unless there was infection."

"So I'm looking for three men, each less an arm, or three similar bodies."

"That about sums it up." Laforet pulled the sheet back over the limbs.

"How recently?"

"The freshest one is no more than three, maybe four days old by my estimation. I'm sorry, I'll know better after I've run a few more tests."

"As far as problems go," Campbell said with a sigh, hands on his hips, "that one's okay."

"Now what about the crate?" said Laforet.

Campbell walked over to it. "Originally one of Chung Hong's and later, it would seem, to have been used by McCloskey's salvage business."

"But that doesn't necessarily mean they were the last ones in possession of it."

"No, no it doesn't. What were they packed with? Straw?" Campbell went over and started pulling out the packing. "It's all straw … I'm catching a whiff of stable."

"I picked that up, too."

"And motor oil?"

"Mm hm."

"Well, it looks like I have a few people to question. Can the crate stay here?"

"Of course."

Campbell was already walking back to his hat. "Are we still on for tomorrow morning?"

"Ah, thank you for reminding me," said Laforet. "Yes, at eleven sharp."

"Shall I bring anything?"

"Can you get your hands on a bottle of sherry?"

Campbell didn't answer; he just pushed his way through the swinging doors.

Chapter 8

LEW TO THE RESCUE

Saturday, August 4

"Lew ... you're not going to believe this." Vera Maude was only inches inside the door at Copeland's and still fumbling through it — her purse strap caught in the door handle — when she said this loud enough for Lew to hear from the back counter. Heads turned. She was early for her shift because she was anxious to bend Lew's ear. She clipped the corner of a table and sent a few copies of *This Freedom* onto the floor. She bent to pick them up and a couple of gentlemen watched. Finished, she slapped the exposed sides of the stack back into right angles and, completing her obstacle course, finally reached the back counter.

"I know," said Lew calmly while re-spooling some gift wrap ribbon, "the president's dead."

"What?" said Vera Maude. She was still catching her breath. "I just saw him." She pulled up the slack in her shoe straps.

"Harding?"

"What? No — the mad bootblack at the corner of London who wears a top hat and calls himself the president."

"No," said Lew as he stretched an elastic band around a spool of twine. "Wait — a top hat?"

Vera Maude shook her head. "Can we back up the trolley?"

Lew pointed his fingers like handguns at Vera Maude. "Go."

"Ready?"

"Ready like spaghetti."

"My uncle Fred proposed to Mrs. Cattanach."

"That's wonderful." Lew checked her expression. "Isn't it?"

"Well, yes, for them, but … he asked me to plan the wedding."

"You?"

Vera Maude stepped back and parked her hands on her hips. "Why does everyone keep saying that … and in that tone?"

Lew had to gently reel her in. "All right, let's start with the way you're carrying on. You may not realize it, but you're having the same reaction yourself, on the inside … but it's coming out."

She attempted relaxing, unpinned her hat, and set it down on the counter.

"You need help," said Lew.

"Damn right," said Vera Maude. She looked over her shoulders. "Is Mr. Copeland in?"

"Lunch in Detroit with clients."

That was some relief. She looked around the store again and then turned back to Lew. "Do you have any experience with this sort of thing? You know, weddings?"

Lew brushed an imaginary particle off his shoulder. "Some."

"Really? What kind?"

"Flowers, I've done flowers — in a pinch. But I know some people who really do have more experience with this sort of thing." He was doing his best to keep things on simmer. "Will it be a church wedding?"

"St. Andrew's," said Vera Maude.

"How many?"

"I don't even know."

"Two hundred? Twenty?"

"Small." She scratched head. "Maybe forty … ish."

"Let's go with that," said Lew. "Ish that is, and that's okay. I've worked with *ish* before. Kidding. We'll have to start with a base and work out … or down. Have you spoken with the bride?"

"No," said Vera Maude.

Lew pressed his hand against his chest. "You need to talk to the bride."

"Lew, this isn't some girl out of —"

There was a jingle from the bell over front entrance and Vera Maude jumped. Not Mr. Copeland, but one of their usual book browsers. She spent hours in the store, asking questions and misplacing books. Maybe every couple of months she'd buy a greeting card.

"You really need to relax," said Lew.

"It's in three weeks."

"Oh, dear. What? Labour Day weekend?"

"Apparently they decided to jump straight from 'someday, maybe' straight into Labour Day weekend."

Vera Maude gently poked Lew's shoulder. "And under no circumstances do you use that phrase in front of the bride and groom."

"What phrase?"

"'End of summer.'"

"Sensitive." Lew paused to let Vera Maude cool. "I was going to say, a row of picnic tables, food served country style ..."

"The flowers. Let's circle back to the flowers, if we may."

There were no real customers about, just the usual lollygaggers performing their usual routine. The only difference was that this morning they got a floor show along with their shopping.

"Off the top of my head," said Lew, "hyacinths. Oh ... maybe not. Put your things away and let's talk between the people."

In Lew's world, in Lew's lexicon, there were people, and then there were "the people." The former were always preferred; the latter to be avoided. He used it to refer to what others called the masses, or the great unwashed.

"I'm still early," said Vera Maude. "Mind if I go out and grab something?"

"Sure, sure."

"Can I get you anything? A ginger ale?"

"No, thanks. You go ahead; I'll watch the fort."

Friday mornings were usually quiet. People tended to be out doing their market shopping. It would pick up after lunch. Vera Maude dashed back out and went back up the block to Andros Brothers' Confectionary. The door was open. She found an empty stool at the counter and planted herself.

"Ms. Vera, the usual?"

"Hit me."

The gentleman came back from the cooler with a frosty bottle of Vernors. Vera Maude slapped her nickel on the counter with a, "Thanks, George." She hustled back to the store, only to run into Copeland at the door. Three complete acts in tweed.

"Ah, Ms. Maguire, right on time."

"Mr. Copeland, I ... yes, right on time."

He held the door open for her.

Lew tried not to look surprised to see him. "Mr. Copeland ..."

"I'm missing a few files."

Copeland walked straight to his desk, found the files, tucked them into his briefcase, and turned to Lew. "Lewis, I'll be returning with a few cartons of books. I'll take a cab up from the ferry, but you will have to help me carry them in, so be prepared. I could telephone from the dock."

"No need, sir, I'll be prepared."

Copeland headed out, this time with two small canvas bags in addition to his files. The staff waited until the door closed behind him before they exhaled.

Vera Maude turned to Lew. "You've got your orders."

"As do you."

"Okay, what's first?" said Vera Maude.

"The fiction bestsellers are in complete ... bad disarray."

"There's a good disarray?"

"Maudie."

"Yes?"

"Just array them."

"Of course," said Vera Maude. "What do I look like?"

"A sweet disarray."

Chapter 9

CANARDS SAUVAGES

Detective Campbell had recently fallen into the habit of not parking his car in front of the address he was visiting. He preferred to park down the block or around the corner, whenever there was a corner to be had. This was how he liked to enter a scene.

He had been assigned violent crime and homicide. He often wondered why, not understanding what they saw in him that made him more suited to this work than any other officer on the force.

He occasionally reminded himself that not every crime scene was a violent tragedy.

He kept walking.

This was a thinly populated area on the fringes of the city, built on the promises of so many realtors and developers, a fringe of roads and avenues that hung from the river, from Riverside Drive, into the only slightly less than wild marsh currently being drained and filled. In this quarter the realtors and developers held sway.

He stepped lightly up the walk and then stopped halfway between the street and the house to observe. She was wearing a coral top with a long blue peacock-patterned skirt. She knelt, revealing the Wellingtons she wore to keep her feet dry. It had rained again, another light shower. She straightened up and adjusted the wide-brimmed straw hat hanging from a loose chinstrap, shading her neck. Her silver-streaked strawberry blonde hair was roped into a large knot and if let loose would have reached down her back. Campbell gave himself a few more seconds.

The day was already turning out to be bright and fine. She was attempting to tame the wisteria climbing the sides of the portico. He thought it looked like a wedding veil. He slid the toe of his right foot slowly across the walk, as if he were rubbing out a cigarette butt. When she turned, he removed his hat.

"*Ah, vous êtes surement* — I'm sorry, Detective Campbell?"

He approached her and she pulled on a couple fingers of her white glove, stained with green, removed it, and presented her hand.

"Eugenie," she said.

Campbell was trying to reassemble everything in his mind, every piece of information he had ever heard about this woman, but all he could see were her smile, her eyes fluttering in the glare of the morning sun, and the smudge of dirt on her cheek.

"Madame Laforet."

"Philippe is in the kitchen. Come."

It was his first time meeting the doctor's wife, and the first time he had ever set foot in their home.

Campbell read the interior. A small foyer; a front room with paintings that resembled stage backdrops; a baby grand piano; two loveseats; a high back chair; and a low table holding down a Persian rug and topped with a vase of fresh cut irises. Not only was there no paper on the walls, but two of them were of different colours, a dull rouge and a clay hue.

"This way," she said.

She led him through the dining room. It was minimally furnished and looked as if it were hardly used — of the four chairs, two of them hugged the nearest corner — unless there were guests.

"Campbell, welcome."

The kitchen reminded Campbell of Laforet's laboratory, except for the fatalities, which in this case were a couple of fowl. White tiled walls, a tray of cutting utensils, enamel bowls filled with innards, and Laforet in a stained apron poised over the table brandishing a chef's knife.

This is where they dine, thought Campbell.

"May I pour you something?" asked Eugenie, walking toward the icebox. "The tea should be cool now."

"That would be fine," said the detective, "thank you." He positioned himself on the other side of the galley, out of harm's way. "I'm sorry if I'm interrupting you. I thought you meant you'd be free when you asked me to —"

"I'm free so long as you don't mind that I keep working."

Eugenie handed Campbell a tall glass of tea with shards of ice floating on top and a thin wedge of lemon straddling the lip.

"Thank you."

"Philippe?"

"No, thank you."

She smiled and made her exit, leaving the men to their business in favour of returning to her pruning. Campbell watched her walk away as Laforet began slicing mushrooms.

"Your wife, Eugenie …"

"She does the cooking during the week and I do the cooking on the weekends."

"A dancer?" said Campbell.

Laforet smiled, still slicing. "She studied ballet, and teaches occasionally at a studio in Detroit."

"A lovely woman. May I ask … I mean, how did you meet?"

"At a cousin's wedding in Montreal."

Campbell took a sip from his glass, set it down, and paid closer attention to what Laforet was doing. "Duck?"

"Soon to be a salmis."

"Salami?"

Laforet set the mushrooms aside. "*Salmis de canards sauvages.* Wild duck, a classic French dish … a hunter's dish."

"Wild? I didn't know they were in season."

"They're in season under the counter at Lancaster's."

Campbell walked around the table to check the recipe, written on a piece of paper standing in the fold of an open book. He started reading it and said, "Anything else I shouldn't know about? The brandy, the red wine …?"

Laforet looked up. "Would you like to stay for dinner?"

"I don't think so," said Campbell. He dropped the recipe back in its place. "Do you have anything else to share?"

Now they were getting down to business.

"You first," said Laforet.

"All right. The Dominion Salt Company records are not all that reliable. They said they'd continue sifting through their rosters. To borrow a metaphor, their employee records were a bit of a rabbit warren."

"How do you mean?"

"I was getting the distinct impression that some of their workers were being paid under the table," said Campbell, "occasionally taking them down a path not of their choosing."

"There are other possibilities."

"Such as?"

"This person was not an employee of the mines, even off the books, but was rather, to put it crudely, *disposed of* in the mines. Hand me that celery."

Campbell picked up the large, leaf-topped head of celery and passed it to Laforet. "Another possibility, I suppose … but it still would have had to been carried out by someone with access to and knowledge of the mines."

Laforet pulled the celery apart, getting to the tender inner stalks. "Unusual."

"Unique."

"Can you splash a bit of water in that cast iron? I think the oven's ready."

Campbell picked up the skillet and ran it under the tap for a second. "This enough? Or too much?"

"Maybe a little too much. Wet the skillet, and then some." Laforet stood by, his elbows bent, hand up, as if he were examining an X-ray before continuing surgery. "That should do; now just set it down here." He dropped the celery pieces into the pan.

"I'm doubting it," said Campbell.

"Doubting what?"

"The idea of it being disposal, as you say." He paused for a moment. "What do you have?"

Laforet was wiping his hands again. "Well, he has a bullet wound in his left leg that went right through, grazing his femur. And you might be right about his being a veteran."

"There's more," said Campbell.

Laforet was saving the best for last. "What we could not see, because of the position he was in, was the trauma on his left side. Both his jaw and neck were broken. It would have been a serious blow."

"With what sort of instrument?" said Campbell.

"Whatever might be handy in a salt mine."

"Might call for another visit."

"May I be excused?" said Laforet.

"Of course. Did he have anything on him?"

"No wallet, no papers, no watch, no rings ... nothing. Just his Essex Regiment tattoo."

"A theft, then?" Campbell perked up. "What sort of valuables could a salt miner be carrying on his person?"

"Only he and his assailant knew," said Laforet.

"The Veterans Association would have him on record."

"What would you be asking them?"

"For starters, has anyone been looking for this man?"

"Good ... but there are other questions."

"Such as?"

Laforet patted the ducks with a towel, preparing to rub them with the fat he kept in a wide-mouthed jar.

"Why take all the trouble?" he said, "I mean, with the burial, such as it was."

"That's a good question."

Laforet arranged the ducks in the skillet, breasts down. "Can you get the oven door for me?"

Campbell pulled it open. It was like a blast furnace.

"Laforet, they'll be reduced to ashes."

"It's only fifteen minutes." He set the skillet down and closed the door. He then poured himself an iced tea, took a long sip, and continued. "Now ... the three arms."

"Yes?"

"Well, we already mentioned the cuts, I mean, that it looked like they were done with some degree of expertise."

"Yes."

"Not butchered, axed, or sawn. No marks from a toothed blade and little to no bone fragment. The cuts were very clean."

"What then?"

"A single, powerful blow."

"With?"

Laforet took another drag from his iced tea and leaned against the counter next to the oven. "Something like a machete."

"A machete?"

"My best guess. Does that tell you anything? Or are you faking some kind of incredulity?"

Campbell set his glass down on the galley and paced one and then two laps around. "I've gone back to thinking that the victims were intended to live, that they were intended to carry this with them, so to speak. And they are still walking among us."

"A cruel and unusual punishment."

Campbell turned to the doctor. "There's that word again."

"Which?"

"Unusual."

"We live in unusual times," said Laforet.

"Is there nothing else about them — the victims, that is — that you can tell me?"

"All roughly the same age — young. I measured the length of the arms and can safely say the men were relatively small in stature, slim but fit. I looked at the fingers, their hands ... they worked hard for their living. Oh, and all three had blood type B."

"Wasn't there anything that set them apart?"

Laforet took another sip from his iced tea. "I was getting to that. There are needle marks inside one of the elbows — not fresh — and on another arm little red splotches that start on the hand and go up just past the wrist, some old and some new"

"A rash of some sort?" asked Campbell.

"Burns, and not from a splash of boiling water but rather hot grease splatter. I've seen it before."

"From a kitchen, possibly a restaurant kitchen."

"Do you know of anyone missing their fry cook?"

"I'll check the help wanted ads. Anything else?"

"No, not right now," said Laforet. "I need more time."

"And some more sleep by the looks of you. One last thing: we spoke in the alleyway that night about the crate perhaps having meant to be found. I'm still playing with that, but maybe we weren't the ones meant to find it." He turned to Laforet. "Perhaps we happened to stumble upon it first."

"Or perhaps it didn't matter who stumbled upon it first, so long as it was found — and soon, obviously. I'm assuming you took note of the businesses that back onto the location."

Campbell set his glass down on the galley. "I did, but I couldn't see any kind of possible connection. I'll have to look again."

Laforet was getting back to his *canards*. "Are you sure you won't stay?"

Campbell knew Laforet was just being polite. "No, thank you. I'd like to get right back to this."

"Very well. Can you show yourself out? I'm keeping an eye on the blast furnace."

"Of course. Thanks for the tea."

Campbell made his way back through the house. Through the dining room window he could see Eugenie still attempting to tame the wisteria. He stepped outside.

"*Trés belle*," said Campbell.

"Thank you. She looks for much attention."

He paused, thinking he had something more to say, but instead simply replaced his hat, wished Eugenie a good day, and tried to remember where he had parked his car.

"*Au revoir.*"

Chapter 10

I HAD AN OCCASION
TO VISIT

Campbell started chasing McCloskey down with various phone numbers. After he went through all of them once he went through them again.

The man is a moving target, thought the detective. *It's intentional.*

At the start of the third go-round he finally caught up with him. McCloskey was at his office now, on the Drive. That's right where Campbell wanted him, where this conversation had to take place because it had to be all above board, not in the darkened corner booth of a diner, a dodgy wrecking yard, or an alleyway. It had to be here. This was the closest thing to McCloskey's public face, and Campbell had to be seen entering the address. It could be a difficult relationship to manage sometimes; the detective often wondered how long they could make it work. In the end it wouldn't be up to the both of them, but up to only one, the one who would finally make the decision.

Campbell resisted looking over his shoulder before opening the door to the building. What he did first, for effect, was pull his notepad out of his inside coat pocket, step back to the curb, look up at the window of McCloskey's office, and fake taking notes.

Coffee ... cigarettes ... light bulbs.

He then proceeded through the entrance and ascended the stairs. On the frosted glass of the only door on the first landing was BORDER CITY EXCHANGE, the name of McCloskey's umbrella organization. Campbell knocked. He could hear someone inside, cursing and slamming desk drawers.

"Yeah," bellowed McCloskey, "c'mon in."

The detective entered and, ever the gentleman, removed his homburg.

McCloskey looked up. "Campbell," he said. He was sitting behind his expansive oak desk, shuffling papers. "Do you know any good lawyers?"

"Is that a trick question?"

"Have a seat and tell me what it's all about. Oh — can I get you anything?"

Campbell sat himself in one of the two chairs McCloskey salvaged from his old boss Lieutenant Green's office. "No, thanks."

"Okay, so?"

Campbell got down to it. "One of our constables found something in the alley behind Pitt, a few doors east of Ferry."

"You could find just about anything there." McCloskey leaned back in this chair. "What was it?"

"A wooden crate, with 'Border Cities Wrecking and Salvage' stenciled on it."

"Really? I hear I'm missing some pistons."

"These weren't auto parts, McCloskey. They were body parts."

McCloskey leaned forward and, folding his hands together, said, "What?"

"Three male left arms," said Campbell, and then he paused. "You know I have to ask."

"I don't know anything about it, Campbell. And you know that's not my style."

"Maybe not yours personally."

"I know what you're suggesting, but none of my boys would do anything like … why would anyone do something like that?" Another pause. "Are you telling me there are three guys walking around the Border Cities missing an arm?"

"You know how many veterans are probably walking around the Border Cities right now missing an arm?"

"True," said McCloskey.

"And I don't even know if they're alive or dead."

McCloskey leaned back again. "Three arms?"

Campbell reached in his pocket for the half-dozen photographs that Laforet had printed for him, and slid them one at a time across the desk towards McCloskey. While he did that he tried to read anything he could off the paperwork on McCloskey's desk. He couldn't resist.

"This one shows the side of the crate with 'Wrecking and Salvage' stenciled on it."

"Yeah, like I said, that's us."

"And that one shows Hong's address label. The crate must have originally come from one of the exporters he deals with."

"Hm." McCloskey examined the images, and without looking up, said, "What else can you tell me about the arms?"

"I can tell you they were very clean cuts, done with some skill. Laforet is still conducting his examination."

"Why leave them in the alley like that? Why not just dump them in the river?"

"Our thinking is that maybe they were supposed to be found."

McCloskey gathered the photos and handed them back to Campbell. "I'm sorry, but I've got nothing for you. If it has our markings on it that means the crate was already sent to its destination. We don't have them lying around the shop, ready to go. It's order-to-order. And what happens to it when it leaves the yard, well, how would I know? It could have been intercepted. And believe me, no one's going to report that."

"Agreed," said Campbell. "Would you be able to tell if it was destined for a local address or a Detroit address?"

"Possibly."

"This is the point where I remind you that I'm not interested in any of your other … activities."

"And this is the point where I tell you that I have no idea to what you might be referring."

That sounds a bit rehearsed, thought Campbell.

The two paused to shuffle the playing cards around in their heads.

"You say you might be missing some parts?" said Campbell.

"It's hard to keep track of things when you're really not supposed to be keeping track of things."

"You don't need a lawyer, McCloskey, you need a shipping clerk."

"Sounds like Hong does, too."

Another pause.

"Can I ask you something, off the record?" said McCloskey. "It's something that might interest you."

Campbell leaned forward, balancing his homburg on his knee. "Go ahead."

"The other night I had occasion to visit the back room at Hong's dry goods place. It was their poker night. Morrison was at the table. Is he up to something or does he just like cards? I mean he looked a little out of place, for a lotta reasons."

"On the record or off, I still can't comment in case it happened to be official police business."

McCloskey set his elbows on the arms of his chair, staring at Campbell.

"Was it?" said McCloskey.

Campbell looked about the room, wondering why he didn't have an office half as nice and well equipped as this one. "He's up to something," he said, "and I have no idea what. That's the truth." He was a little embarrassed to admit it.

"Have your conversation with Hong," said McCloskey, "and then tell me anything you think I need to know. Maybe we can piece something together. So Laforet has the crate?"

"At the hospital. And it's evidence."

"Gotcha. Are we done?"

Campbell looked at this man and wondered how long before, like it or not, he was running the Border Cities. Campbell had the feeling that, now more than ever, his day would be made of life-changing choices and decisions.

"We're done." Campbell pocketed the photos, stood, and showed himself to the door. He took his time down the stairs, going over everything in his mind, filing it, making sure he didn't lose any of it.

Back on the street, he looked up and down the Drive and checked the skies. The wind was changing and the cloud cover was breaking up.

Chapter 11

HOUSE CALLS

"Goddamn squirrels."

"You didn't," said Linc.

Jefferson was at the wheel. "I missed."

"You were aiming for it?"

"How can you possibly aim at something like that?" said Jefferson. "That thing doesn't even know what direction it's going."

"So you weren't aiming?" said Linc.

"'Course not. What do you think I am?"

"What if you ran over it?"

"You gonna hold a dead squirrel against me?" said Jefferson.

"I might." Linc returned to his notes. "Says 'Tuppy.' The address is 34 1/2."

"Who lives at 'a half'? I never understand that," said Jefferson.

"Yeah, 'cause you're living your life to the fullest."

"That I am."

"Stealing headlights and rear-view mirrors?" said Linc.

"Why you riding me like this?"

Linc had his elbow on the open window frame, drum-rolling the edge of it with his fingertips. "Me and Moll had a fight last night."

This was something new. Jefferson glanced between his partner in crime and the road, looking out for squirrels. "Yeah?"

"Yeah." He paused. "She says I don't take her out."

"What do you mean?"

"She says her girlfriends … their boyfriends take them out every weekend. Sometimes even during the week."

Jefferson wasn't in a relationship, at least not a steady one. "So you never take her out?"

"I didn't say never … she did. Sometimes I take her out, regular times."

Jefferson was hoping to glean something out of all of this, something that might enable him to understand women. "So why not more often?"

"Maybe I don't like going out so much. Maybe I like staying in at the end of the day."

"So take her back to our place."

Linc took his arm off the window frame. "Our place?"

"Sure, why not?"

"Well, for one thing," said Linc, "you're there."

"I could make myself scarce."

"And for another thing, have you seen our place? It looks like it got rolled down a hill."

When Jefferson was finished checking addresses he said, "So take her to the pictures."

"Maybe I'm waiting for something I might wanna see."

"Geez you're tough to please sometimes. Maybe it won't be something you want to see."

Linc was shaking his head. "I get pleased just fine."

"Keep telling yourself that. I maybe don't know as much about women as you, but I do know that you don't know pleasure until you've learned how to please someone else."

"Can we drop it?" said Linc.

"Give and take, that's all I'm saying."

"I'm sorry I brought it up."

"What was the model again?" asked Jefferson.

Linc went back to his notes. "A 1918 Studebaker Type 19, a Model HS Light Four."

"This is lighting you up, isn't it? What, you got the collector's card?"

"Wait for it." Linc smiled, holding up his finger.

"What?" said Jefferson. It was indeed lighting him up.

"That's not all."

"What? What?"

"Open ... touring."

"Shut up. Hey, isn't that it?" Linc was pointing to a house on his side of the street.

"Yeah," said Jefferson, as he pulled over. "You grab the blowtorch and I'll grab the saws and the tool bag."

They shuffled to the front door and Linc gave it a knock.

"You want them folks out back," said the woman who caught their drift. And then the boys caught hers: a stained and tattered housecoat, and a host of houseflies buzzing all around her. Jefferson almost wished he had something to share. Linc casually pressed the back of his hand against his mouth. "They're the ones with the vehicle," she said.

"Tuppy?"

"Yes," said the woman.

Jefferson touched his hat. "Thank you, ma'am," he said, handing the woman his business card.

She studied it. "I don't know from no auto vehicles."

"Well," said Jefferson, "keep that in case you see a stray you need taken down."

Linc glanced over. He thought Jefferson needed to work on his pitch. "Out back, you say?"

"Yeah, out back."

The boys touched their hats again and went around the corner. They spotted the Studebaker. It had been turned into a four-wheeled planter, the centrepiece of the back garden and spilling over with perennials. Their jaws dropped. Linc almost dropped the toolbox. Behind them, a screen door squeaked open.

"I see you found her."

How could anyone miss? thought Linc. *Someone please explain white folks to me.*

"Sir," said Jefferson, "what exactly did you want us to do? I mean —"

"She's all yours, so long as you take her away — all of her. Just make quick work of it."

Tuppy was standing on the back steps in his undergarments, holding a bowl of puffed rice, mashing a spoonful between his gums, milk dribbling down his chin.

"What about the … well, it's got a garden growing out of it," said Linc.

"That was the miss's. She passed on in the springtime, bless her soul. I'm not much of a gardener. Take what you want of the foliage."

"And the rest?" said Jefferson, still slightly confused.

"Well," said the man, "I guess just put the loose dirt in the yard, and everything else — the combustibles, that is — can go in those oil barrels."

The boys turned to look at where he was gesturing with his spoon. Two oil barrels that looked accustomed to seeing smoldering rubbish while being gazed upon by the master of the house and his drinking buddies.

"We'll get to it, sir," said Linc.

The man saluted them and returned inside to finish his puffed rice and what Jefferson guessed was a rye chaser.

"Okay," said Jefferson, "let's chop her up and get out of here."

"The wheels are half in the ground," said Linc. "Did you see a shovel anywhere?"

Jefferson pointed to a vegetable patch. Rows of carrots, radishes, kale, and parsnips.

"That's some strange salad."

The boys got to work.

"Hey … we bring any buckets or pails?" asked Linc.

"Yeah, two buckets. Why?"

"Some of these flowers look real nice. What's that one?"

"Yellow and gold … Black-eyed Susans," said Jefferson. "Where you gonna plant them? In the bathtub?"

Linc was too busy to answer, already distributing the Studebaker's dirt along the garden beds and replanting some of the flowers. He took a moment to lean on his shovel. "What did Tuppy say? His wife passed on in the spring … and he was no gardener?"

"Yeah, why?"

"Nice-looking garden."

"So? Let's get to chopping," said Linc.

"Do we want the whole thing?"

"Yeah. Why not? He's offering it up. You start on the engine and I'll work on the body."

They'd have to make two trips to the salvage yard with the remains of the dismembered Studebaker. If they could have found a way to tow the thing wholesale to the yard, they would have done just that.

"How much you figure we'll get for this?" said Linc.

"Her guts were well preserved. I don't know; let's let Mud figure that out."

Tuppy appeared, now dressed in a suit and with his comb-over back in place. The boys barely recognized him.

"I'm going to be stepping out for a short while. By the looks of things you won't finish before I get back. We can settle up then."

A couple hours passed and then Tuppy came around through the backyard, looking slightly disheveled but with a smile on his face. "You guys almost done? I thought you'd be done by now."

"We're just finishing up," said Jefferson, throwing a side-glance at Linc.

"Do you want us to tidy the rest of the garden mess? We didn't get to —"

"No, no it's fine," said Tuppy. "Thank you, boys, you did a great job. Such a relief."

"A relief?" asked Linc.

"AAAAHHH!"

"What the hell?" said Jefferson, turning toward the voice that came from around the side of the house.

"Tell me that isn't ..." said Linc.

"It is," said Tuppy.

"Mrs. Tuppy," said Jefferson.

"She's not dead?" asked Linc.

"Very much not so," said Tuppy. "Boys, you've done me a great favour."

"What have you done?" Mrs. Tuppy picked up a garden hoe and started waving it around, enraged. Not quite an axe or a pitchfork, but intimidating nonetheless, and able to do some damage.

"Jefferson," said Linc, "we got everything?"

"Everything we came for."

"Then let's skedaddle."

"Hop that fence and let's run through the yard next door."

Mrs. Tuppy was taking swings, wielding the hoe over her head like it was some sort of medieval battle weapon. Tuppy grabbed an ashcan lid and raised it in defense. Linc and Jefferson paused for a moment on the other side of the fence, taking in the spectacle, and then made for Betsy.

— *Chapter 12* —

THICK WITH PEOPLE

Detective Campbell knew he wouldn't have as difficult a time tracking down Hong as he did McCloskey. It was Saturday, his dry goods place would be bustling, and he was known for being very hands-on with his business. Campbell walked east along the Drive after leaving McCloskey's office, keeping his head down and comparing the cracks in the sidewalk with the cracks in his thinking. He knew that the coffee and cigarettes, along with other things like lack of sleep, were eating through him.

Is this the way it's going to be?

He knew there were other things he could probably be doing besides telling himself to *get used to it*, but he just couldn't think of them.

People were hustling in and out of the shops. Campbell had to pause at the Avenue as the constable on point duty directed the pedestrian and vehicular traffic. Campbell gave him a nod and the constable returned it. It was a manageable chaos. The ferry whistle tooted, car horns blared, and babies wailed from the comfort of their bouncing buggies. Campbell somehow managed to cross the street without incident.

He paused in front of the Canadian Bank of Commerce building to look over at the British-American Hotel and down Ferry Hill towards the dock. It was thick with people, all seemingly with two arms. McCloskey's point about the veterans was a good one. There were still so many scars, prosthetics, wheels, and canes. Once again distracted in thought, Campbell continued along Riverside Drive.

After he passed the Davis Building, people and machines became a bit more scarce. Travellers toting luggage made their way up from the train station towards the King George. If they continued further east on foot, their destination was likely the Empire Hotel at Windsor Avenue, which sort of marked the end of the downtown. He observed the travellers begin to separate, heading to their respective lodgings, and wondered how much they really knew about the Border Cities, about what went on in the streets and roadhouses at night.

Maybe they heard rumours and are here to learn more, he guessed.

There were several Chinese establishments before that block: Hong Wick Company, grocers; Low's barbershop; Chung Hong's dry goods place; and of course the Chinese Nationalist League. Though there were other Chinese businesses in the Border Cities, this hub was the best qualified to be called "Chinatown."

Campbell entered Hong's place and found it bustling indeed. Hardwood floors, walls lined with shelves overflowing with products, counters on both sides and along the back. The ceiling was strung with banners sporting Chinese sayings, punctuated by paper lanterns, mostly red. A green-and-yellow paper dragon, almost the length of the space, hung from the ceiling.

Inside the door, to Campbell's right, were sacks of rice piled in a pyramid about four feet high. To his left was an arrangement of open wooden crates displaying imported tableware packed in straw.

Campbell went deeper into the store, taking it all in. It wasn't his first time visiting the establishment, but those previous visits were for personal reasons. This was different. He walked in with new eyes.

"May I help you?" asked a young man from behind the counter. He wore a black mandarin shirt with frog buttons.

"I'm here to speak with Chung Hong."

The young man looked around and said, "He is not in."

Campbell showed the young man his badge. "I just want to ask Mr. Hong a few questions."

The young man studied the badge. "One moment," he said, then disappeared through a wide door leading into a room at the rear.

Where the poker games must take place, thought Campbell.

Hong came out first, straightening his vest. "Detective Campbell."

Campbell was slightly taken aback. "Have we met, Mr. Hong?"

Hong's young protege reappeared.

"No," said Hong.

Campbell would rifle through his mental file cards later. "I'd like to ask you a few questions, Mr. Hong … privately."

"Certainly." The young man lifted a hinged section of the countertop and held it in place. Campbell followed Hong into a back room.

"I'll be brief," said Campbell.

"Please sit," said Hong.

Campbell glanced around the room before pulling out one of the chairs around the table. "One of our constables made a discovery last night, and it has raised not just a few questions, some of which regard this establishment."

Hong furrowed his brow. "Yes?"

"It was a crate, almost identical to the ones you are currently using in a display at the front of your store. It was found in the alley between Pitt and the Drive just this side of Ferry."

"Go on."

"It contained three severed arms."

Hong's expression upon hearing this was a little different than McCloskey's — his jaw slackened and his face changed colour. Campbell pulled the photographs out of his coat pocket and spread them on the table like he was laying out a royal flush. Hong studied each of them closely.

"This is terrible," said Hong, pulling a small packet of cigarettes out of his vest. "Do you mind?"

"No," said Campbell.

Hong pulled a matchbox out of his other vest pocket. He dragged the little stick across the side of the box and held the flame to the end of his cigarette. Blue smoke swirled up toward the lantern that hung over the table. Without taking his eyes off the photos, he reached for the overflowing serpentine ashtray and slowly dragged it toward him.

"Mr. Hong, have you ever seen anything like this before?"

"No," he said.

"Do you have any idea what it might mean?"

"No, I don't."

"Seen any young men missing an arm recently?"

Hong nodded. "I have a stock boy."

Campbell's eyebrows climbed halfway up his forehead. "You have a one-armed stock boy?"

"Yes," said Hong. "He's very good."

"How did he loose the arm?"

"A mining accident in British Columbia."

"Very unfortunate. No, these are recent."

"How recent?"

"Just a few days. Oh." Campbell quickly checked his wristwatch — beginning to think that he should start wearing more than one — and said, "The coroner is still conducting his examination. I'm due to meet with him shortly." He stood up and extended his hand. "Thank you for your time, Mr. Hong."

"Always happy to co-operate, detective. Help yourself to an almond cookie on your way out. Homemade."

"Thank you." Campbell walked through to the front of the store, turning heads. He could feel everyone's eyes on him. He smiled and nodded at the young man behind the counter and the young man nodded back without a smile.

Campbell walked up to his apartment on Arthur to get his car. He didn't want to be late for Laforet.

— *Chapter 13* —

IT'S A DATE

It was only the middle of the afternoon and McCloskey was already looking for a break in the action, if paperwork and telephone conversations could be called action. He rang up Vera Maude at the bookstore and asked if she felt like doing something that evening.

"Yes," she said. "Yes, we do gift-wrapping."

"What?" said McCloskey.

"We also make local deliveries."

He finally remembered that she wasn't allowed personal phone calls.

"Maudie, deliver yourself over here after your shift."

"You're welcome … good day, Mr. McGillicutty."

Wanting to avoid running into any co-workers, Vera Maude decided to take a roundabout way to McCloskey's place. She took Park Street to Church, dropped down to Chatham, and then across to Dougall. She figured she shook anyone that might be on her trail. She was back to reading detective magazines in her free time, and less than halfway to McCloskey's, she started to feel nervous. It wasn't like she hadn't been out with him before. But this felt different for some reason. When she arrived, he was sitting on the steps, finishing a cigar. The thick air held down the smoke.

"What took you so long?"

"I took a wrong turn," she said.

"I'll say — you're arriving from the opposite direction."

They stood on the first landing of the stairs that climbed the outside of McCloskey's apartment block, LaBelle Terrace. Being a sort of alcove, it sheltered them from the hot, humid breeze blowing off the river. A light summer rain was on the way but was taking its own sweet time.

"Well, I know how much you like the movies," McCloskey said. "Do you feel like catching one?

"Yeah, sure," she said. "I just happen to have on my person …" She pulled out the entertainment section of the *Star* from her purse, unfolded it, and turned to the movie listings. McCloskey tried to read it over her shoulder. She could feel his breath on her neck and tried to concentrate.

"Hey, look — 'Relax in the Cool Comfort of the Allen.'"

"What's the picture?"

"*The Enemies of Women*," she said. "Doesn't look too promising."

"Okay, what else?"

"Let's see what's at the Walkerville ... *Woman With Four Faces*, and there's a vaudeville: *The Juvenile Follies*. It says, 'Comedy — Packed With Laughs.'"

No comment from McCloskey. "And the Capitol?"

"*Without Compromise* ... also with a vaudeville revue ... the Drake Sisters headlining, and some jazz jugglers."

"Don't think so; that stuff's not really for me." McCloskey straightened up and turned his gaze towards the intersection, thinking. He watched three cars try and negotiate the crossing and then he turned his attention back to Vera Maude.

"Why don't we just go for dinner?"

Vera Maude, relieved because she really couldn't see McCloskey sitting patiently through a movie, refolded the section and tucked it back into her purse.

"Sure ... where?"

"I know a place."

I bet you know lots of places.

"Not far, and nothing fancy. It's actually a house. They converted their front room into a sort of café. It's small, and usually quiet. They serve proper meals, and they're good people."

"Good people? And here I thought you didn't know any."

"Ha. So that suits you?" said McCloskey.

"Suits me fine."

"It's just up Pelissier. We can walk it."

"Together?"

"Mostly, I guess. Yeah, of course together."

They had both been trying to avoid being seen too often together in public, each for their own reasons. McCloskey still didn't want Vera Maude getting tangled up in his complicated life, and Vera Maude didn't want to be seen by her friends, colleagues, or family hanging out with a man who was rumored to be a gang leader and a threat to the peace.

"Oh, wait."

"What?" said McCloskey.

"I should call Uncle Fred."

"Right … upstairs. You make your call and I'll fetch my umbrella."

When they reached his door, McCloskey pulled his keys out of his pocket and jangled them around until the right one fell between his thumb and forefinger, the one with the most scratches on the cuts and the greasiest bow. He jabbed the lock and tickled the tumblers. Vera Maude went straight to the phone, woke a sleepy operator, and finally got through.

"Uncle Fred? … Yes, it's me … No, but I'm going to be late … No, you go ahead and … Yes … Is Mrs. Cattanach there? … Oh good … Okay … Bye."

She hung up the earpiece and set the phone back on the little table.

"Everything okay?"

"Everything's okay," said Vera Maude. "Lead the way."

They headed back down the stairs. The rain was closing in.

"We'll start up this way." McCloskey broke into his stride.

"Hey, don't walk so fast."

"I'm not walking fast," he said, "this is normal walking."

"Try walking like that in a tube skirt that's almost to your ankles."

"So wear a shorter skirt."

Vera Maude looked up to see if he was serious. She was thinking he was.

"I should have asked you this first. Maudie, you like borch?"

"I may have voted for him in the last election. Do you mean *borscht*?"

"The soup."

"Yeah, I know, but around our house we just call it cold beet soup."

"It's nice in the summer," said McCloskey. "Very refreshing. I'm liking it."

Another side to this man. "Are you turning into some sort of gastronome?"

"A what?"

"It means you've got a keen interest in food and good cooking."

"Well, we've been working on the menu at the club. They keep throwing new things at me."

"Sounds like a food fight."

Their arms dangled for a bit; their fingers brushed and then McCloskey took her little hand in his rough boxer's mitt and said, "Are you okay with this?"

"Yes," she said. She was loosening up a little.

They walked in silence for a while, admiring the homes and the front gardens, each wondering what the other was thinking.

"They serve it with this amazing bread."

"What?"

"The soup."

"Ah."

The house was south of Wyandotte, on the west side, a two-and-a-half-storey green clapboard affair that, when walking right past, one would never suspect that it served the best meals in this quarter of town. They didn't have a sign or a sandwich board, but McCloskey knew it. It was almost like a speakeasy.

The woman who greeted them inside the door recognized McCloskey right away. She was as wide as she was tall and wearing the same floral pattern apron she tied around her waist every morning as soon as she got out of bed. Strictly old country.

"Chack, come here and sit down." She found them a table. "So, Chack, who is your friend tonight?"

Tonight? thought Vera Maude. *What am I, the Saturday night special?*

"Babushka, this is Maudie; Maudie, Babushka."

"Such a pretty one. Also, she looks very serious. Nice to meet you Muddy. Chack, what do you want for you and this pretty girl?"

"We'll start with the" — he glanced at Maudie — "*borscht.* And then, well, what's the kitchen been working on today?"

"For you, I still have left something special ... a *kulebiaka.*"

Vera Maude looked at McCloskey for some help on that one, but McCloskey was back in unfamiliar culinary territory.

"What's that?" he said. He didn't mince words.

"Salmon and cod, rice and mushroom, dill, all wrapped in delicious pastry. You will like."

It almost sounded like a command.

"Sounds wonderful," said Vera Maude.

"We'll have that," said McCloskey.

"And to drink, to drink," said Babushka with, her palms pressed against her cheeks and her eyes rolling, "I have chilled *kompot* I make just this afternoon." She saw their blank stares. "Fruits — ripe, ripe, ripe — strawberries, blueberries, raspberries, plums, and I don't know what else, simmered, made even more beautiful and sweet. I will bring you some." And off she went, a babushka on a mission.

"She's something else," said Vera Maude. "Is that her real name?"

"It's what she tells everyone to call her." McCloskey looked carefully around the room, checking out the diners. There was no one he recognized and no one seemed to be eyeing him. That was good. He was beginning to like places like this more and more.

At the same time, he was beginning to realize that his face and his reputation could quickly spoil things for the proprietors and their guests, and he might have to move on to another establishment soon. He was only just beginning to realize how he could unwittingly ruin things for other people — besides the maître d'. But he had to be careful; he needed Vera Maude. Sitting here with her, he saw things being pushed to a sort of tipping point. He told himself he could maintain the balance.

"So Uncle Fred won't be dining alone this evening?"

"No," she said, "he has Mrs. Cattanach's company. Oh, that reminds me, I'm getting some help with the wedding plans. My friend Lew has some experience with this sort of thing."

"Lew … bookstore Lew?"

"Yep, the Lew and only."

"What's he know?"

"Well, for starters he knows flowers. And he knows people who know more than he does about everything else. I'm a little out of my league here. I'll just try to pull it all together, make sure the bride and bridegroom get what they want, and that it's something special, you know, a day to remember."

Babushka returned with a couple of small mason jars brimming with the *kompot*, a few shards of ice floating on top. "I'll be right back with the soup," she said.

McCloskey and Vera Maude tasted their drinks.

"Delicious," she said. "It tastes like summer."

"So you're feeling a little more confident about pulling this off?"

"*Pulling it off?* Hey, I'm not the one standing at the altar. The pressure is on them."

"That wasn't your tone yesterday morning."

"I know. I flew off a bit. You know me. But I've had a day to calm down and think about it." She plucked a raspberry out of her drink and popped it in her mouth. The juice dribbled down her chin but she caught it before it stopped traffic. "I'm happy for them. They should be together."

Babushka returned and set down two floral-patterned, wide-lipped bowls on the table. The vines in the pattern reached out of the soup and held onto the edge of the dish.

"What a beautiful colour," said Vera Maude.

The soup was pale-purple velvet. Babushka smiled and then resumed her rounds. There wasn't an empty seat in the place and she was starting to turn people away. It was the dinner rush. Her grandson, Yevgeny, was busing tables as fast he could.

"Anything else new?" asked Vera Maude. She was enjoying herself.

He looked around and, in a low voice, said, "A certain detective we both know came across three severed arms in an alley off Ferry Street."

"Jack, I'm eating!"

"You asked."

Still, she was intrigued. "How did you find out about this?"

"The detective had a few questions for me." McCloskey rested his spoon and said, "The limbs were in a crate with our markings on it."

"Your markings?"

"The salvage yard's."

She looked up from her soup. "Oh.... Oh?"

"I don't know what to make of it. That's what's-his-name's beat."

Vera Maude's spoon hovered mid-flight. "So you know nothing about it?"

"Nothing," said McCloskey, looking her in the eye.

She couldn't read him. He seemed to be made of a combination of things, things one had to ignore and things one never wanted to forget. She'd leave him tangled for now.

Babushka came back for the soup bowls, saw the two were deep in conversation, leaning across the table towards each other, and smiled. She probably thought it was something deep and romantic when actually it was something violent and sinister.

After the *kulebiaka*, some homemade peach brandy served with a wink, and the bill, McCloskey persuaded Vera Maude into dropping by a speakeasy that was also in a house in the neighbourhood, but not before slipping a few folded bills into Babushka's palm.

"Thank you, Chack. I like her. You be a nice boy."

"You know me."

"Yes, I do."

The partially overcast sky made for a dusky, late summer evening. They walked hand in hand.

"Good thing I don't have to work tomorrow," said Vera Maude.

ACT THREE

Chapter 14

KICKING THE GONG AROUND

Monday, August 6

PLOT TOLD OF CHINAMAN IN DOPE CASE
Claims That He Was "Framed" By Orientals Here

Claiming that he was the victim of a deep Oriental plot, Sun Yen Chen, or Chen Su Yen, a Toronto

Chinese, pleaded not guilty yesterday afternoon before Judge W.E. Gundy of having morphine in his possession. Despite all protestations, however, Chen was found guilty and remanded for sentence.

In giving evidence in his own behalf, Chen told a highly sensational story. He informed the court that when he came to Windsor, it was to say goodbye to his many friends here as he intended to return to the land of his fathers.

RECEIVED WARNING

Previous to coming here from Toronto, he said, he received a letter of warning from a friend in Chicago who warned him that the Windsor Chinese were a bad and desperate lot, who would not hesitate to "frame" him. And in this respect his worst fears were realized. Someone, he declared, filled his pockets with cans containing morphine, and it was this that got him into trouble when the police searched him at 117 Sandwich Street East, where he was staying.

On each can, marked in Chinese characters, was the name Li Yun. According to Tom Wu, Chinese interpreter, Li Yun is the name of a firm of opium exporters in China; one of the largest in the business.

ESCAPED TO TORONTO

The accused was arrested by members of the RCMP detachment, who produced evidence to show that premises held by Chen in Toronto had been raided by the police and a quantity of opium secured, although Chen had never been caught in the police dragnet at the time of these raids. Chen was represented by Roscoe Rodd, while W.H. Furlong acted as prosecutor for the Federal government in the absence of William M. Egan. Chen will be sentenced Saturday.

Ung Lee Pong, on whose premises RCMP officers found a quantity of opium prepared for retailing, was found guilty of unlawfully possessing narcotics. He will receive sentence Saturday.

"That's the detective I was telling you about." He spoke in a loud whisper.

"Where?"

"There," he said, pointing with a gnarled, curled index finger, the full finger being rude, or so he had learned from his mother, who had always told him that it was not polite to point. "Him, the fellow with the chair groaning under him … yet still holding some regard."

They were two elderly men, one a retired clerk from the jail and the other his new friend from the lodge — Prince of Wales No. 52. When they first met at a recent smoker held to welcome new members, they discovered their mutual interest in the courts. The retired clerk said he attended whenever he could, and invited the initiate to join him sometime — when the case looked particularly interesting — and they'd make a day of it. They compared calendars and found some openings, a few of which happened to overlap. The retired clerk said he would keep his ear to the ground and his eye on the newspaper. He was flexible. They exchanged calling cards, one printed on vellum and the other hand-written on a gift tag. The ex-clerk touched the brim of his panama, and the initiate nodded. After checking with their social directors — their wives, that is — the ex-clerk telephoned the initiate and a date was set.

The two had met at the courthouse early that day, only to find the room almost full. The folding chairs would get a good polish today. Drug smuggling cases were the latest addiction amongst the general populace, providing some fresh entertainment, a departure from the now-routine Prohibition violations currently ranking in the crime index alongside milk bottle theft. The lodge men found a couple of chairs towards the back, not side-by-side but one behind the other, the ex-clerk in front.

"Are you sure?" said his friend, his hand on the other's shoulder.

"I've been coming here often enough to know." This was his territory.

The initiate furrowed his brow while lifting himself ever so slightly from his chair in order to gain a better view. He made like he was straightening the seat of his trousers, as if that would be any less conspicuous. He sat down and reported. "It looks as if he's doing a crossword."

The ex-clerk rose, conspicuously this time, found the same angle, lifted his spectacles, and with one eye closed, squinted the other as if he were peeping through a keyhole. He then sat back and turned to his friend. "Yes … yes it does, doesn't it?"

"He might not seem as if he were all that interested in the proceedings, and yet …"

"And yet what?"

"And yet it's as if he were taking notes."

"A keen observation." The ex-clerk was suddenly disappointed in himself, realizing that as much as he liked to think so, he was perhaps not one for details, and it was all in the details. His shoulders sagged a bit under the weight of self-doubt, and he wondered many things.

The ex-clerk kept seeing Morrison here because the detective was maintaining a close eye on his investment, an investment that was beginning to go south, and when an investment such as the accused started to unexpectedly tank, one sometimes had to help it along to its estimated demise. The exit strategy was all timing and execution.

Morrison was indeed gently stabbing and scratching at the crossword with his pencil, not filling in answers but composing a message buried in numbers and letters and little black squares.

Six Down — Li Yun.

When court adjourned, Morrison waited for everyone to clear out before taking his leave. To him, it was like waiting for a backed-up sink to drain. He feigned preoccupation with his crossword while walking to the nearest streetcar stop.

Standing there, looking west down the Drive, he waved his folded newspaper as if hailing a cab. There was a man standing one corner up who removed his hat and started fanning himself with it. When the distant car approached, the man boarded. When the same car stopped in front of Morrison, he also boarded. The detective found the man near the back and sat himself two seats over on the same bench. Morrison set the folded paper down between them, lit a cigarette, and then got up and staggered towards the front of the wobbling car, gripping the hand straps like they were vines dangling from the ceiling of a jungle.

"Detroit Street," he said.

"Short trip."

Morrison smiled but it wasn't all sunshine. The driver caught Morrison's drift: *Mind your own goddamn business.*

"Yes, sir."

When Morrison disembarked, the man he had been sitting near picked up the newspaper and unfolded it to reveal the crossword. He started working the letters and numbers, occasionally looking up from the paper to stare out the window to let his own wheels spin. When he knew he had it, he refolded the newspaper and tucked it into the back of his belt, under his jacket. He'd ride the car all the way downtown, or as long as the driver would have him, avoiding eye contact or doing anything that might leave an impression.

He always had to know how to play it, figure out just what the situation called for. He knew that's why the detective chose him. He could either be that whom the *gwai lo* would pretend did not exist, even after they had passed him on the sidewalk, or he could be the stranger he allowed them to abuse, even vilify. He could be either a standout or he could make himself invisible.

It was a pleasant day, a rarity during this particular season, and he considered getting out of the car and walking the rest of the way, but by riding a car with so few passengers, less people would see him. And these ladies were too polite to stare.

Today, I am not here.

Meanwhile, Morrison doubled back, walking west along Riverside Drive, passing several homes until reaching a vacant building comprised of a storefront and a single residence up top. The previous owner had lost the business and it was now in the hands of a realtor who just happened to be located a few doors down. This realtor and his brother-partner had been in Morrison's scopes for some time. The detective was tipped that their house movers were moving more than furniture. They were also moving cases of illegal beer and liquor, using vacant properties as showrooms and depots. It was convenient for them and difficult for the cops to follow. But Morrison was patient, and he knew how minds like this worked. He had watched, saw the pattern, tracked their routine, and let them dig themselves in deeper before swooping in. He'd informed the brothers that he had enough evidence to send them to court on numerous charges, and that this little bit of embarrassment would likely cost them the business they inherited from Daddy, who would probably also cut them loose. What did Morrison want? For the price of leaving them alone he wanted access to the same vacant properties for brief periods, and the occasional case of rye.

"What are you going to use the properties for?" one of the brothers had asked.

"Yeah, we're still responsible."

"Official police business," had been Morrison's reply. He thought that should be more than enough for them.

In actual fact the properties were being used for anything other than official police business. Morrison had his own apartment downtown, but he liked to keep it clean, meaning there was never any booze there; he did not arm-in-arm any women by; he never invited any other police over; and he did not bring any of the petty thieves, drug addicts, and smugglers he kept company with over for sodas. He needed another location or, even better, a succession of temporary ones. That's where the realtors came in.

The dwelling upstairs could be accessed either by the stairs at the side of the building or through the store, and there were two ways to enter the store: through the front door or the receiving door out back. Morrison always used the latter.

He resisted the temptation to look over his shoulder while he rummaged through his pockets for the keys. He visited the place during the day infrequently, doing so only to keep up the appearance of a legit operation. The store was empty save for the fixtures. The entire inventory had been sold off. The only things on the shelves were dust halos where the cans used to be.

Creaking stairs carried Morrison up to the apartment. It was furnished with the basics, ready to show. He checked his watch. His friend should be downtown by now, delivering the coded message in the crossword. He should be getting a phone call shortly. He removed his hat and peeled off his overcoat, tossing them on the chesterfield. There was a bottle in the cupboard above the stove and a dirty tumbler in the sink. He poured himself three fingers and, with the bottle still in hand, went to the window overlooking the street. It was a nice neighbourhood. He let himself become distracted by passersby and wondered what might be occupying their minds. He used to feel like he was getting closer to people, getting to know their hearts and minds, but lately he was feeling like he was drifting even further away. He wondered if he might be losing sight of things. The small part of him that was still a detective, enforcing the law and cracking cases, suddenly felt a little disappointed in himself. He shook it off.

Times change, people change.

He tossed back what was left in the tumbler, poured another, and sat himself down next to the phone, setting the bottle on the floor. There would be no conversation. There didn't need to be. He could tell when a caller was either nodding or shaking their head.

Chapter 15

THE BLACK CANDLE

Campbell's latest printed and bound acquisition was a copy of Emily Murphy's *The Black Candle*. He had left a special order for it at the store and as it turned out, a fellow bookmonger of Copeland's in Detroit had a slightly used edition taking up space on one of his shelves. Booksellers in the Border Cities and on the other side of the river often helped each other out when it came to their customers' wants and needs. Agreements were made over long lunches and sometimes short reaches under the table — meaning open agreements were occasionally superseded by offerings mentioned on notes tucked between the pages of books: *A customer recently brought a certain title to my attention. I thought it might be a welcome addition....* Booklegging could sometimes be a more profitable sideline.

The detective had been up all night reading *The Black Candle* and now flipped back and forth, rereading passages he had flagged with little yellow slips he always had at the ready. Slips for the most important passages got a dot of LePage's on them to hold them in place. Having just run out of the yellow pads he'd been lifting from the department, he now resorted to strips cut from faded envelopes from the bottom of his desk drawer.

Letters unwritten, letters never sent.

After rereading the first section of the book, he turned back to the preface. He tended to read in loops, and was even known to occasionally read a book from back to front.

> Six years ago, when appointed a Police Magistrate and Judge of the Juvenile Court of Edmonton, the capital city of the province of Alberta, I was astonished to learn that there was an illicit traffic in the narcotic drugs of which I had been almost unaware, and of which the public was unaware.

Campbell jumped ahead.

> Although there are over two million drug addicts on the North American Continent, and a vast outnumbered army who live by exploiting them, I cannot find that any volume dealing with the subject generally has ever been published.

He set the book down, lit another cigarette, and watched the dawn light creep over the still river, smooth as glass and unsuspecting. Purples and oranges were in a fierce competition on the horizon. It was Campbell's favourite kind of morning. The switch in his table lamp was broken, so in order to turn it off he had to unscrew the bulb. The only thing that kept him from a good first-degree burn was spit and a greasy handkerchief. He pivoted his chair away from the window, propped the book up on his chest, and continued reading.

> All honest men and orderly persons should rightly know that there are men and women who batten and fatten on the agony of the unfortunate drug-addicted-palmerworms ...

He lifted his gaze from the page for a moment, letting it float in the middle of the room. *Locusts?*

> ... and human caterpillars who should be trodden underfoot like the despicable grubs that they are.

Maybe what we need is an insecticide, thought Campbell.

> And all the folk of gentle and open hearts should know that among us there are girls and glorious lads who, without any obliquity in themselves have become victims to the thrall of opiates ...

And thus endeth the sermon. Campbell paused to rub his tired eyes and then brought them back into focus by playing them around the staggered piles of books rising from the floor. His thoughts turned to bookcases and how he could ever possibly manage to get one up the stairs.

If I could assemble them in the apartment ... why couldn't it be done? So simple. Focus now, focus, focus ...

> It was found that opium was being brought to America in chests of tea; in coal-bunkers; in the beams of the vessels; under the stairways; behind panels in the saloon; in water-tanks, and even in the ship's piano. Sometimes, it was smuggled by means of nutshells ...

This was beginning to sound vaguely familiar to Campbell. How soon, he wondered, before we went from nutshells to piano cases filled with tins of the stuff.

He could hear a body coming to life on the other side of the shared wall, rising with the sun, shuffling about, and hitting the shower.

Theobald, Edmond, machinist ... at least according to Vernon's city directory. Now back to Ms. Murphy.

He adjusted the book on his chest until it rested on a shirt button.

> Chapter IV: Opium.
> Opium is the juice of the white poppy (*papaver somniferum*) and is the sap which exudes from incisions made on the outside of the capsules when they have attained their full growth after the fall of the petals. The poppy was well known to ancients, its cultivation mentioned by Homer, and its medicinal properties by Hippocrates.

Morphine is an alkaloid of opium — that is to say, its active vegetable principle having alkaline properties.

Codein is a derivative of opium.

Opium and its derivatives are distinguished by a flavour that is acrid, nauseous, and bitter.

Opium is smoked, morphine is taken hypodermically, or by the mouth. Hypodermic injections are more favoured by the users of this particular drug in that they become intoxicated without the disagreeable effects of the substance. Then, too, when morphine is swallowed, it takes longer to produce its solacing effect.

Contrariwise, the use of the hypodermic needle is attended with dangers from an infected solution or from a dirty needle. Frequently, morphine habitués will insert the needle into their arms without the precaution of rolling up their sleeves. This infection results in the form of abscesses.

Surely, thought Campbell, *Laforet would have read about this in the medical journals.*

He wondered if the doctor had already treated any such cases. He should inquire. Still, there are the clouds and fog that descend upon —

"The unknown users." The words came out of him like a breath. He read on.

Last year, a young bride of three months who had married an addict, and had herself become one, was charged with having opium in her possession unlawfully.

During the trial, she became hysterical and began to beg piteously for morphine of which she had been deprived from the day previously. She complained of intense neuralgia, chills, thirst and abdominal pains. Finally she collapsed. Surely, the soul of her was "full of scorpions."

Campbell set the book down again, got up, and stood at the window as if he had been commanded to. He blew smoke at the glass and flicked some ash into the saucer perched on the radiator grill. He looked down at Arthur Street, not exactly new to him but not quite home, seeing men in their factory clothes, half of them stoop-shouldered, feet dragging, coming home from their shifts; the other half moving in the opposite direction, clean and dry, bright-eyed and caffeinated, ready for endless hours of repetitive motion. Campbell wondered how they did it. He tilted his lean frame over the radiator, rested his forehead against the windowpane, and let his arms dangle. He stared down at what passed for a garden.

I don't know how they can tell what's a weed or not. Weeds flower, too.

He had forgotten about the lit cigarette in his hand. He twisted what was left of it into the saucer, hot ash mingling with cold, and returned to his study of the garden, though he could feel his interest fading. Back to Ms. Murphy's opium den.

That this Ring has its runners directly across Canada is evidenced by a communication received recently from Chief-Constable William Thompson of Windsor, Ontario. "There is," he says, "every evidence that there is a drug organization from the continuous endeavors to transport drugs from Montreal to border cities, and across the line to American cities, namely Detroit, Pontiac, and other places within close range of our border. I also had information to the effect that 'dope' crosses at our own border and is taken through to Chicago."

This statement is borne out by Sergeant A. Birtwhistle of the Royal Canadian Mounted Police who declares that prominent men in commercial and club life in Windsor are at the head of a Ring which is supplying drugs to peddlers. It is altogether likely that these men receive the bulk of their supplies from Montreal as suggested by Chief-Constable Thompson.

Campbell tucked another strip of yellowed envelope between the pages and closed the book. He needed another coffee. He made his way to the kitchenette, opened the lid of the coffee can, closed his eyes, and took a whiff.

Acceptable.

He got the Flavodrip going and stood over it while it made its gurgling noises and blew off steam, and then he looked around the kitchenette. He was thinking that he could put all of these cups, plates, pots, and pans in the bathtub, fill it with hot, soapy water, let them soak, drain the tub, and then run the shower over them. He could clean the place up.

Yes, he thought, *that just might work. And after that, I could start having my dinners delivered to me, a minor inconvenience for the establishment, but maybe a small gratuity would make it worth their while.*

His lack of sleep was starting to catch up to him. He refilled his cup and made his way back to the table, already a little brighter than when he left it. The morning sun climbed quickly this time of year, eager to get the show on the road.

> It is said that the ringleaders' names in Montreal were obtained through the death-bed confession of Mrs. William Bruce, aged 24 of that city in February of this year.
>
> Mrs. Bruce and her friend, Dorothea Wardell, aged 21, were found unconscious on the Montreal express, near New York City, by a Pullman porter, suffering from overdoses of heroin.

Campbell gently blew ripples across the surface of the hot, black brew, took a sip, and set the cup down. He then reached for his cigarettes and got one going with his trusty Ronson. He stared at the flame for a moment, thinking about the spoon and the needle. And then he studied the smoke twirling up from the glowing tip of his Player's. He was having a flashback, back to his childhood.

"What's the last thing you remember?"

The faces in the wallpaper.

Campbell wondered if the drugged state was like having a fever, falling asleep, silhouettes swimming, flying all around you, and then waking up in a crisp, colourless hospital ward, lying in a pool of one's own sweat.

> The girls received emergency treatment but the Wardell girl died on the way to the Bellevue hospital.

Mrs. Bruce recovered sufficiently to tell
her story to the deputy-police commissioner in
charge of the drug squad.

Campbell thought he might have had more in him, but this
was enough for now. That part of his brain, whatever it was, was
winding down now. He closed the book and finished his coffee
and cigarette over the view of the river. He looked east. The
orange shades had won out, and the first vessel of the morning
was making its way into the strait.

Like a pair of shears cutting through satin, he thought.

It looked to be a canal freighter, long and low. Campbell set
his cup down and grabbed his binoculars off the windowsill. He
wondered what she might be carrying. There appeared to be a
few men on deck, and seeing how they already seemed to be busy
with their tasks, he thought he ought to get moving. He set the
lenses back down and made his way towards the bathroom. Time
to shower and start the day, try and turn it into something, or at
least get something out of it.

"Flower of dreams," he muttered to himself as he unbuttoned
his shirt.

Smuggled in a nutshell.

When he removed his trousers he could almost stand them
up. It was time to send them to the cleaners. He dialed up some
water from the taps and let it warm before stepping behind the
curtain and letting the water run over him. Rubbing himself with
the bar soap, he stretched out his arm and considered the blue
veins inside his elbow. When the steam came, he lay down on the
floor of the tub, eyes closed.

Morpheus. And what about the insomnia, the sleep deprivation?
He wondered. *What does it, can it do to one's brain?*

He opened his eyes.

One begins to see things.

He closed them again, and tried to focus on the sound and feeling of the water on his skin. He began to drift.

Cold water — the hot having run out — woke him a few minutes later. He turned off the taps and looked for the time on his bare wrist.

Damn.

He managed to climb out of the tub without slipping on the floor.

Chapter 16

THE SNAKE ISLAND GANG

McCloskey figured the smugglers had to be operating in a thinly populated area somewhere downriver, so they started their search in Ojibway. The three of them — McCloskey at the wheel, Quan with his elbow out the passenger window, and Li-Ling wedged between them — slowly cruised south along Front Road.

A map was stretched across the dashboard. McCloskey had picked it up at a roadside stand advertising fresh produce and live bait. The exposed section featured details of the shoreline and islands along the length of the river from Sandwich all the way down to Lake Erie.

The first landmark McCloskey came upon was his family homestead. The yard had become so overgrown he almost missed it. He stole a few quick glances through the gaps in the scrub. It was boarded up, safe and sound, though probably a warren for any variety locals, two legs or more. The front porch appeared to be intact but in need of some attention, as did the roof.

Maybe some other time, he thought.

McCloskey told Li-Ling to ask Quan to point out anything that looked even remotely familiar — a barn, a shed, a windmill, a bend in the road, a canal, anything. The problem was that so much of it looked the same, especially if you weren't from these parts. And if you were from here, you might be of even less help because it could be like driving through the same daydream over and over again.

Betsy chugged along. McCloskey had to wave ahead every vehicle that came up behind them. Even a truck pulling a trailer stacked with rows of gold-and-green hay bales passed them. This was a little embarrassing for a guy who usually sped around town in a fiery, lightweight Studebaker. He began to dread the thought of eventually being overtaken by an old lady riding her bicycle to church. To be fair, Betsy was in need of a good tune-up. McCloskey would get Mud on that as soon as they got back into town.

"Ask Quan again if he recognizes anything."

Li-Ling asked and Quan just shook his head.

McCloskey was beginning to wonder if they had any real chance of finding his target. "He did see the place in the day, right? I mean, when it was light out?" The bootlegger was still getting used to the idea of his young protege not always grasping his rapid-fire speech or certain turns of phrase. Also, as quick of a study as Quan was, he was still a little self-conscious about his accent.

Li-Ling rephrased the question for Quan.

"Yes, Jack," replied Quan.

McCloskey smiled and kept rolling along, past strip farm after strip farm, neat little rows of corn and what looked to be radishes running from the road all the way to the river. Approaching LaSalle, Front took a bend and you could make out the head of Fighting Island about a mile downriver. McCloskey pointed across the dashboard. "Okay, ask him if he recognizes that island."

Li-Ling asked Quan. He squinted at it, examined his surroundings again, and shook his head.

"Tell him to keep a close eye on the island and the farms along the shore here." Smugglers, like McCloskey and his boys, liked to work the long ribbons of islands that cleaved the river into channels from here to the lake.

The land between the road and the water began to narrow, lending some variety to the landscape. McCloskey thought that might help. It was also a little more picturesque. If he had a cameraman perched on Betsy's flatbed they could be making a nice travel reel for Pathé right now. They passed through LaSalle.

"Ask Quan how long he was in the boat. Was he in it for a long time?"

"He says shorter than China."

"*Shorter than China.*" McCloskey could tell Quan and Li-Ling were losing interest. If Quan's English was better, McCloskey could be teaching them a camp song to pass the time. McCloskey spotted the head of Grass Island. On the map it resembled the head of a great water snake slithering between Fighting Island and the shore. He nudged Li-Ling and pointed. She in turn nudged Quan.

"What about that island?"

Quan squinted at it. He shook his head. And then he looked again.

McCloskey had the feeling Quan recognized something. He had an idea. "Li-Ling, tell Quan to watch out the back window."

Quan gave McCloskey a curious look and then complied.

McCloskey kept glancing over at him. Quan seemed to be staring intently, examining his surroundings with new interest. It had occurred to McCloskey that it might be more likely that Quan had seen the property as he approached from the south, not coming from the north out of the Border Cities or west from inside the county. When they crossed the little bridge over Marentette Drain, Quan started bouncing in his seat. He stuck his head out the window, repeating the same phrase over and over again.

"Jack — Quan says it is here."

"Where?" asked McCloskey, gearing Betsy down to a crawl.

Quan discreetly pointed towards a farmhouse in the distance, closer to the shore.

"Are you sure, Quan?"

Quan turned to McCloskey and nodded. He suddenly looked paler. This place meant something to him. McCloskey stopped, looked up and down the road, and examined the property. No one seemed to be around; it was dead quiet, except for the sound of ducks overhead. A dirt path bordered by wild-looking shrubs lead from the road to the house.

"Li-Ling, there's a canvas on the flatbed. I want you to get under it."

She climbed down out of the truck and up onto the flatbed. The canvas smelled of motor oil and stable. She held onto the pickets, making sure she still had a view outside. McCloskey reversed and then turned up the path. Tall weeds brushed the underside of the truck while shrub branches scraped the sides. *This is a lot of cover*, he thought to himself.

He had a clear view of the house now. It was smaller than his family's, and maybe a little newer. Still, an old clapboard box covered in peeling paint covered in dead fishflies. The path skirted the house and appeared to go all the way to the shore, presumably to a dock. McCloskey pointed to the house and said to Quan, "Here?" Quan nodded. Then, touching the boy's shoulder, he gestured to Quan to get down under the dashboard.

McCloskey stepped out of the truck and checked inside the front panel of his greasy overalls. He had cut a hole in the bottom left-hand corner of the large pocket, just wide enough to accommodate the barrel of his Webley. His cover would be that he was answering a call to either pick up some unwanted auto parts or chop a vehicle on-site; he hadn't decided yet. He pulled his cap down further, walked up the verandah, opened the screen door, and gave the solid one hanging behind it a few quick raps. No answer. He repeated. Still no answer. It was unlocked so he let himself in.

Men live here, and only men, thought McCloskey. The signs were obvious. In the front room there was a ratty chesterfield and a low table covered in dirty dishes and spoons standing in open cans, with flies darting all around. The next room was a small dining room with a table covered in a pyramid of boxes. There was clothing strewn about. McCloskey stepped lightly through this room and into the kitchen. Strangely, there was no evidence of food here. An empty sideboard, an icebox, a long table in the middle of the room with several empty Mason jars scattered about, a map on the wall, and a what looked to be mail bags piled in the corner. This looked like it might be the strategy room. McCloskey heard a screen door open behind him.

"Who the hell are you?"

McCloskey turned. "I'm here to chop the T."

"The what?" asked the young man, a stoop-shouldered beanpole in long johns and rubber boots.

"Border Cities Wrecking and Salvage. We got a call from a place fitting this description saying they had a Model T they wanted chopped and hauled away."

"We ain't got no T, and I don't know no Border Cities ..."

"Wrecking and Salvage. You sure?"

"Sure I'm sure."

At that point the man stuck his head out the back door.

"Perc! Perc, did you put word out about an auto parts pickup or the like?"

The man shook his head, mumbled something, and then went out the door. McCloskey followed. He needed to learn a little more about these guys.

There was a narrow stretch of ground not more than eight or ten yards long sticking out into the river, with a slip on either side and a boat in each — a low-slung skiff on the left and an outboard on the right. He looked up and down the shore and saw much of the same.

"Who are you?" asked Perc.

"Jake, from Border Cities Wrecking and Salvage. Like I was telling your cousin here, we got a call to come out and chop an old T for the price of a cold beer." McCloskey was taking a shot in the dark with the beer remark.

"Don't know nothing about it," said Perc. "And he ain't my cousin."

"Figure of speech," said McCloskey. There was a pause. He let the two continue sizing him up. "I guess I'll have to settle for the cold beer then."

"What makes you think we got beer?" said the first one.

"Seems natural, I guess," said McCloskey, looking around. They were getting suspicious, and rightly so, he thought.

"Tommy, why don't you fix our man here up with an ale?"

Tommy left the scene and entered the cellar below the house by way of two big wooden doors.

"You're from the city," said Perc.

"Actually, born and raised just up in Ojibway."

"Huh," said Perc, "practically neighbours."

Perc was eyeing McCloskey but good now. Tommy resurfaced.

"Here you go … uh …"

"Jake."

"Right, Jake."

McCloskey took a swig from the bottle. "I suspect you boys see a lot of action around here."

"More questions," said Perc.

"Only making conversation," said McCloskey. "If there were any, well, that's something I might like to get in on. I know the shore … and I got connections in town."

"What kind of action you looking for?" said Tommy.

"The same kind of action my pa was into. You know, moving things."

"Moving things," said Perc, rubbing the bristle on his chin with the back of his hand.

Perc and Tommy sat themselves down on two of several milk crates set in a circle around a small firepit dug in the sandy earth and started a quiet discussion between them. McCloskey wondered how Quan and Li-Ling were holding up. He'd have to move this along. He finished his beer, tossed it into the ashes of the firepit and reached in his overalls for his weapon. He pulled it out and started waving it around like it was nothing. The boys' jaws suddenly hung loose.

"Now, before we enter into any kind of an agreement, I'd like to have a tour of the facilities."

The men froze.

"Stand up, boys, I got people waiting for me. Oh, by the way, this is a Webley .455. It makes a big noise and even bigger holes. Make one wrong move and it'll all be behind you." Alternating the barrel between the two men, McCloskey turned his head toward the front of the house. "Quan!" He waited and then shouted again, "Quan Lee!"

Quan tentatively came around the side of the house. He saw McCloskey holding the gun, and the two men who had taken him for his boat cruise.

"These men?"

Quan nodded. Judging by the expression on Quan's face, there was no doubt in McCloskey's mind.

"Okay, boys, take me on a tour of your cellar. C'mon now," said McCloskey, waving his artillery, "don't be testing my patience. You, the uglier one, you lead the way." There was a split-second beauty contest and then Perc — inarguably the ugliest of the two owing mostly to a shortage of teeth and a lack of hygiene — lost out. He rose first and led the way. Tommy, standing tall now in his long johns and rubber boots, McCloskey, and Quan followed close behind.

Sturdy wooden stairs led down to a dirt floor partially covered with pallets. A few bare bulbs hung from the ceiling. There were several cases of beer, more mailbags, and more opened cans with spoons standing in them.

"How's business?"

"We do all right," said Perc.

"Shut up, frog lips," said Tommy.

"And when you don't have any beer to move, then what?" said McCloskey.

The two men looked at each other for an answer.

"Recognize my friend here?" McCloskey continued, pointing at Quan.

"I dunno … they all look the same to me," snorted Tommy.

"This is funny?" said McCloskey. "As funny as how he recognized the house and you two? You greasy sons of bitches who robbed him and his travelling companion of their money, took them for a ride in your outboard, and dumped them in the river somewhere near the Westwood. Quan here made it to shore. His buddy didn't. How much was that worth to you?"

Silence. The two smugglers just glanced back and forth at each other. McCloskey fired a round into the pallet they were standing on and sent some wood chips flying. Quan jumped. It was so loud it caused dust to fall from the ceiling.

"Fifty bucks," said Tommy.

"Each?"

"Each," said Perc.

"Okay, let's start there. I'll take a hundred bucks — and I don't accept cheques or promissory notes."

"We don't have it," said Tommy.

Another round, this time between their heads and into the exposed brick behind them. There were flying chips of masonry. The two slack-jaws blinked this time.

"I figure you're at least smart enough not to keep your profits and working capital up in the house, so it must be down here somewhere, maybe in one of these cans. Get it, or I blow a hole through those cases of beer — your only real assets."

Perc fetched a coffee can down from one of the many shelves. The bills were loose, just jammed inside. Perc peeled out what amounted to a hundred dollars and handed it to McCloskey.

"Good. Half for Quan, and half for the Chinese Nationalist League. Now, I'll take the beer."

"What?" said Tommy.

"Each of you grab a case. I've got my truck parked out front."

"That's not fair play," said Perc.

"Yeah," said Tommy, "you got your refund on the yellow coons, so how do you figure on the beer?"

"Compensation."

"What?" said Perc.

"This has been a distraction, boys, keeping me a little too far from my day-to-day, if you know what I mean. I'm feeling the loss in my pockets. This is compensation for my time and trouble." He stooped to pick up two of the mail bags. "Now get moving."

McCloskey waved the Webley around a bit more and got the brothers moving. When they reached the truck with the first load McCloskey pulled back the canvas.

"C'mon down, Li-Ling. Everything's fine."

"Another one?" said Perc. "They're overrunning the county."

"Go get the rest of the beer, you two. Li-Ling, come out back with us. I want to make sure Quan knows what's happening."

Li-Ling looked unsure about what to make of any of this.

When they finished loading the beer onto the truck, McCloskey asked Li-Ling and Quan to cover it with the canvas and secure it with ropes and chains.

"Now let's have a look at your watercraft." McCloskey marched the two men back out to the slips and Quan and Li-Ling followed. "Ask Quan which boat it was."

Quan pointed to the outboard, confirming McCloskey's hunch.

McCloskey blasted a hole through the hull of the other, the skiff, and it immediately began to take water.

"Shit," said Tommy.

McCloskey tossed the mail bags into the outboard. "Get into the boat and climb in the bags."

"What?" asked Perc.

McCloskey raised the Webley. "You heard me."

The two men climbed into the boat. McCloskey handed the weapon to Quan and Quan's hands trembled. When the boys were in the bags, McCloskey climbed in and pulled the drawstrings tightly over their heads.

"What're you doing?" asked Tommy.

"Yeah," said Perc.

McCloskey started the outboard and climbed back out. He took the Webley back from Quan, who looked grateful to get it out of his hands. Li-Ling and Quan watched McCloskey take aim at the two men. Quan reached out to hold Li-Ling, shaking his head. Li-Ling looked away.

McCloskey fired, and put a hole in the boat.

"What the hell was that?" shouted one of the men.

"The hole is about one inch above water level. It's going to take a little work to get out of those mail bags, so don't rock the boat too much and you might make it." McCloskey aimed the boat downriver and gave it a push. He then tucked the Webley back in his overalls and turned back to Li-Ling and Quan.

"You two hungry? Because I could eat."

Quan Lee and Li-Ling just looked at each other.

"I bet you never had grilled corn on the cob. C'mon, I know a place."

They boarded the truck and took the same positions on the bench. McCloskey was twisting the steering wheel in his grip, and he could feel Quan's and Li-Ling's eyes on him. They were asking the same question he was asking himself.

Why? Why did we go this far?

He was seeing it more and more, the angel on his right shoulder and the devil on his left.

Defend them, said one.

Take the city, said the other.

Chapter 17

THE WEDDING PLANNER(S)

Uncle Fred, Mrs. Cattanach, Vera Maude, and Lew were seating themselves around the dining room table at Uncle Fred's, to the sounds of shoes shuffling and then chairs settling into position.

"So, like I told you," started Vera Maude, "I've enlisted the aid of Lew here to help us out with a few details; the flowers, for instance. He's also got some experience with certain aspects of the wedding ceremony."

Not with anyone older than Confederation, thought Lew. "You both must be very excited. I'm glad to assist in any way that I can." He smiled, trying to calm those who appeared uneasy. That included just about everyone.

"I'll be overseeing everything," added Vera Maude. "You will both have final approval, of course."

The groom looked like he already had pre-wedding jitters, even though he was the one who had proposed. Mrs. Cattanach appeared calm on the surface but her gentle hand-wringing was giving her away.

Lew was searching for ways to bring it back to the couple and their bond. "May I see the ring?" he asked.

Mrs. Cattanach looked at Uncle Fred, who nodded, and then held her hand out toward Lew. He didn't touch it; he just held his gaze on the band.

Simple, but tasteful, thought Lew. "Lovely, quite lovely. May I ask where you got it?"

"Sansburn-Pashley. I bring them my pocket watch occasionally for cleaning, and I had been admiring this bit for some time."

This bit.

Mrs. Cattanach cleared her throat. "Maybe I should make us some tea before we get started."

"That would be nice," said her fiancé.

Vera Maude and Lew each chimed with a "Yes."

Off went Mrs. Cattanach into the kitchen. They listened to the clatter of chinaware and spoons for a moment before Uncle Fred broke in with "So, Lew, I understand you work at the bookstore with Vera Maude."

"Yes," said Lew, smiling, "partners in crime, I guess one could say."

"Crime?"

"Just an expression, Uncle Fred."

"Right." Uncle Fred paused. "You say you have some experience with this sort of thing? Married, are you? Or maybe you have a special someone in your life?"

Vera Maude and Lew caught each other mid-glance.

"Married? No," said Lew. "And as far as that special someone, well there's always someone special just around the corner, isn't there?"

Lew felt a gentle tap on his shin. Before he could return the favour to Vera Maude, Mrs. Cattanach arrived just in time with her tray of tea paraphernalia.

"Ah," said Uncle Fred, rubbing his hands together. "Let me pour."

Lew let his eyes wander. It was a modest apartment, but it had certain effects that seemed to catch his attention, though he didn't, and wouldn't, say as much — the lace over the linen tablecloth, the curio cabinet wedged in the corner, the plate rail that ran just below the ceiling, to name a few.

"Very nice, very homey, Mr. Maguire," said Lew.

"Oh, why thank you, Lew. Though I can't take all the credit, you know," he said, glancing at Mrs. Cattanach. "And please, call me Fred."

"Vera Maude," said Mrs. Cattanach, "I know you only take sugar. Lew? Cream?"

"No, thank you, nothing in mine," said Lew. "Now," he began, "I understand that both the ceremony and the reception are to take place at St. Andrew's. Is that correct?"

"That it is," said Uncle Fred.

"We had originally wanted something simpler," said the bride-to-be, "maybe at a friend's house, maybe at one of Fred's niece's or nephew's in the county, but when Reverend Paulin heard about our plans, well, he insisted. You see, I do a lot of work for the church."

"Ah," said Lew. "And the date?" He pulled his notebook out of his jacket pocket.

"That would be Saturday, September first," said Uncle Fred.

Lew jotted that down. "And there's going to be a luncheon?"

"Something relaxed and informal," said Uncle Fred, "like a church picnic."

Lew stopped his pencil. "Outdoors? You're not concerned about the weather?"

"Well, I suppose we could take it inside if we had to." Uncle Fred looked at Mrs. Cattanach. "Right?"

"Yes," she nodded, "certainly."

"It's always good to have a plan B," said Lew. "And how many are you expecting? Have invitations gone out? People do make plans quickly for the last weekend of the summer, you know."

Vera Maude stepped in. "Um, no, invitations have not gone out just yet. And Lew, remember you and I talked numbers and I said about forty."

"Forty?" repeated Uncle Fred, setting down his teacup. "Who are they?"

"Well," said Vera Maude, "I was thinking about family, and friends of Mrs. Cattanach's from the church … too many?"

Uncle Fred looked at Mrs. Cattanach. "I guess we should give that some more thought."

"The sooner the better," said Lew. He made a few more notes before continuing. "I've brought some things for you to look at." He unzipped the satchel resting on his lap and pulled out what looked to be a portfolio, setting it on the table. "Let's talk bridal bouquet first." He looked at Mrs. Cattanach. "Would that be all right?"

"Yes, of course," she said and took a sip of her sugary cream with a hint of orange pekoe.

Uncle Fred slid the tea tray further down the table, leaving Lew enough room to open the portfolio and lay it flat in front of Mrs. Cattanach. Inside were loose sheets of hand-coloured florist sample images.

"Now, roses, of course, standard issue. But what I've been hearing and seeing a lot of lately is Ophelia roses mixed with lily of the valley."

"I like those," said Vera Maude.

"Yes, those are nice," agreed Mrs. Cattanach.

"Of course we wouldn't want anything to clash with your gown. Did you have anything in mind?" asked Lew.

"Well, I was thinking of just wearing my —"

"May I suggest a crepe de Chine? That's also something we're seeing a lot of this season. For a colour, how do you feel about salmon pink?" Lew also had some images of dresses in the portfolio. He pulled them out. "Oh, that reminds me — we should also open a discussion about the menu and the cake."

"We should?" said Vera Maude in a whisper and barely moving her lips.

It was beginning to sound to Uncle Fred like they were planning a grand ball. "Um, Lew, how much is this going to cost?" Someone had to ask.

"Not to worry, Fred. I can get you some deals."

"Lew," Vera Maude said, "why don't we save the menu and the cake for our next meeting? I think we've left the bride- and groom-to-be with enough to look over and think about."

"Yes," agreed Mrs. Cattanach, "certainly a lot to think about."

Lew managed to hide most of his disappointment. "Of course," he said, closing the portfolio. "I'll leave this with you."

"That's no trouble?" asked Uncle Fred.

"Not at all."

"More tea?" asked Mrs. Cattanach.

"Not for me," said Vera Maude.

"Me neither," said Lew, "but thank you."

"It was a long day at the store," said Vera Maude, "and I'm fading here."

"Yes," said Lew, "the place was a madhouse. Mondays can be like that. Thanks for the tea, Mrs. Cattanach and enjoy your evening, you two."

Vera Maude got up first and walked Lew down the stairs to the front door.

"Lew, you need to try to slow things down a little here before Uncle Fred and Mrs. Cattanach call the whole thing off or elope to Niagara Falls."

"Too much too fast?"

She nodded slowly. He looked slightly crestfallen.

"I'm sorry. I just get so excited."

"You're very sweet."

He smiled and said, "It's going to be wonderful."

"I know it will," she said. "And I'll have you to thank."

"Talk to you tomorrow?"

"Talk to you tomorrow."

Chapter 18

YOUR RIDE JUST LEFT

Business was booming at Border Cities Wrecking and Salvage and that could make for some interesting challenges, as in the boys were having difficulty balancing supplies of liquor and auto parts. In any given week it could flow either way. The preference was to have more parts than booze, otherwise their front organization would start looking like just that.

"We've got a cellar full of rye we have to move," said Shorty. "We can't just have it lying around like this, not when we've got customers waiting and cops sniffing around like they have been lately. I don't know what's brought them around all of a sudden."

"We've probably just been added to their rotation," said Gorski.

"We need more parts — and quality stuff this time."

"Quality stuff?" asked Mud. "Why *quality stuff*?"

Mud and Shorty were facing off, as they often did, from opposite ends of the long workbench.

"Because our contacts are telling us that when we're shipping crap parts it looks a bit too much like packing material, which we all know it pretty much is, but that's not the point."

"So what do they want?" said Mud.

"No Fords," said Shorty, "at least not for a little while. They want to see some high-end stuff in the mix, and newish."

"And where are we supposed to get that?" said Gorski.

"Yeah," said Mud. "Buy the cars off the dealer's lot? There go the profits, so you know we won't be going down that road. Then … what?"

Shorty was thinking, pacing around the greasy workshop. And then his dashboard lit up. "No, we go to the roadhouses, the racetracks, and look for Michigan plates … no, forget the racetracks … we have to do it at night."

"And when a car gets reported stolen, where's one of the first places the cops look?" said Gorski.

"We bring our catch straight back here — no joyrides — and we chop it up, pronto. Maybe we can count on them not reporting it if they've just come staggering out of a roadhouse smelling like a distillery. Mud, you know how to boost a high-end Studebaker?"

"With my eyes tied behind my back."

It was no secret that the majority of auto thefts were perpetrated by Detroit-area autoworkers. Boys easily distracted by shiny objects. All they needed was one minute and a few inches of wire. Almost none were stolen for keeps — many were resold — the rest, well, joyrides and chop shops.

"All right," said Shorty, "we'll leave here at ten. Gorski, you stay here and have the fence out back ready for when you hear us come knocking."

Shorty and Mud decided to try their luck first at the Island View Hotel. They would take Riverside Drive east to the edge of the city, make their score, and then wind their way back, first through side roads and then the back streets into the city's heart. There would be no speeding.

The parking lot was jammed with vehicles large and small, old and new. Mud felt like a kid in a candy store. They didn't see any Studebakers, but they did spot a sweet-looking Packard with Michigan plates parked near the Drive.

"Yeah," said Shorty, "that one. You think you can do it?"

Mud was rubbing his chin. "This year's model ... lemme see."

Shorty watched his back. All of the action seemed to be inside: no one out for some fresh air, no petting parties, and no security detail. *That might change after tonight*, thought Shorty.

It took a minute but as soon as Mud got the engine going he didn't hesitate, settling in and motoring it as smoothly and quietly as he could out of its space. Shorty approached, Mud gave him the thumbs-up and the former jumped back in his own vehicle and followed Mud out of the lot and onto the Drive. Mud then geared up and lit a cigarette.

"Sorry, I have to do this."

It was dawn; McCloskey had been out all night but wanted to check on things before cruising back to his apartment and sleeping the morning away.

"What the ...?"

"We scored some parts," said Shorty, smiling, "the kind of stuff the clients have been asking for." He and Gorski were standing there in their dirty shirtsleeves, each with a wrench in hand, sweat streaming down their grease-smudged faces. Mud Thomson was the only one of them who had his own pair of overalls — having actually worked in a factory — and looked, as always, like he was trying to keep his cool.

The parts were strewn about the floor and hanging from the rafters on hooks. Auto carnage. A butcher's shop cutting up rubber, glass, lead, and steel.

"What was it?" said McCloskey.

"A Packard." Shorty smiled.

McCloskey hesitated. "Where'd you get it?"

"The parking lot at the Island View."

"You stole a brand new car?" McCloskey was examining the parts like a meat inspector, wondering why he had a bad feeling about this. "This can't be all of it. Where's the rest?"

"The less easily identifiable parts are hidden in the yard," said Shorty, "and the panels, bumpers — the exterior parts — are in the cellar."

"Are the crates ready?"

"Ready," said Shorty.

"How many?"

"Six, maybe seven, depending."

"All right," said McCloskey, "let's get that rye out the door, and all the parts you can fit in the crates."

A few hours later McCloskey came storming back into the shop. He unfolded the newspaper he had in his hand and, flipping to The Third Page, said, "Did you guys say you got that car at the Island View?"

"Yeah," said Mud.

"Do you know who it belonged to?" asked McCloskey, looking up from the paper.

"No ... who?" said Shorty.

"A Packard executive's son." McCloskey was searching the column. "Here ... it's right here."

The boys tried to digest this. It was already causing Shorty some pain.

Gorski was the first to speak. "Does he want his car back?"

McCloskey almost hit him on the nose with the rolled-up newspaper. "No, he wants you to send him the odometer reading. Of course he wants his fucking car back."

"He admitted to coming out of a Windsor roadhouse? A well-known joint?" asked Shorty.

"He admitted to meeting with his real estate brokers about buying some property on Riverside Drive," said McCloskey.

"Shit," said Gorski. "What're we gonna do?"

"Did you ship those crates off?"

"Yeah," said Shorty, starting to look a little queasy. "There turned out to be seven."

"A lot left, I bet," said McCloskey.

"A fair bit."

"Well that's a fair bit of trouble then, isn't it, boys? Hey — what'd you do with the seats?"

"They're in my living room," said Gorski.

This time McCloskey did hit him with the rolled-up newspaper.

"At least we moved out all the rye, Jack. And the Packard came free of charge."

McCloskey glanced sideways at Shorty, resisting the temptation to slap him with the newspaper as well, but that wouldn't look good in front of Gorski and Mud, who he outranked. "Let's hope it stays that way," said McCloskey. "Mud, did you claim your trophy?"

Mud hesitated. "Yeah."

"Find out where this guy lives," said McCloskey, "and mail it to him."

Mud collected licence plates.

"We're not pulling anything like that again, right?"

"We were just improvising, Jack."

"I want you to make all of those exterior parts downstairs — everything you couldn't fit in one of our regular shipments — disappear. Here's an idea: tonight, dump those parts off at Windsor Auto Wreck. Make it fast but don't be sloppy. Bring a pair of bolt cutters … and a steak in case they have a dog in their yard. When you're done, phone in an anonymous tip to Windsor Police."

"Will do," said Shorty.

McCloskey stepped out. Shorty was left wondering where Jack's head was right now. Was it that big of a deal? Then he thought maybe it wasn't Jack; maybe it was him. Maybe he was misreading things.

"No more of this *just in time delivery* crap," Shorty said to the room. "Let's start stockpiling parts right now. Get Linc and Jefferson out scavenging some more — but let them know they have to keep it clean or they're out of work. Pay them by the pound of scrap. By the end of next week I want to be tripping over auto parts just to get to the front door."

The place emptied and the crew went to work. Shorty rested his hands on the edge of the workbench and leaned against it, tired, his nose burning from the fumes of the place, his mind just as cluttered. He bunched up the newspaper in his hands and threw it against the wall.

What do you want, Jack?

Chapter 19

ACCIDENTALLY ON PURPOSE

Wednesday, August 8

Campbell was sitting at his desk, going over some notes and examining a new batch of photos from Laforet. He was putting the salt mine case on the backburner and concentrating on what he and the doctor were referring to as "The Case of the Three Arms." He swore to himself he would think of another tag for it by the end of the week.

At least he gave a semblance of concentrating on the papers before him; thoughts of Morrison continued to intrude. Even

McCloskey was asking what Morrison was up to. What made it that much more irksome for Campbell was that, like the branch of a tree, this big question kept leading to a lot of little ones, some of them regarding members of the department.

Something told him that perhaps he should have been paying closer attention to the inner workings and social dynamics of police headquarters. It was true he didn't give his colleagues much consideration and had never gotten chummy with any of them. For one thing, he thought it unprofessional. For another, he had no idea how to go about it. Always the shy and awkward one, he was aware he didn't mix well. He found his own way and just kept to his work, which his superiors must have been satisfied with because he never received any complaints and had never been called on the carpet. He was respectful towards the constables and always seemed to have their full co-operation whenever he needed them. Though there were a few that worked close to the street, like Bickerstaff, with whom he felt a certain affinity. He always made a little more time for those men.

This moment of self-reflection was interrupted by Morrison walking past Campbell's door in the flesh. It was unusual to see him darkening the halls this early in the day. He was becoming the card in a gin game that one kept discarding and somehow kept picking up, over and over again. *Maybe*, Campbell thought, *I should hold on to it this time. What is he up to?*

Campbell had always known that Morrison had a different relationship with the streets than he did. He supposed this in turn meant that Morrison had his own methods and approach. The two of them, thought Campbell, ought to complement each other.

But what if Morrison had other reasons for taking his particular tack? Have I been turning a blind eye towards him? And who else might I have been turning a blind eye to?

He closed his folders, got up from his desk, stretched his back, and headed for the break room. On his way there,

Campbell started thinking maybe he could make a ritual of doing a walkabout through the office every day, combined with a few trips to the break room; approach headquarters the same way he approached the streets of Windsor. It occurred to him how much latitude he was given in regards to his whereabouts. He was never given a hard time about working from home or elsewhere. He wasn't avoiding police headquarters; it was just that so many of his resources were in his apartment, at the library, or on the street.

Maybe they're trying to keep me out of headquarters, on a long leash. Am I right where someone wants me?

More self-doubt. He shook it off.

In the break room there were a few staff and constables chatting together, catching up and sharing stories. He recognized their faces but remembered none of their names. He nodded to the ones that looked his way and said, "Good morning." He made his way over to the coffee station and poured himself a cup. Some of them stopped talking, others continued in a low murmur. What Campbell didn't realize was that he himself was a bit of a mystery to the force, just not one that any of them was interested in solving.

He turned to leave and nodded at those who happened to look his way. He thought he'd take a circuitous route back to his desk and see who else he might run into.

"Morrison."

"Campbell."

They almost walked into each other as they rounded the corner in the hallway. Campbell barely managed to keep from spilling his coffee on Morrison's shirt. Now that he had his attention, Campbell had to think of something to say.

"Sorry about that."

"In some kind of hurry?"

"No, just anxious to get back to my desk. I've got a couple of cases making me itch."

"Oh."

"How about you? Working on anything interesting?"

"Not really," said Morrison.

"Say, I've been reading a lot about the drug smuggling situation. Are you in on any of that?"

"What d'you mean?"

"Well, you've been involved in some of those cases before, I was just wondering if this new wave of activity was something you might be tangled in."

"Tangled?"

"Yes, you know … keeping you busy."

This is isn't going very well, thought Campbell. *How am I going to extricate myself from this before I start sounding like an even bigger fool?*

"The normal busy," said Morrison, "and untangled. I have to make some calls."

"Of course. Don't let me keep you."

The detectives parted. When Campbell got to his office he closed the door, set his coffee mug down, and stood at the window with his hands on his hips. Staring blankly at the intersection below, he reflected on how his first attempt at a hallway conversation might also be his last. He sat behind his desk and re-opened the file folders.

Not interested in my cases, short answers … and did he bristle slightly when I brought up the drug trafficking activity?

Campbell had to try to block Morrison from his mind and focus on the severed arms. He got his magnifying glass out of his top drawer and began to study the new images more closely.

Morrison didn't return to his desk to make any phone calls. Instead he turned around and headed right back out into the street. He needed to think; he also needed to meet with a couple of people. He reached in his coat pocket for his Camels and his matches, and once he got one going he cut over to McDougall, heading straight down toward the river.

What's Campbell up to?

Chapter 20

SUNKEN TREASURE

Shorty was already onto his next scheme: retrieve the cases of rye lost in February when the Model T had fallen through the ice near Fighting Island. All they needed was a boat. Luckily he had a contact out in Kingsville who did some smuggling, island hopping back and forth across Lake Erie to Sandusky. He had a thirty-foot fishing trawler that could probably loosen the T and hoist the cases up. All that Jones — the smuggler — would ask for was a small cut. Shorty would negotiate "small" after they assessed the rescued goods.

They — Shorty, Mud with his tool bag, Gorski, and Linc, their swimmer — drove out to Jones's dock early Wednesday morning. They found him out there doing whatever it was fishermen do with their nets when their nets haven't got fish in them. The vessel had been christened *Last Call* with a bottle of sacramental wine, part of a case that had never made it to church.

"Shorty Morand." Jones extended his hand and Shorty took it, despite the wet and the smell. "How's your boss doing? I haven't seen him in a dog's age."

"You know Jack. He likes to keep busy." Shorty introduced Jones to the rest of the fellows.

"Now, about that 10 percent," said Jones. "I hope I made it clear that that was 10 percent of the street value, not 10 percent of the bottles." Jones knew he couldn't get as much for the bottles as these guys could, what with their living in the city and having the right connections.

No, thought Shorty, *you didn't make that clear, and thanks for bringing it up in front of my boys.*

"Right, 10 percent of street value. Am I supposed to bring you a receipt after we move it all?"

"No need to do that; I'll just check in with Jack."

Shorty could feel the boys' eyes on the back of his head. "Sure," he said, "now let's get moving."

They piled aboard *Last Call* and Jones got the old coal engine going.

Chug chug chug …

"How long do you figure it'll take to get there?" Mud asked Jones.

"About forty minutes. I could do it faster but we don't want to be attracting any attention. It's bad enough that we're sailing in the opposite direction as everyone else."

"I noticed," said Mud as they cruised past Cedar Beach.

When the sun was rising over their starboard side, Shorty knew they were out of Lake Erie and heading upriver. He continued pacing the platform with Mud sitting on his tool bag nearby. Gorski and Linc were on opposite sides of the deck, taking in the view. The only sound right now was the low, steady rumble of *Last Call*'s engine and the bow slicing though the rippling water.

Shorty paused to look over the port side. "Hey … hey, Jones," he said, pointing. "Is that it?"

"No," shouted Jones from the wheelhouse, "that's Bois Blanc. You city boys have to be a little more patient."

"I'll be right back," said Mud. "I want to see this from Jones's point of view." Mud climbed the stairs. The first thing he sighted was a beverage container on the window ledge.

"Hey … what's in the Thermos?"

"Brandy. Help yourself."

"Thanks." Mud unscrewed the top and took a swig from it. He made a face like he just swallowed a mouthful of bleach.

"What the hell kind of brandy is that?"

"Plum. Homemade. Best kind."

Mud looked at the man. "Should I be taking the wheel?"

"No — these waters coming up take some serious navigating. You have to know what to look out for."

They were approaching the Navy Yard in Amherstburg. Jones noticed Shorty with his arm outstretched again, pointing.

"Listen," said Jones, "wanna bet here comes Shorty with more of his fool questions? I told him to only bother himself with the islands on the port side."

"Jones … that one?"

Mud smiled and took another swig from the Thermos.

"No," Jones shouted, "that's Crystal Island. A few more minutes and we'll be there. Relax and enjoy the fresh air, boys."

"What if someone else already got to it?" asked Gorski. "Or it got run over or something?"

"And what if we score, huh?" countered Shorty. He didn't need Gorski bringing everyone down like he so often did.

"There's no harm in trying, is there?" said Linc.

They were all chewing on that when the old man called down again. "River Canard's to your right," he said, "and that means the tail of Fighting Island is what's on your left. The river's gonna narrow as we near the head; I'll be wanting some direction from you boys soon."

Jones slowed *Last Call* and Shorty bound up the stairs to the wheelhouse, which, being more like a closet with three walls, meant that Mud had to return to the deck. "I'm guessing our target is about twenty yards from the island's shore," said Shorty.

"Guessing?"

"It was covered in snow and ice then; it'll hardly look the same now. Can you slow it a little more? Hey, Gorski, Mud: gimme a shout if you recognize anything." They had been with him that morning back in February.

"The T was closer to the island," said Mud.

"I think you're right," said Shorty.

"I can't get much closer," called Jones, "or I'm going to hit that sandbar."

"You see a sandbar?" asked Shorty. "The T took a nosedive into a sandbar."

"Anyone who knows these waters knows about this sandbar. Why, it can't be more than five yards —"

Scrape.

"I think we found her," shouted Mud, pointing directly below the bow.

"Jones, drop anchor before you crush the T and our cargo."

"Out of my way, city boy, and hold the wheel steady."

The old smuggler's feet only touched about three steps on his way down to the deck. He scrambled to the windlass, unlocked it, and let the weight of the anchor do the rest.

"Whoa! Did I just hear a clunk?" Gorski asked.

"Jones!" said Mud.

"What?"

"I think you just dropped the anchor on the T."

"No, no, no ..." moaned Shorty.

They all froze for a moment, gazing down into the not-so-clear waters.

"Yep," said Gorski.

They turned to Linc.

"Good thing I brought my swimming goggles," he said.

"Your what?" Gorski asked.

"They come in handy in this river," said Linc as he pulled them out of the hip pocket of his baggy overalls.

"I don't know from no swimming goggles, but those ..."

"Look like motorcycle goggles," said Mud.

"They are ... or at least they were." Linc smiled and showed them off before donning them. "I replaced the leather strap with a length of rubber fan belt ... and around the edge of the eye cups ... pieces of rubber hose from an old acetylene headlamp."

"Let me see."

Linc handed them to Mud who examined them closely. Gorski leaned in.

"Nice, huh?"

"What did you use to ... I mean ... the adhesive ..."

"I don't know what it is; some concoction I got from a guy downtown who fixes bicycles tires."

"Waterproof?" asked Mud.

"That's what he told me. They've been tested and they work."

"Yeah, nice. You should go into production." Mud looked impressed. He handed them back to Linc.

"So how about a demonstration?" asked Gorski.

"Yeah, Shorty's probably getting a little anxious up there."

"Okay," said Mud, "you're on."

Linc stripped down to his drawers and dropped toes first into the water, hardly disturbing it. The others watched and waited, trying to interpret the shadows and occasional glimmering below.

Their diver surfaced, climbing a narrow length of net that was their ladder. He caught his breath and then delivered his report. "It looks like the anchor dropped into the chassis, not through the body. It's tangled in the suspension and rear axle. The front wheels and most of the hood are buried in weeds and sand."

"And the crates?" Shorty had just come down from the wheelhouse.

"They look solid."

There was a collective sigh of relief.

"All right," said Shorty, "let's bring her up."

"And just how are we going to do that?" asked Gorski.

"Whaddya mean, *bring her up*?" said Jones.

"If the anchor has a good bite on the T, why don't we just haul her back to Kingsville?"

"All the way to Kingsville?" said Mud.

"You're daffy," said Jones.

"Okay," said Shorty, "here's another idea: can we swing this boom around and load the crates into the net?"

"You're going to have your man go back down there and load how many crates into the net?"

"I counted six. Shorty ... I can't manage loosening those crates *and* loading them into the net. I haven't got that much air in me."

More ideas were tossed around but they were just swimming in circles.

"Okay, okay, how about we quit the hypothetical for now and just start with trying to pull her out of the sandbar?"

They all nodded in agreement and Jones headed back up to the wheelhouse.

"Mud, I want you working the windlass. Take up any slack there might be in that chain right now, then lock it and we'll have Jones wiggle her out … and keep it tight while he's working."

"Right."

"Give me a signal." Shorty positioned himself halfway up the stairs to the wheelhouse. When he got the sign from Mud, he called up to Jones, "Okay, but slowly."

Jones nodded and then gently started to pull on the T. He didn't want to tug at it — pull, rest, pull, rest — because he thought for sure that would wrench the car apart. Dark, heavy smoke was billowing out of *Last Call*'s stack again. The old river rat was walking a fine line.

There was movement and Mud took up the bit of slack.

Jones continued pulling, pretending not to notice how the ship was listing, its frame creaking and moaning. And then the ship snapped back, though not quite right. Shorty almost fell down the stairs while the other boys steadied themselves and, looking down again, could see that the vehicle still appeared to be intact.

"Well I'll be damned," said Mud.

Shorty had Jones stop the engine and then went back down to join his crew.

"Now what?" asked Gorski.

"Mud, do you think the windlass and a couple pairs of hands could lift the car to water level?"

"Shorty, we're talking twelve hundred pounds of steel and rye."

"Not to mention the sand and water," said Gorski.

Jones could sense a fight brewing, so he made his way down the stairs and toward the bootleggers. He seemed to be hearing pieces of a plan that worried him.

"Whoa," he said. "Whoa, whoa." He was willing to go along with them on this, but to a point. After all this was his tub. "You're gonna capsize my boat. Either that or rip the windlass off the deck boards."

"We'll take it slow," said Shorty, "and we'll create a counterweight with everyone — except for Linc and Jones — and everything portable moved to the starboard side."

"What'll I be doing?" asked Linc, thinking he already knew the answer.

"You're going back down for the crates. You won't be all that far from the surface this time — and you come up for air between each crate, right?"

Mud grabbed Linc's shoulder and said, "You come up whenever you need to."

"And when it's looking like *Last Call* has had enough, this expedition is over," added Jones.

"Okay. Now let's get to work," said Shorty, and the others started moving all of the portable cargo to the other side of the boat.

McCloskey was thinking what an unusually quiet morning it was when his phone rang. It was Elias Jones, one of his suppliers out in Kingsville. There was some small talk and catching up and then McCloskey asked the old man why he was calling.

"What're you selling today, Jones?"

"This comes to you free, Jack; I already got my recompense."

"Come again?"

Jones then launched into a tale of the early dawn fiasco of a recovery mission that almost cost him *Last Call* and McCloskey one of his crew.

Linc had successfully retrieved four of the crates, but when he got to the last two, at the bottom of the footwells, he discovered the crates were almost crushed and half filled with sand. He tried to wrestle free the few salvageable bottles when, while looking for some help from the running board, he slipped and put his foot through the net. This wouldn't have been so difficult to overcome, except in his panic to extricate himself he got the ropes of the net somehow tangled behind the rear wheel.

Mud had been counting down the time of each of Linc's dives, and when this last one seemed to be going on a few seconds too long, the non-swimmer broke from the group of counterweights and jumped into the river. Mud saved Linc; Linc saved Mud; and no one saved those few loose bottles.

"Jesus," was McCloskey's reply. "So what happened with the T — and the *Last Call*?"

Apparently Mud had volunteered to take his hacksaw to the chain. But if he were successful, that would have meant Jones was out an anchor.

"And I wasn't going to have that," he said.

Linc wasn't about to go back in the water, so they all agreed to try dragging the old car, hoping to get into a tug-of-war with whatever it might snag and then gently pull the rear assembly right off the vehicle.

"It didn't work," McCloskey guessed.

"It sort of worked."

Last Call and her anchor did indeed manage to pull the rear assembly off, and Jones was keeping it as proof, along with his damaged windlass. He kept one of the three cases of rye.

"My apologies, Elias."

"Make sure you see those two other cases, Jack."

"Thanks. And send me the bill for the windlass."

Minutes after McCloskey set the phone down, Shorty walked into his office.

"Morning, Jack."

"Morning, Shorty. So, what have you got for me?"

Chapter 21

NO SUBSTITUTIONS PLEASE

Thursday, August 9

Several new pieces of furniture had been added to Shady's, including a few round tables large enough to seat eight, each with a revolving server at the centre. McCloskey got them from the same place in Detroit that had outfitted his office. Claude the maître d' helped pick them out. He had a good eye and he knew a fair price.

Seated at one of these tables were Vera Maude, Li-Ling, Bernie, Pearl, Claude, and Shorty. McCloskey got the group's attention and was ready to make his opening remarks. Quan and the new sous-chef — Sing, recently lured from the kitchen at Essex Golf and Country Club — stood next to him, hands folded, looking a little nervous.

"Thanks for coming. All of you — Quan included — have no doubt tried out at least some of the Chinese cafés or diners here in the Border Cities and found that some are good, some not so good. Regardless of the quality, what they're doing seems to be working because, well, they're all still in business. That's fine; let them stick to their tried and true. All the better for us because, in my opinion, this leaves the door wide open for a place like Shady's, where we'll be offering the same — but a little different. Quan tells me what he's going to be serving up today are traditional Cantonese dishes, some influenced by what he picked up in kitchens in Montreal and Toronto, along with other dishes made unique by a local twist he's putting on them. I believe that with this menu, combined with the new entertainment bill — courtesy of Pearl and Bernie — we'll be on track to making Shady's the Border Cities' hottest new food and entertainment venue. Quan, Sing, I hand it over to you."

McCloskey took the empty seat between Vera Maude and Shorty. He looked around the table. There were skeptical faces, stone faces, and a couple of eager and anxious ones.

This would make for an interesting poker game, thought McCloskey.

"Jack," whispered Shorty, "have you given any more thought to your idea of Shady's being dry?"

"Shady's *is* going to be dry." McCloskey let a flattened hand glide over the table. "End of discussion. I'm not running any speakeasy and this isn't a roadhouse."

"And you still think they're gonna come?"

"Yeah, Shorty, I do. Now don't go spoiling my lunch."

Quan was wheeling out a multi-tiered cart from the kitchen laden with covered bowls and serving platters. Sing loaded them onto the revolving server while Quan, in his best English — with Li-Ling filling any gaps — described the dishes, pointing at each one with his chopsticks.

"Egg rolls … chicken and sweet corn soup … frog legs with ginger and garlic … pork chop suey … a seafood chow mein with crisp noodles … almond chicken … Chinese spare ribs … pig's feet … shrimp fried rice … moo goo gai pan … egg foo young … bowls of rice …"

It was a small feast.

"And now," said Quan, "*sik faan!*" But before taking his seat between Li-Ling and Bernie, he remembered one more thing: "Oh … tea!" He called Sing back out and gave him a few instructions. Sing disappeared once more into the kitchen and returned with a smaller cart, a tea wagon of sorts.

"Oolong, green, and ginger," said Quan while Sing poured.

"Jack," said Shorty, "what are normal people gonna eat?"

Normal people, thought McCloskey. *I'd like to meet one someday.*

"Don't panic, we'll still have some roadhouse on the menu. You know, roast chicken dinners, steak, French fries —"

"Who wants to try the soup?" asked Vera Maude, her fingertips on the server.

Claude signaled.

"Here it comes." She spun it over to him.

"I can't work the sticks," said Pearl.

"Maybe you just ain't got rhythm," said Bernie.

"Seriously?"

"I think the chopsticks work with this food," said McCloskey. "It just takes a little practice."

"Hey," said Pearl, watching him. "Where did you pick that up?"

"I've been getting lessons."

"Like this," said Li-Ling, and she demonstrated for Pearl.

"When you hold them … you learn how to be gentle and when to … make tension. Like Mr. McCloskey said, the food sometimes will tell you." Li-Ling reached over and positioned the chopsticks in Pearl's hand.

"And what's all this stuff?" asked Bernie.

Again, Li-Ling jumped in, and pointing with her chopsticks at the little bowls, explained, "Soy sauce, black bean sauce, sriracha — very hot — and chili oil."

"What's this?" said Shorty.

"Shrimps," said Li-Ling.

"Doesn't look like it," said Pearl.

"Delicious," said Claude.

"You know, I never thought I'd like this stuff," said Bernie.

"This one I'm not crazy about," said Vera Maude.

"Oh yeah? Which one's your favourite?" Bernie asked her.

The conversation began to spin like the server at the centre of the table. McCloskey watched and listened. He and Quan kept making eye contact. A glance at Sing from Quan and Sing was refreshing everyone's tea.

McCloskey was the first to raise his cup. He thanked Quan and Sing for the wonderful meal, and Li-Ling for her guidance. He then glanced back at Quan. They had rehearsed this one.

"*Yam sing!*"

Following that, the sous-chef drifted back into the kitchen with his cart stacked with empty bowls and dishes, returning with plates of almond cookies and another confection balanced on his arm. The guests helped themselves to the treats.

"Quan … what do we have here?" asked McCloskey, holding up one of the curious little triangles. It looked like a thin wafer about the size of a small saucer that had been loosely folded. The wafer had what looked like a maze pattern pressed into it; a maze folded on itself.

Quan smiled and said something to Li-Ling, who nodded and began to explain to the rest of the group.

"It is called a prosperity biscuit or prosperity cookie. Quan first saw them in Vancouver where Chinese immigrants — some from Malaya — made cookies like this. They called them love note cookies, or *kuih kapit*. Legend says lovers passed notes to each other this way. Also sometimes the cookies have notes that impart wisdom or foretell events. Break yours open … please."

Everyone cracked open their prosperity cookie and found a narrow slip of paper with something printed on it. They unfolded them and read. The room was silent for a moment.

"Do you believe this stuff?" said Pearl to McCloskey.

"What's it say?"

"*I learn by going where I have to go.*" She was quick to dismiss it, but he caught her discreetly tucking it into her cigarette case.

"Pearl," said Bernie, "I'm not sure what it means, but I'd come back to this joint just to get another one."

"Are you going to share?"

"*There's no such thing as an ordinary cat.*"

Vera Maude joined in after she put on her cheaters. "Mine says … *You are going to have some new clothes.*"

She immediately looked at what she was wearing. So did everyone else at the table.

"You look fine, sweetheart," said Pearl.

Vera Maude was reading something in the flapper's tone.

The group started getting their things together and making for the door, thanking McCloskey for the free meal. He listened to them discuss the meal, their notes of wisdom, his vision for the club, and Shady's prospects as he again complimented Quan and Sing, thanking them for a job well done. As soon as the two turned back toward the kitchen, McCloskey turned back toward the door and managed to catch Vera Maude before she made her exit.

"Maudie … Maudie, can I talk to you for a minute?"

She said her goodbyes to the others and returned to the table.

"Sure, what?"

"Maudie, we need a menu."

"It looks like you've got one, Jack," she said, smiling. "I think you've really got something here, the whole package."

"Thanks, Maudie, but that's not what I mean. Here, sit down." He pulled a chair out for her. "I'm talking about the actual menu, the card, the whatever-it-is that people read so they know what to ask for and what they're eating. It's all about the details now."

"Gotcha."

"Can you sit down with Quan and Li-Ling on your next day off and work on something together? Like I said, I want to make people feel comfortable, so make it something fun, something that will draw them in, something …" He was trying to find the words.

"Hey, how about Chop-Shop Suey?"

He squirmed a little and wondered himself what exactly it was he was asking for. "Not exactly, but I think you might have the right idea."

"Okay, I'm in."

"Great. And can you do me a favour?"

"What?"

"Leave Bernie out of it."

"Okay … so, why?"

"Because I also don't want it … to be a kind of joke."

"Oh … okay." Vera Maude looked slightly confused. "Anything else?"

"Yeah, are you doing anything this afternoon?"

"Depends," said Vera Maude. She was still getting used to changing tracks when it came to talking to this man. "What did you have in mind?"

The contractors, who had been sitting on the back of their flatbed truck eating their lunch, must have gotten their cue when Pearl and the Follies came out of the building because they re-entered the club, ready to get back to work, with silly grins on their faces and a sideways glance for Vera Maude.

"Hi, boys."

The foreman nodded. "Mr. McCloskey."

Chapter 22

CROSSWORDS

Campbell bracketed his eyes with his hands and pressed his face against the glass to stop the glare. He examined the menu card in the window, making the clientele on the other side feel not just a little uncomfortable over their club sandwiches and coffee. The bottom of the menu card read:

> *The Businessman Knows* — *that the most delightfully quiet, cool and restful place to enjoy his lunch is here.*

He hadn't checked in at Osterhout's in a while. *Yes*, he thought. *Yes, lunch for a change.* He always had to remind himself to eat.

An older gentleman walked out just as Campbell was about to enter. His face was unmistakable to the detective, with its high, pink cheekbones and bushy white eyebrows combed straight up, giving the man the appearance of being in a perpetual state of shock.

"Mr. Gerald."

"Ah, young Campbell."

Mr. Gerald shifted his cane from one hand to the other — an affectation, Campbell was sure — so that the two could press palms. Gerald was a friend of Campbell's father. They were members of the same lodge — the Prince of Wales, Campbell thought it was.

"How are you keeping, sir? I haven't seen you in ages."

Campbell noticed how his vernacular changed whenever he spoke to one of the old guard or his college professors. It was like a reflex, or perhaps a defence mechanism.

"I'm well, very well, thank you," said Mr. Gerald.

"Keeping busy, then?"

"Yes, yes — oh, and with something that might already be of interest to you, I'm sure: I've been attending court cases over in Sandwich. Found a fellow from the lodge who's also quite keen on taking in the proceedings."

"Any wagering going on?"

"Oh!" grinned the old gentleman. "No, it's just fascinating stuff. And a different view of the city, I should say."

It felt like this was turning into a conversation, so Campbell moved out of the way of passersby trying making the most of their lunch break. Mr. Gerald followed Campbell's cue, also shuffling over.

"I'm sure it is," said Campbell. "Do you attend very many?"

"We try to attend as many as we can, health and weather permitting, of course. A lot of interesting characters have been taking the stands these past few weeks. But some of the spectators can be just as interesting, let me tell you."

Campbell chuckled politely.

"Say," said Mr. Gerald, "speaking of characters, do you have a detective on the force — at least I think he's a detective — a blimp of a man, slightly unkempt?"

Campbell smiled. "That sounds like Detective Morrison. Did you see him there this morning?"

"Yes, as a matter of fact I did."

"He must have been testifying."

"No, no, he just sat there doing his crosswords, as always."

"His crosswords?" Campbell lowered his voice and hoped Mr. Gerald would follow suit. "How often do you see him there?"

"Not that often ... only for certain types of cases it would seem."

This detail piqued Campbell's curiosity. "Oh? Which types of cases?"

"Oh, the ones involving those nasty drug smugglers. Now there's a bad lot. I hope they all get what's coming to them, especially the one today that for some reason seems to think he's above the law. Then again, so many of that kind do. You know who I'm talking about, don't you, young Campbell?"

Campbell's wheels were turning. "Detective Morrison must be doing some research, or following up on cases."

"You would know."

I'd like to know more, thought Campbell. He looked around at the automobiles and citizens going about their business along the Avenue. *Yes, I'd like to know more.* He extended his hand. "It was nice catching up with you, Mr. Gerald."

Campbell was already leaning away.

"Weren't you going in for some lunch?"

"I was, but I just remembered some work I was supposed to have finished up first. Hope to run into you again sometime, sir."

"The same, young Campbell."

Again with the "young Campbell," thought the detective, *as if I were still in short pants. Why do our elders insist on freezing us in time?*

"Good day."

They touched their respective chapeau brims.

"Good day."

Almost walking into traffic, Campbell headed straight back to the police station. He thought he'd check the files on recent drug smuggling and possession cases to see if anything jumped out at him. It wasn't really his area, but lately he'd been thinking more and more about how he should pay closer attention.

And then that question popped into his head again: *What's Morrison up to?*

He walked along the Prince Edward Hotel side of Park Street, crossing at St. Alphonsus.

And that sound? He nodded at a couple of constables he passed coming down the stairs. *It's your stomach, you fool, eating itself.*

ACCUSED CHINAMAN SAYS "NO CAN CATCH"

Su Men Yen, typically Chinese, pleaded not guilty in police court this morning in illegally possessing narcotics. Yen was arrested last night when Sergeants Burns and Begg found him at 50 Chatham Street with 17 decks of opium in his possession. Yen asked for bail and was informed that $1,000 cash would be sufficient to secure him his liberty.

"No can catch," replied the accused, and he was led below.

Chapter 23

DRIVING LESSONS

"Did you ever stop to think maybe I don't want to know how to drive a car?"

"You should know how to drive a car."

"Let me rephrase that: I don't think I need to know how to drive a car."

"Maudie, everybody needs to know how to drive a car."

"Are you shilling for Ford now, or did you just buy a dealership?"

McCloskey leaned back. "You need some water in your rad."

"My who?"

"C'mon," said McCloskey, "give yourself a chance."

"At what?"

The first thing he needed to do was calm her down. The roadster was parked in the middle of the grounds of the Jockey Club, on the fringes of the Border Cities, a place he figured Vera Maude could do the least amount of damage with an automobile, compared to the heaps of damage she could do on city streets. McCloskey knew a couple of stable boys here and they let him on the grounds in exchange for not asking them for any tips on the bullet work pulling stretches on the straights, whatever that meant. These boys had their own language.

McCloskey had convinced Vera Maude to come out here on the pretense she would get to pet a few horses, maybe even pose on one and have her picture taken for a calendar. McCloskey kept the calendar idea to himself. If it happened, he'd hang it in the garage at the Wrecking and Salvage.

"Jack … seriously, I don't know about this."

"You're just going take it once around the track. Easy stuff. What're you gonna hit?"

"Don't even say that! Jack — what are you trying to do to me?" She was bouncing in her seat, twisting her grip on the steering wheel and staring straight ahead as if it were mere seconds before the gun at Indianapolis.

"Maudie, would you calm down?"

"It's a killing machine," she muttered.

"What? Where did you hear that? Look, no one's around, no other cars, and nothing in your path. The worst you might do is take out a length of fence."

"Worst? Jack, you really are setting me up, aren't you?"

"This isn't a five-pin bowl, Maudie. I'm right here, right next to you. In fact … tell you what." McCloskey made sure the car was in park before he stepped out of the vehicle and walked around the grille while Vera Maude resumed bouncing in her seat.

"Holy shit … Jack!"

"C'mon, slide over a little bit."

She wiggled her hips in the other direction and he leaned in, holding the door half closed.

"What are you doing?" She had a new, fresh look of panic on her face.

"Relax. One step at a time; you're gonna get used to the pedals and the wheel today, that's all."

"What's happening?"

Improvising, mostly.

"I'm going to stand on the running board, with the door open so that I can jump in if I have to. I'll get her in gear — low gear — and then, like I said, all you're gonna do is steer. Let's just leave it at that for now."

"This is crazy…. Is this how you learned to drive?"

"No," he said. "I taught myself how to drive one Sunday after church. My pa was sleeping one off and I got a little ambitious and accidentally backed his truck into the shallows. It looked like it might actually slip further into the drink but I jumped out and tied the front bumper to a tree. I was a quick thinker."

"Can you tell me how that ended after we do our lap around the track?" said Vera Maude. "I'm choking on the fumes."

McCloskey steadied his feet on the running board and tightened his arm around the door's open window frame. "Do you see that gap in the fence we came through?"

She squinted at it. "Yeah."

"Hey — did you bring your cheaters?"

"In my purse."

"Put them on."

Without looking, she fished them out and adjusted them on her face. He wondered why she hated wearing them. He thought about that calendar again.

"I'm going to put the engine in gear now, and you're going to take us toward that gap."

"Which pedal makes it go?"

"That one." McCloskey pointed. "I'll handle the clutch and the accelerator."

"The whats?"

"Okay ... go."

The roadster lurched forward. McCloskey wrapped his other arm around the driver's seat.

"Are you all right?" shouted Vera Maude. The volume really wasn't necessary.

"I'm fine ... just keep both hands on the wheel and aim between the goal posts."

"The what?"

"Just try to make it through the gap."

It was twice the width of the car; she had to make it. And she did. The wheels hitting the track surface startled her, and she had to adjust her grip. "Whoops."

"You're fine."

A couple of the groomers came out of the stables to catch the action, leaning on their rakes, silly grins on their faces.

Vera Maude took the first turn.

"That was good," said McCloskey, "but don't take the next one so tight; you've got lots of room here." They were on a long stretch now. "I want you to play with the wheel a little bit here, get a feel for it."

"Like this?"

She started gently working the wheel back and forth. McCloskey momentarily lost his footing on the running board and had to resist the impulse to grab the wheel back from her.

"That's good," he said. "Okay, you got your next turn coming up. Remember what I told you."

"Not too tight."

"Just ease yourself into it and don't force it. Let the car and its push and pull do some of the work for you."

Vera Maude took it a little wide and McCloskey almost spilled into her lap.

"Was that better?"

He straightened up and caught his breath. "Better. Now, before this next turn, as you approach it, move a little to the right first and then just before the curve, start turning the wheel to the left."

Her hands were losing their grip on the wheel. "Got it."

McCloskey braced himself. The stable boys were leaning on the fence now, their necks craned.

It was a smooth, balanced, well-executed turn. Everyone, participants and spectators alike, relaxed a little bit.

"Okay, Maudie, you're in the home stretch."

"Woo-hoo, giddy up!" She paused. "Are we going to be driving back into the grounds?"

McCloskey thought for a moment. He realized she would have to brake, stop, and reverse. And while he could do some things for her from where he was standing, those weren't any of them.

"When I grab the wheel and give you the go-ahead, you're going to slide over and I'm going to jump into the driver's seat."

For the first time during the lesson, Vera Maude took her eyes off the road and turned to McCloskey. "Really?"

"Yeah, just be ready."

They motored along down the home stretch. One of the stable boys was pumping his rake in the air like a hockey stick and the other was whistling loud and hard.

"Almost," said McCloskey. "Almost."

Vera Maude shifted her bottom in the seat, preparing to make her move.

McCloskey grabbed the wheel. "Now," he said. He moved his right leg in too soon and got it tangled briefly with Vera Maude's left. He jerked the wheel.

"Shit. Maudie, move your leg out of the way!"

"I'm trying to, but … my skirt."

"Don't worry, I've got my eyes on the track. Now slide over."

"Jack — the fence!"

"I see it."

Vera Maude completed her manoeuvre over to the passenger seat and straightened her skirt. McCloskey stole a glance when he dropped into the driver's seat. He pulled the door closed with his free hand and then worked the clutch and the gearshift until he brought the roadster to a stop.

The stable boys applauded and McCloskey wiped his brow with his shirtsleeve.

"That was fun," said Vera Maude. "When can we do it again?"

Chapter 24

OCCIDENTAL

Laforet dissected cadavers with bone chisels, articulators, knives, scalpels, and snips. In between cadavers, when he was bored or held up by forces beyond his control, he occasionally used his words to take apart the living. A nurse once referred to it as verbisection. Some got off easy while others went away with a limp of sorts.

His cheek rested in the palm of one hand while the other hand slowly drummed a clipboard with a pencil, which made a sound like water dropping from a leaky gutter. This was also the tired, impatient Laforet sitting at his desk waiting for laboratory results, which suspended all of his other activities. Roger Smith, the newest orderly at the hospital, was seated across from him. He was being bounced around the hospital, told to become familiarized with the doctors' and nurses' responsibilities and how the facility generally functioned. Their conversation, if it could even be called that, was beginning to wander.

"In this case, Smith, I prefer Chinese," said Laforet.

"To what?"

"*Orientals*," said Laforet.

"But they clearly …"

"Yes, clearly they." Laforet straightened up. "You might have an oriental rug, go out for an oriental dinner, maybe have a taste for oriental costume, but when it comes to the people …"

"But I always thought …"

"Smith, whenever I hear someone utter that phrase I know right away that they themselves weren't responsible for any of the thinking but rather conveniently left that difficult, messy business up to someone else. Try using the word as an adjective, not a noun."

"Oriental?"

"Yes."

"Well," said Smith, "that puts things in a different light, doesn't it?" He paused for a moment. "So what are we then?"

Laforet resumed drumming his pencil on the clipboard.

"You could say we're occidentals," he said. "Not to be confused with the many accidentals I've delivered into the world over the years."

"We're nouns, then?"

"Yes. Except you, Smith; you are an adverb."

Quan and Li-Ling had just left Laforet's lab. Quan had had an altercation with a few young men who didn't feel he was giving them enough room on the sidewalk. He was pulled by his lapels into an alleyway off Chatham Street where he received a brief lecture, a black eye, and a split brow.

"There," one of the thugs had said, "now people will know how badly you misbehaved."

Quan had been on his way to the market, but after his altercation had turned around and headed straight to the laundry. Out of his good eye he could see the looks he was getting along the way. Li-Ling cleaned him up as best she could but he obviously required a few stitches. She walked him to Grace Hospital, knowing that in his condition they wouldn't be let on a streetcar and the cabbies would drive right past them. Even Gladys at hospital reception hesitated. Luckily, Laforet was heading toward the front desk, having been informed that a package had just arrived for him: supplies he had been anxiously awaiting. When he saw the bloody handkerchief Quan held against his eye, and the look on Li-Ling's face, and Gladys's perplexed face, he asked the pair to come downstairs to his lab immediately, where he would have a look.

"Does your friend speak English?" the doctor had asked Li-Ling as they made their way down in the elevator.

"Quan is learning."

"From you?"

"Yes," she said.

When they had reached the lab, Laforet gave Smith a few instructions and then asked Quan to sit down as he wheeled a light stand over, so that he could properly assess the damage. "Not as bad as it looks," he said. "That's the way it usually is with injuries like this." He got to work. "Some doctors might think it was none of their business. I don't happen to be one of those doctors." He finished cleaning the wound and was about to start with the stitches. "Can you tell me whose handywork this is?"

The young couple looked at each other.

Quan carried one calling card: *Border Cities Wrecking and Salvage*. McCloskey had given it to him when they were all at Woo Hong's place. He took it out of his pocket and handed it to Laforet.

"If you run into any trouble ..." McCloskey had said to Quan upon giving him the card.

Quan said, "Trouble."

Laforet examined the card. "Is this Jack McCloskey's card? Did he give this to you?"

Yes on both counts.

"I have to ask, did he do this to you?"

"No, no, doctor, not like that at all," said Li-Ling.

"Who then?"

"Boys on the street," said Quan.

Laforet knew what to infer from that. "And whose phone number is this on the back?"

"My father's laundry."

Laforet gave the card back to Quan. He was torn. It was against his better judgment to encourage Quan to become further entangled with McCloskey, but then Quan might need someone like McCloskey in his corner. He might mention all of this to Campbell. He just needed to figure out how to frame it for him.

The doctor finished with the stitches and gave Quan's brow one final, quick daub with some cotton. "And where are you going now?"

"The laundry," said Li-Ling.

"The market," said Quan.

Laforet walked them to the door of his lab, stopping at his desk to pick up one of his own cards.

"Take this," said Laforet. "Now you know where to find me."

That was almost a half hour ago now, thought the doctor as he checked his pocket watch. *I hope Quan made it safely to the market this time.*

"You can tidy up now," he said to Smith.

"The young man — Quan, was it? — said 'boys on the street.' What did he mean by that?"

"He meant the boys out there roaming the streets who feel it is their duty to let people know whether or not they are welcome in this city. Boys with nothing better to do with their sorry selves."

"Looks to me like maybe they're not welcome," said Smith, examining the bloody cotton balls and bloodstained white enamel dish. "Were you born here, doctor?"

"Yes."

"I thought I heard an accent."

"My father was Quebecois. It was a bilingual household."

"But English was the mother tongue."

"So to speak. We're all the same on the inside," said Laforet. "Trust me. I've seen it for myself. Those could be anybody's guts in that jar."

Quan and Li-Ling walked together down London Street and parted at Bruce Avenue, just before the laundry. She would tell her father everything that happened, but she did not want him to see Quan or see her with him; not like this. Quan told Li-Ling he would tell McCloskey the same.

He cut down Bruce to Chatham Street, determined to complete his errand at the market. The sun was higher now and he wished he had something to cover his eyes. He saw people wearing those dark glasses that were becoming popular. He made it safely to the Avenue, and at the corner came upon a tobacconist that had eyewear like that on display in his window.

Belvedere Smoke Shop. He tried sounding the words out in his head. He entered, and immediately began looking through the selection in the showcase.

"May I help you?"

Quan smiled and nodded, still nervous with his English. He pointed at a pair of glasses in the front row.

"Please," he said.

"One dollar," said the salesman before removing them.

Quan pulled out his wallet, unfolded a crisp bill, and placed it on the counter. The salesman set down the glasses in front of Quan and Quan tried them on. They fit fine and looked good in the mirror the salesman was holding, and were large enough to cover most of his purple badge.

"They suit you," said the salesman. "Have a nice day."

Feeling a little better and less self-conscious, Quan jogged alongside a streetcar as it crossed the Avenue. He followed that with an optimistic stride until just before Goyeau.

No.

"Well, well, well. Look who it is."

They pulled him into a laneway.

"I thought if we spilled a little blood you might have gotten the message. Maybe what we need to do now is break something."

Quan closed his eyes and heard a *crack*, followed by another *crack*, and another. He opened his eyes slowly and saw that two boys had fallen, now writhing on the cobblestone. Quan looked up and saw a man that could have been one of his own countrymen, only bigger, broader.

Mongolian.

The man brandished a long, metal pipe that he seemed to make collapse into itself and then disappear up his coat sleeve. Quan recognized the work of the Mongolian: he had not struck their faces or hands, and judging by the way the victims were holding themselves, had instead hit their knees, elbows, and ribs. He had seen this work before. The giant left the two able thugs to carry the two crippled ones away. He did not utter a word. The thugs made their way out of the scene.

The Mongolian, if that was in fact what he was, rested a heavy hand on Quan's shoulder.

"Quan Lee," he said, "you need a friend like me."

The Mongolian took Quan's hand and pressed it against his barrel chest. Quan swallowed hard. This was the second time today Quan wished he was somewhere else other than the Border Cities.

ACT FOUR

Chapter 25

NEAR-DRESSED REHEARSAL

Tuesday, August 14

Only after a rush of meetings and late-night telephone calls, bleary-eyed reviews of design renderings, and arguments that must have resembled the antics at the Paris Peace Conference, did they finally finish reconfiguring and realizing the look and layout of the new Shady's.

More than a few conversations took place behind the scenes between McCloskey and the contractors concerning delays, broken promises, and who needed to settle their tab before the doors could be thrown open. After some pressure was applied in both directions they got to the point where someone — no one was quite sure who — could confidently schedule a walk-through.

McCloskey arrived well before the others in order to check things out and prepare for any legitimate concerns. The designer, a young man who had come recommended by way of a source working in Albert Kahn's hive, conducted the tour. He was just starting out but already gaining a reputation, specializing in those smooth, welcoming interiors that made an impression and kept customers coming back for more.

"Mr. Jack?"

McCloskey was pacing the sidewalk in front of the building, almost impossible what with the workers shouldering in and out and the hustle and bustle of lunch hour on the Avenue. He had half an unlit cigar clenched between cheek and molars, thumbs tucked into belt, and mind in high gear. He was trying to shift down, to not feel so much like he was turning a corner at top speed with only two wheels touching the pavement. He was getting rundown, working through all of these above-board channels, straddling the worlds of order and his usual ordered chaos.

The designer came up behind him, his fingers pressing McCloskey's shoulder.

"Mr. Jack?"

He turned sharp. "About time; I gotta meet with people as soon as yesterday, people with less patience than me. Can we get — what's your name again, kid?"

"Palladio."

"Paula Joe?"

"Palladio."

"Lead the way."

Dust was settling in the foyer, which was about the size of a freight elevator and illuminated by a trio of stepped pendant lights that resembled inverted cocktail shakers. The floor was new — black and white tile in a chevron pattern pointing toward the bottom of the stairs. There was something about the glass brick bordering the floor that caught McCloskey's eye. He bent down.

"Marbles … how'd you do this? You've got some thumpers, mashers, and tom bowlers down here."

"Yes." The designer smiled, thrilled that his client noticed these details.

"And more than a handful of peewees."

"Come, Mr. Jack, and see more."

There were framed photos along the wall up the stairwell.

"Who are these people?" asked McCloskey, pausing at the first one.

"They are having a good time, yes?"

"Who are they?"

"I found them dancing in a newspaper."

McCloskey continued his ascent. "You pulled these from local papers?"

"Good?" asked Palladio.

"Yeah," said McCloskey, fixated. "Very good … really sets the mood. These clubs on both sides of the river?"

"*Si.*"

They followed the cream-coloured walls up the turn in the narrowing stairwell, their hands gliding along the carved black railing. Approaching the top floor landing, guests would be greeted by a painting on the door.

"What's that?"

"Like Kandinsky, no?" asked Palladio.

"Like what?"

The designer's presence had a way of calming the man who signed the cheques where others had only taken note.

"What do you see?"

McCloskey felt like he was being tested. He hesitated, turned and glanced sideways at Palladio, who was standing three steps below and grinning from ear to ear, and finally said, "I see jazz … I see a jazz band."

Colours, shapes, and rhythm, maybe a face or two; instruments that looked as if they had been bashed around and broken up. It was busy but somehow everything came together inside the jamb.

"Yes."

"So on to the main event."

McCloskey opened the door and was almost completely overwhelmed. His eyes roamed the place, taking in all of the details.

Shady's occupied the entire floor, which included a mezzanine and a fully equipped stage left over from the previous tenant. Claude's station, an oak podium, was to the left of the entrance. Once a guest got past Claude, a hostess would show them to their table. Booths lined the left and the right walls, with a half-dozen round tables in the middle — three facing the stage, then two, and then one nearest the entrance.

The stage was about two feet off the main floor — a minor elevation. To the right a spindled staircase with a filigree of copper vine wound up to the mezzanine, repositioned so that, if they wished, the girls could use it in a dance number. On the opposite side of the stage was a short passageway to the kitchen. The dressing room was behind that. It wasn't pretty; it still doubled as a receiving deck for shipments hoisted up from the alleyway. It needed some finessing, as did a few other areas in the club. Sometimes the end work was like trying to detail a truck while it was travelling down the road at forty miles an hour.

"So … you like, Mr. Jack?"

"I like, Mr. Palladio." McCloskey grabbed the designer's hand and gave it a shake. "You and your people did a great job here."

"Thank you, thank you, Mr. Ja—"

"Okay, what did I miss?" Pearl almost swung the door off its hinges. Her girls trailed behind her. They all stopped in their tracks as soon as they got a good look. There were gasps all around.

"Mr. Jack, I have to go."

"You don't want to show the girls around?"

"But I think they have something to show you."

Vera Maude arrived presently with Bernie in tow.

"You're right," said McCloskey. "Thanks again — will I see you later?"

"Maybe, after I see a man about an … *aquario*."

"A what?"

"Ciao!" Palladio made his exit.

"Jack, this looks wonderful!"

"Thanks, Maudie. I wish he could have stuck around long enough to hear that."

"Was that your designer?"

"Yep. Hi, Bernie."

"Hi, Jack."

Pearl approached. "Jack, we should get started."

"Okay, let's grab some seats. What is it you've got for us today, Pearl?"

"We just want you to see how things are coming together so far."

"Right," said McCloskey. "Say, is anyone in the kitchen or at the bar? I could use a —"

"Ginger ale?" asked Vera Maude.

"Oh yeah, a ginger ale."

"Your rules, remember?"

"I remember just fine. Now can we get on with this?"

"Okay, Jack, so it's going to be a little rough. We're thinking we're going to open with Bernie — surrounded by the girls in their costumes — saying a few lines and welcoming our guests. He then leaves the stage and the girls do their first dance number, at which time I come out and sing a tune. Got it?"

"Got it."

Pearl went backstage and returned shortly with the girls. Bernie found his mark.

"I know I don't need to worry about the licensing inspector," said McCloskey, "but what about the morality squad?"

"Is it their outfits? Jack, that's only what they wear to practices and rehearsals. Besides, we're all friends here, right?"

"Not yet; you haven't introduced me."

McCloskey didn't notice the look he was getting from Vera Maude.

"Okay, line up, girls. Jack, this is our lead, Miss Ardis Breeze. And this is Ethel, Jo, Clare, Genevieve, Zoe, and Ivy."

"The roster changed," said McCloskey.

"We're still the Windsor Follies," said Ardis, and as if on cue, the girls took a short bow.

Bernie appeared, making a show and flapping his way through the curtain at the back of the stage.

"Looks like you've got a tough act to follow, Bernie," said McCloskey.

"I'll just be riding on their skirt-tails, Jack." He went back into character. "Let's give a nice hand to the Windsor Follies … and I'm only talking applause; please keep your hands to yourself. Aren't they wonderful? Ladies and gentlemen, welcome to Shady's."

Bernie's turn in the spotlight consisted primarily of jokes that sounded like they came from the *Starbeams* column in the paper — tame stuff, not too broad — as well as his own reviews of current vaudeville shows in the Border Cities. He had a few colourful things to say about Carmen Excella's performance in *The Versatile Lady*, now halfway through its run at the Capitol. At one point McCloskey leaned over Bernie's empty seat to ask Vera Maude, "Am I paying for this?"

"This is what you wanted," said Vera Maude, gesticulating. "A show, some variety."

McCloskey straightened up in his seat. "Not this."

Judging by the slight shift in Bernie's expression, Vera Maude thought their master of ceremonies might have heard the exchange. Undeterred, Bernie kept things moving. "Maybe we can coax the Follies — in their own inimitable style — into escorting out our first act of the evening."

Bernie got the applause going. The girls came through the back curtain, grouped in a close circle and wrapped in pink gauze. Once they were front and centre, the circle opened to reveal Pearl in a knee-length glittering white frock.

"Ladies and gentlemen," said Bernie, "Miss Pearl Shipley."

"Thank you, Bernie. Here's a little number I learned on the coast; it's called 'Another Rendezvous' … Jack, I thought I'd open with the encore."

"That's a bit presumptuous," said Bernie to the imaginary audience before stepping back into the wings.

Pearl tuned her pipes and the Follies unfolded and waved around her like flowers in May. McCloskey was already seeing problems but he wasn't going to say anything until the ladies were through their routine. With her hands on her hips and a twinkle in her eye, Pearl started to sing.

> *I got me another rendezvous,*
> *A meet-up halfway to the moon.*
> *He'll take me the rest o' the way*

And I'll have to remind him
It's all just play.

I like a sweetie on the side,
Someone who can provide a thrill,
Maybe some confide,
And turn me inside — out.

"And this is where we have a short musical interlude," explained Pearl, "you know, no vocals." She moved about the stage and hummed a few bars before getting back to the song.

I got me another rendezvous,
A meet-up halfway to the moon.
He'll take me the rest o' the way.
Those will ask and I'll remind them
It's all just play.

I'll work me up; he'll dress me down.
My lil' swing could sink this town.
Loose me 'fore I'm found,
Wrap this commotion and remind me
How it's all just play.

Pearl took a bow and Bernie reappeared.

"Ladies and gentlemen, how about a hand for the Border Cities' own Pearl Shipley and her Windsor Follies."

The talent wiggled their way backstage to the dressing room. Bernie followed but did not contribute to the wiggling.

McCloskey applauded, saying, "That's more like it."

Vera Maude was surprised at his reaction. "You didn't think it was too … risqué?"

"I don't know. Maybe she can leave it until the end of the night, after the old folks've left and gone home to bed. We wouldn't want to upset their sensibilities." He turned to Vera Maude. "Is there going to be more of that variety stuff for me to see soon? I hope she's working on that."

Vera Maude knew when McCloskey had had enough of something and needed to move on. Sometimes he had the patience of an eight-year-old.

"Yeah, it's going to be fine, Jack. Bernie told me about some of the other acts Pearl's been seeing. Bernie said she might have a juggler."

"A juggler? You're kidding, right?"

"A redhead. She'll be a hit."

"The juggler's a girl?"

"Yeah, so?"

"What's she juggle?"

"Live squirrels. I don't know."

McCloskey stood up and straightened his tie and jacket. "I've got a meeting."

"You're leaving? What do you want me to tell them?"

"Tell them anything you want; tell them they still have jobs," he said, and out he went.

"Heartwarming," said Vera Maude. She checked her watch. She was due at the bookstore in ten minutes, and before she left she would probably have to have a word or two with Bernie.

Futz.

Chapter 26

THE INFORMER

This was the first drug smuggling case to be heard in the courts since Detective Campbell had run into Mr. Gerald on the Avenue. Campbell thought of contacting the gentleman and asking him if he could telephone from the visitor's desk and let him know if Morrison was in attendance, but he thought he should leave Gerald out of it, for a number of reasons, the main one being that he didn't want the man jumping to any conclusions and then going around spreading false rumours and muddying the waters. Campbell knew his type; they could get a little too excitable very easily.

The detective arrived early for the proceedings, entered the courtroom quietly, stealthily over creaking floorboards, and made sure Morrison wasn't already there — he wasn't — and then made his way out the way he came, crossing the street and climbing back into the Essex where he changed hats, slumped down in his seat, and observed the intersection of lives at the corner.

He continued checking his watch, waiting, and then checked it again, like it would tell him something new and change the course of his life. It was almost time for the proceedings to start and there was still no sign of Morrison. He thought he knew the make and model of Morrison's car, but maybe he missed it what with all the usual morning activity now mixed with the fresh buzz of the courthouse. Campbell remembered Mr. Gerald's comments about the kind of attention these particular cases were garnering.

There could be a magazine, something for the newsstands.

A streetcar approached from the east, behind Campbell, and stopped at Brock. Commuters shuffled and waited patiently to board, the tail of the queue huffing and puffing like they had run to beat the car to its bell, while passengers were exiting in their own style.

Morrison.

Campbell slid lower in the car seat.

Arriving by streetcar. This is something other than detective work, he thought. *Slow deceptions in broad daylight.*

Morrison crossed and Campbell waited until he was out of sight before stepping out of the Essex and making his way towards the building. He was one of the last to enter. Flashing his badge at security, he asked about the session and then made the *be quiet about this* sign with his finger against his lips. "I'm not here," he said.

"Yes, sir," whispered the clerk, catching the detective's drift.

He was one of those loud whisperers and Campbell gave him a look that said something akin to, *and please stop talking.*

Campbell rolled his gaze back and forth across the room and spotted Morrison. His head was down and it appeared as if he might be working at something, perhaps one of those crosswords that Mr. Gerald had mentioned. Campbell had seen enough. He exited the building and headed straight to his vehicle. This was quick-thinking time.

If he came by streetcar, he ought to be leaving by streetcar ... but I have to see him board.

Campbell exited his four-wheeled change room, crossed Brock Street diagonally, and feeling only slightly ridiculous, positioned himself behind a tree at the edge of St. John's Cemetery, where he had a clear view of the front of the courthouse and the streetcar stop. Nothing but squirrels to blow his cover.

And then what?

He decided that if he saw Morrison board the car, he would run back to the Essex and follow it, waiting a few blocks before he pulled in front of the thing and brought it to a stop.

I'm a Windsor Police detective following an important lead ... tailing a suspect who might also be a danger to the public at large.

A bit dramatic, but under current circumstances Campbell was feeling the urge to do a little pushing against legal and social boundaries. It was becoming more and more about boundaries for him.

The streetcar crossed Mill Street. Campbell waited for a gap in the oncoming traffic, passed the streetcar, and pulled in front of it before it reached Detroit Street, waving his arm. The car ground to a halt and Campbell stopped, jumped out, and approached the side door, flashing his badge.

"Detective Campbell. I'm sorry to interrupt your route but I'm working on an important investigation. This won't take but a moment."

And then what? thought Campbell. *More improvisation.*

"She's all yours," said the driver.

Campbell made his way up the aisle, nodding at passengers, making apologies. None of them even remotely resembled Morrison. He walked back up to the front of the car.

"Excuse me, but did you take on a passenger at Brock, a rather stout fellow in an overcoat and hat, perhaps a little unkempt, maybe holding a book of crosswords?"

Now how would he get that? thought the detective.

"Why yes," said the driver.

The roving conductor chimed in with, "He's one of our regulars."

"Where did he get off the car?"

"Mill, right before you passed me on the left. You must have been distracted with the oncoming traffic."

"Yes," said Campbell. "Yes, I must have been." He thanked the driver, wished him a good day, and apologized again for the inconvenience. The detective stood on the sidewalk and watched the streetcar pass, continuing toward the downtown.

He saw me, thought Campbell, *and damn it, he was watching me. A half-baked plan if ever there was one.*

ACCUSED CHINAMAN GAVE INFORMATION TO OFFICIALS

Su Yen Men, Chinese, 50 Chatham Street, appeared before Judge W.E. Gundy this morning on a charge of illegally possessing narcotics. During the hearing of the evidence, Sergeant Burns, in reply to a question put by prisoner's counsel, A.A. McKinnon, stated that Men had supplied the police with information as to Chinese who were selling opium in Windsor.

"Did he ever receive the money from the fines?" asked Judge Gundy.

Sergeant Burns stated he did not know, but believed he had in one case where he had acted as an informer.

A.A. McKinnon, on behalf of the prisoner, objected to all the evidence on the ground that officers raided Men's house with a search warrant that was not in accordance with the Act. The officers had a search warrant to search for liquor issued by Inspector M.M. Mousseau, a justice of the peace, and prisoner's counsel stated that in the case of narcotics, the warrant must be issued by a magistrate.

Judge Gundy noted the objection, but did not sustain it.

Sergeant Begg stated that the opium was found in envelopes concealed in a bed in which Men's 13-year-old son was sleeping.

"The envelopes were sealed when we found them," declared the sergeant.

"Did you think they contained liquor?" asked the prisoner's counsel.

"I did not know what they might have had in them," replied the officer, but after being pressed for an answer admitted that he did not think the envelopes concealed any liquids.

W.H. Furlong acted as prosecutor for the crown, and the case was not concluded.

Chapter 27

IN CASE OF EMERGENCY

Wednesday, August 15

"But why?" asked McCloskey.

He and Vera Maude were standing on the southwest corner of Wyandotte and the Avenue along with about a half-dozen rather anxious-looking citizens.

"The other day you insisted, for what reason I can't even remember, that I learn how to drive a car. Well, I think you should learn how the rest of us get around."

"Yeah, but why? I got wheels. If I ride one of these … things," he said, gesturing to one of the streetcars passing on the opposite side, "I guarantee you I'll never ride another one of them again."

"It'll give you the chance to see the city through other people's eyes," said Vera Maude.

"Other people."

She squinted as she looked up at him. "Yeah, people like me."

"Sounds like I'm getting some kind of lesson. Seems these days I'm always getting a lesson."

"You're only noticing that now?"

"Do I get a turn driving it?"

"Driving what?"

"The barn on wheels."

Vera Maude rolled her eyes. The barn was approaching. "C'mon, Jack. Hey — you got change?"

"Change of what?"

"Change … you know, coin." She paused to examine her shoes. "What was I expecting? First rule is you have to pay a fare."

"I thought first rule was I gotta stand in line."

"All right — second rule."

"I don't think I've carried coin since I was twelve years old," said McCloskey. A penny here and a nickel there, and then he was borrowing, stealing, and smuggling. He skipped the begging part. McCloskey pulled his money clip out of his jacket pocket. It could barely contain his walking-around money for the day.

"Jack!" She grabbed his wrist and looked over her shoulder. "Put that away."

"What? Why?"

"I'll pay your fare."

"All right. I'm good for it, you know." McCloskey put the clip with its wad of bills back in his pocket. "I got paid yesterday."

"I don't want to know about it."

The streetcar slowly came to a halt. It looked like there was now about as many people waiting to board as there were getting off. McCloskey looked at their faces, their clothes, their bags and briefcases.

Vera Maude was right; he didn't know these people. She paid the conductor. All the seats were taken, so they stood near the back, each clutching a dangling leather strap. McCloskey actually preferred this to sitting down. He could look around, occasionally bend down and get a view of the street if he wanted, and keep an eye on …

"Maudie, what's …?"

A heated exchange drew McCloskey's atetntion back inside the car.

"That man just took her seat," said Vera Maude. "He practically shoved her out of the way to get it. Did you see that?"

While he may not have been up on his public transit etiquette, McCloskey thought he knew a bully when he saw one and moved in.

"Jack …" said Vera Maude.

It was turning into a bit of a commotion.

"And who the hell are you?" asked the man.

"Manners," said McCloskey. He was trying to hold his temper but this situation was beginning to look like nonsense. "I think the lady has claim here. Let's be respectful."

"Are you calling me disrespectful?"

McCloskey always wondered where people like this guy got their nerve.

"Jack … Jack …" Vera Maude repeated.

"What are you going to do about it?" said the man.

"Jack, please."

"Maudie, can we somehow put the brakes on this infernal thing?"

She took a deep breath, plucked the emergency cord, and braced herself. The car came to an abrupt halt and McCloskey balanced himself, bent down, and grabbed the fellow's ankles.

"Hey!"

"This is your stop," said McCloskey as he yanked the man off his seat. His head first hit the top of the bench, then the edge of the seat, and finally the floor. He seemed momentarily stunned but he managed to grab onto a pole as McCloskey dragged him down the aisle. It was no use. McCloskey just kept pulling. Passengers were getting out of the way, trapping the driver and conductor at the front of the car.

Vera Maude plucked the cord again and again. She wanted to make sure the streetcar didn't start moving until Jack was finished whatever it was he was doing, but it looked like the driver was trying to clear an intersection.

McCloskey continued backing up toward the side door. Vera Maude followed. The man's head hit every step down, but before he was knocked unconscious on the curb, McCloskey picked him up by the lapels and dropped him on the sidewalk, leaving him moaning and groaning. Some pedestrians stopped in their tracks. A woman screamed.

McCloskey looked down at Vera Maude, who was standing beside him with her mouth agape, speechless.

"Is it always like that on that car?" he said.

"Wha— no, Jack, of course it isn't."

Some people walked faster, more stopped and stared from a safe distance. McCloskey straightened up, held his hand across his brow, and squinted into the near distance.

"I'll never be allowed on a streetcar again. How will I get to work?"

"Aw, you can get whatever streetcar you want, Maudie," he said. Then he put his fingers in his mouth and whistled.

"What are you doing?"

He waved. "Our ride's here."

"What ride?" Vera Maude looked like there had been a script change that no one had told her about.

A shiny blue Lincoln sedan pulled in front of them.

"Shorty," said McCloskey. "He's been following us."

"Shorty? Who's Shorty and why was he following us?"

"Because I told him to." McCloskey opened a door for Vera Maude. "Now get in before the cops show and I have to unroll a few of these felons."

The two settled into the back seat. "Shorty, Maudie; Maudie, Shorty."

"Miss Maudie." Shorty touched his hat and they sped off.

"That was fun," said McCloskey. "We should do this again sometime. Say, Shorty, a day like this and you're riding around without the top down?"

"I thought you'd like us inconspicuous."

"Ah, right."

"That and I didn't want the leather too hot."

Vera Maude closed her eyes, rested her elbow on the edge of the open window, and pressed her palm to her forehead.

"Hey," said McCloskey. "You wanna go to the beach?"

Chapter 28

BE OUT OF TOWN BEFORE SUNDOWN

JUDGE TELLS CHINESE HE HAD BETTER LEAVE BORDER

Changing his plea from not guilty to having opium in his possession, to guilty of smoking opium, Su Yen Men, 50 Chatham Street, formerly employed by the Windsor police as informer, was fined $10 and costs by Judge W.E. Gundy in the Windsor police court today.

The case against Su Yen Men was heard yesterday afternoon in the Windsor Police court, when he claimed that he had been "framed" when officers found opium in his home. Through his lawyer, he told the court that he had given information that resulted in several Chinese being fined for illegally possessing narcotics and he believed that it was some of these men that had placed the opium in his house. Today, however, he admitted that he had smoked opium.

In imposing the fine, Judge Gundy stated that he had taken cognizance of the fact that W.H. Furlong, acting as prosecutor for the crown, had recommended leniency in view of Men's efforts on behalf of the police. He told him, however, that his usefulness as a detective had been destroyed, and, considering his relation to other Chinese in the Border Cities, he would do well to look for another field for his endeavors.

"Our business is done."

Men's fortunes were indeed fading.

"What you mean?"

"You, me, we're no longer in business," said Morrison.

The detective was checking out a new piece of real estate, but he already had the feeling that it wasn't going to suit his needs. It was a furnished house on the west side of Caron Avenue, a few doors south of the Drive. Something about it just didn't sit quite right with him. He thought maybe it was the location. He had told Men to meet him on the back porch around noon; he said he'd be the one with his feet up, puffing on a Player's and tipping a flask. And sure enough that's just how Men found him.

"I do good work; I work for you from Detroit now."

"No, Men. It's getting too messy, too complicated. I'm streamlining my operations."

Men leaned back on the rail, waving the smoke from Morrison's cigarette away from his face.

"Streamlining? I do that too," he said.

The detective drained the flask and cleared his throat, which was thick with nicotine-laced phlegm. He wiped his mouth with the back of his wrist. "Men, I need you to get lost or I'm going to get you lost. Get me?"

There was location, and then there was location, thought Morrison. He was back to looking around the property. He liked the proximity to the Drive, Pitt Street, the railway, and the ferry, but maybe it was too convenient for some and too much of a risk for him. *Yeah*, he thought, *time to have another meeting with the realtors*. They were slipping.

Or maybe it's the market.

"What you want?" asked Men.

No, this isn't going to work, thought Morrison. *Look at all these ladies hanging their laundry in the middle of the afternoon.*

"Like Judge Gundy, I want you to disappear." He stood up, accidentally tipping over his chair. "It's simple." He pulled his wallet out of his inside pocket and pinched some bills between two fat fingers and handed them to Men. "This is your severance and travelling expenses. Understand?"

Men nodded, though he didn't understand, at least not entirely.

"Go to the Westwood — you know the Westwood, right? — and ask the bartender for your delivery. Got that? Give him half this, then do what he tells you. Hear me?"

Men stared at the bills in his hand, probably more money than he had ever held before. He nodded.

"Go," said Morrison, "and tell the bartender that you can't wait until dark — that'll cost extra."

"To where is my delivery?"

"Across the river ... then you'll be free."

Free to check out the accommodations in the Wayne County jail, thought the detective through his haze of rye.

It was time to move on.

Chapter 29

THE SPIDER AND THE FLY

It was while standing on a dusty sidewalk downtown listening to car horns go off, triggered like so many babies crying in a nursery, that Morrison turned and spotted him making his way up Victoria Avenue through the low-hanging billows of engine exhaust.

Morrison would occasionally stand on a random street corner for several minutes, not waiting for something to happen so much as seeing what caught his attention. What caught his eye this afternoon was an ill-fitting, out-of-season suit, and the stiff-necked over-the-shoulder glances of the man inside it.

A Chinese. Unusual on this stretch, thought Morrison. Curious, he decided to follow.

The dust cleared, Morrison picked up his pace, and got a better look. If he didn't know better he'd say the suit was pulled off the "unclaimed" rack at a laundry. The subject touched his shoulder with his chin again but was still pretending not to see Morrison; he just kept making like he was checking the traffic and the others on the sidewalk, waiting for his chance to cross the street.

Why so nervous? Where you heading?

And then the Chinese puzzle-stepped off the walk, continuing in the direction of …

The library?

Morrison stopped in his tracks, waiting a moment before climbing the steps, holding back just far enough. There were children keeping cool in wedges of shade on the lawn. A little girl tented a picture book over her head, squinting at him as he passed.

It felt slightly cooler inside, though it may have simply been the power of suggestion. Morrison spotted his man but maintained a distance. He held a few membership cards, but not one for this joint. He buttoned the top button of his shirt, straightened his tie, and brushed the crumbs off his lapels in an attempt to look slightly less derelict. Still, he got looks from the librarians as he galumphed his way through.

He thought the place looked like a small temple: columns, marble, carved-wood desks, and a chain of islands down the main aisle that could easily serve as altars. He would normally have presented his badge as a courtesy but was getting in the habit of keeping it in reserve. He also didn't want to send the staff into a panic. Morrison thought they looked a little tightly wound.

The detective did a poor job of making himself look busy while his subject made an inquiry at one of the windows. He pretended to read the postings on a bulletin board and happened to look over just in time to see the staff member point the young man in the direction of an adjacent room.

Morrison avoided eye contact with the librarians as he followed his subject into the children's section. The detective couldn't have looked more out of place, and he knew it. He was sure he was scaring the young readers. He watched the man peruse the shelves and survey what the small group around the table was reading. He would occasionally smile and nod or bow to one of the youngsters. Morrison was beginning to wonder if he wasn't on to something else here. He picked up a discarded copy of *The Curlytops on Star Island* and started casually flipping through it. His Chinaman pulled a few books off the shelves and then sat down at an uninhabited table. He opened one of the books and started reading, occasionally glancing over at the children who were trying to figure him out, as was Morrison. He noticed one of the librarians already had her hand on one of the telephone extensions. Morrison had a knack for setting genteel folk on edge.

The celestial must have been satisfied with his choices because he gathered his reading material as Morrison watched, following him to the main counter where he checked them out. Morrison dropped his *Curlytops* copy on one of the islands and followed the young man out the doors, down the stairs, and across the lawn to the corner of Park and Victoria. He was looking behind him, obviously aware and very suspicious of Morrison.

After he crossed Victoria he began walking faster, no doubt looking a little conspicuous. The young man wanted to shake his pursuer but had little idea how to go about it. He slowed, making it easy for Morrison to catch up with him.

Morrison reached out, put his hand on the Chinaman's shoulder, and, startled, the young man dropped his books: *The Wonderful Wizard of Oz* and *Aesop's Fables*.

"That's library property."

The Chinaman bent down and picked them up out of Morrison's shadow. Morrison then grabbed his arm and pulled him into a garden separating two nearby houses.

"Do I know you?" asked the detective. "You don't look familiar."

The Chinaman shook his head.

"Show me your papers."

"Papers?"

"You know what I'm talking about."

"I do not have with me."

"What's your name, boy?"

"Lee, Quan Lee."

Morrison squeezed Quan's arm tighter. "You're shaking. You got something to be nervous about? You don't have any papers, do you?"

Quan said nothing.

"That's an answer," said Morrison. "No papers. Okay, let's hold that card for now. What's with the books?"

"I learn English."

Morrison was trying to decide what questions to ask, how much he wanted to know, right now, and how much he wanted to leave on the table. "You're working, or you have a ... sponsor, a benefactor, someone paying your way? Got me?"

"I am working."

Morrison's eyes widened and he snapped his fingers. "I remember ... you were there that night at Hong's, with McCloskey and his runt Shorty Morand. You remember me, don't you?"

Quan answered with his eyes.

"You do. Now listen, my good boy: my name is Morrison — *Morrison* — and I'm with the Windsor Police." Morrison showed Quan his badge. "But you're going to forget all of that. Understand?"

Quan nodded slowly.

"Don't worry, I'm not going to turn you in — but I do know people in immigration — and Mounties. I have a feeling you know who the Mounties are."

"Mounties." Quan nodded.

"You could be very useful," said Morrison, "and do good for yourself at the same time."

"Useful?"

"Jack McCloskey must not know we spoke. We will speak again, or I will contact my friends in immigration. Where are you flopping? Sleeping like? At McCloskey's?"

"No, not at Jack's."

"Where?"

"A room. On top Allies."

"Allies? That diner near the Walkerville Theatre?"

"Yes."

"Huh. Okay, Quan Lee, I'll have other work for you soon, very soon," said Morrison. "I'll find you when I'm ready for you."

Chapter 30

FINAL AUDITIONS

McCloskey leaned back in his chair and, looking over his shoulder to Pearl seated behind him, said, "Remind me again, am I paying for this?"

She gave the back of his head a gentle smack. "Hush and pay attention. This is what you been asking for, remember?"

Every day McCloskey had been asking Pearl how things were coming along with the entertainment portion of opening night. She kept putting him off and putting him off, until yesterday when she informed him that — after, in her words, whittling down her talent roster — she would be holding her last round of auditions mid-week.

So here they were, not even started yet and McCloskey was already fidgeting like a kid in church. Fortunately it was all going rather smoothly. Pearl told everyone to be at the club no later than six, giving everyone enough time to finish up with their daytime commitments and maybe grab a bite to eat — though there would be refreshments.

One of Pearl's chorus girls, Susie, handled the talent when they arrived, holding their hands in the dressing room until Pearl gave her the cue to bring one of them out. The first hopeful was a woman who was here to unveil her trademark "Salome's Dance," a routine she had been performing on stage since the coronation (which coronation, no one was sure). Apparently she had even taken the act to London and New York, where it was well received. Unfortunately the act was looking a little dated, as was Salome. The cringe-worthy act was like watching your auntie perform a burlesque show. McCloskey expressed his dislike with a hand signal behind his back. Pearl thanked the woman and told her she would be in touch.

The next act was a husband and wife team. The husband did some comedy bits — one with a ventriloquist dummy that kept falling apart, and another as a clumsy juggler. His wife played the straight man the whole time. Pearl told McCloskey that the duo could add some laughs and a bit of physical comedy to the show. They were a "maybe."

The third act was a former professional baseball player. He delivered a mildly amusing monologue about his days on the diamond, and then did a short song and dance number. McCloskey liked him and thought he might be a hit with the crowd. Perhaps he could even be persuaded to deliver some prognostications on the rest of the season. He was a "definite maybe."

There were a few other artists that got their chance to impress the owner of the club. The only standout was Li-Ling's father, Woo. He played a Chinese guitar, or *ruan*, that had a big round moon face and four strings. McCloskey had his reservations but Pearl insisted he give Woo a listen. She said it could really tie together some of the Oriental themes McCloskey already had going on in the club. Woo played a couple of traditional folk songs, impressing McCloskey so much that he made Woo promise to be a part of their bill for opening night.

That left one more act.

"Susie — our tap dancer Mr. Piedmont, please."

"Coming right up."

Susie disappeared through the stage's back curtain and then reappeared with a smiling, nattily dressed young gentleman with a peg leg.

McCloskey turned all the way around in his chair this time. "Wait — you were serious? A one-legged tap dancer? Did you save the best for last?"

Pearl shushed him. "Just watch ... and listen."

McCloskey turned back around. "Mr. Piedmont, is it?

"Rufus Piedmont, sir, but usually I just go by Peg Leg."

"You lose it in the war?"

"No, sir, a cotton gin accident when I was twelve."

"And that's when you decided to take up tap dancing?"

"Tap, yes, but I been dancing since I was about five years old."

"Please, go ahead," said Pearl.

Peg Leg bowed and then launched into a fiery routine that had both McCloskey and Pearl spellbound. He was nearly acrobatic at times, his routine ending with him landing in a front split, peg leg forward. The room was dead silent for a moment, and then McCloskey started a round of applause. Turning to Pearl, he said, "Make sure we get him for opening night."

"You got it, Jack."

"Thank you, Mr. Piedmont."

The dancer sprung back up. "Thank you, sir."

"Mr. Piedmont, Susie will make sure we have all of your contact information."

"Yes, sir." Piedmont mopped his brow and made for the dressing room with Susie.

"What do we have next?" asked McCloskey.

"That's it, Jack."

"What do you mean *that's it*?"

"Short notice," said Pearl. She was hoping Peg Leg would have been enough of a distraction. "People are booked, touring, on vacation —"

"There must be some other —"

"Sorry, Jack."

"So that's it? Some show."

Pearl had been conversing with bookers on both sides of the river, and even tried to catch a few acts live on stage. She knew it was going to be tough, and she also wanted the right mix of talent. The only guidance from McCloskey was that there be no minstrel acts. She thought that was a given. It was tough and she herself began to have some doubts. She kept that to herself though, and kept the bookers' doubts about Shady's to herself, too. People were already telling McCloskey that the concept — a combination of Chinese and roadhouse food; entertainment with no burlesque and no booze — would never fly. Pearl told him that he had to trust her, and that she had a feeling in her gut that it was going to take off. She had to stay strong, especially while McCloskey continued to have these misgivings.

He was about to go stomping out of the joint when Pearl grabbed him by the arm. "Jack, I'm telling you this is going to work."

McCloskey knew he would eventually break out of his funk. He was just in a mood. He needed a drink.

"I can do this," she said. "You fill the house and I'll give them a show like they've never seen. If they don't like it, well then, you can always turn the place a into a five-pin bowling alley."

She got a smile out of him. That was good.

"I feel like I've invested more than just money into this place. Pearl, I really want it to work. I need it to work."

"You think I don't?" She pressed her palms against his cheeks. "Just leave the entertainment to me. Who knows … I might have a little something extra for you up my sleeve."

Chapter 31

SALT MAN

Thursday, August 16

He had come down to police headquarters of his own volition, proceeding straight to the front desk and asking to speak to a detective regarding a certain matter. He looked a little lost.

"Any detective in particular? Which matter?"

He pulled a square of yellow paper out of the inside pocket of a well-worn jacket, unfolded the dusty sheet and held it in front of the duty sergeant's face. The grit got everywhere.

"Oh, it's Detective Campbell you're after."

"Yes — is he here?"

"What's your name, lad?"

"Burke, sir."

"Burke."

The duty sergeant jotted down the name and the time somewhere in the margins of his blotter and then went back to the ledger opened over it. He looked over the edge of the tall desk and said, motioning blindly toward a uniform standing nearby with his hands in his pockets, "Yes, Mr. Burke, the detective is in."

"Sir?"

"Constable, show this gentleman to our conference room."

"Right."

Dirkland led Burke down a couple links of hallway to the so-called conference room while the sergeant rang up Campbell and informed him that he had a guest, a young man from the salt mines.

"He had his papers with him, and that pamphlet with your name on it. Sir, if I may say —"

"Where will I find him?"

When the detective arrived in the room he excused the constable hovering at the door and joined the young civilian at the table, pulling out the chair opposite him.

"Burke, is it?" said Campbell, folding his hands.

"Yes, sir."

"Relax, mister. Am I to understand you know something about our victim?"

There were six other men from the mines who had paid Campbell a visit since he had started his search for answers.

"Yes."

"So …?"

"Well, I saw the bulletins posted in the offices and on the grounds, asking if anyone knew anything. And if they did know something, well, they should go to Windsor's police and ask for you." Burke reached in his pocket and unfolded the paper again. The creases looked like they had been getting a good workout, as if he had been rehearsing this moment. "It's all right here."

"Ah. I'm familiar," said Campbell.

"I had a feeling — no, I knew — but I needed to know what everyone else knew, what everyone else saw. There were photographs. How could I face anyone?"

Campbell unlocked his fingers.

"Just what exactly have you come to tell me, Burke?"

The miner looked for his reply somewhere over the detective's shoulders, in a corner of the ceiling.

"That I killed him, sir."

Out of the half-dozen other interviewees, this was the first real confession Campbell had heard; not that he was expecting one. He pretended not to notice.

"Can you tell me a little bit more about that?"

"He saved my life," said Burke.

"In the mines?"

"In the mines? No, in the war, sir. I carried him to a quiet, undisturbed place, scraped out a small grave with my helmet. I didn't have much time. I was only able to dig out so much. I fit him in it —"

"Somewhere in the field?"

"In the mines," said Burke.

Campbell was trying to gather and assemble. "Who was he?" he asked. "He had nothing on him."

Burke pulled an envelope — a pay packet — out from his coat pocket, opened the end of it and spilled its contents onto the table. "This is what he had on him."

There was coin, a Dominion Salt identification, a wallet with a couple of bank notes, and a pocket watch of little or no value, as tarnished and dead as its owner.

Campbell searched for a name.

"Fitzsimmons," he said.

"Jim he was to me."

"You didn't tell anyone?"

"How could I?"

Campbell could tell that the soldier was about to break down.

"No one else knows you're here?"

"No one."

The detective was having trouble figuring out which minefield he was treading through.

"How did it happen? Underground, I mean."

"Well … we were shedding away —"

"Where exactly?"

"Near where you found him."

"Uh huh." Campbell pulled out his notebook and a tiny pencil and started jotting notes. "I'm listening … but how? I mean, how did you happen to kill him? Was there a weapon handy that you used?"

"I told you, detective …"

"Yes, you did tell me."

"It was an accident."

"You were a prisoner of war, Burke."

Burke swallowed hard. "I was."

"And Fitzsimmons?"

Campbell walked Burke down the labyrinth of halls towards the exit, pausing near the front desk, and was caught by the duty sergeant.

"Any help, detective?" said the duty sergeant.

"Yes and no," said Campbell.

"Should I expect to see him again?"

Campbell's mind was somewhere else, somewhere below the river.

"Could you phone Dr. Laforet and have him meet me in my office as soon as he is available? I'll be waiting. Tell him it's about our salt man."

When he arrived, Laforet was escorted to the detective's door. The doctor nodded to Bickerstaff and waved him away with his hand.

"Why are you so nasty to my constables?"

"Aren't they used to it?"

"I don't encourage it."

"So, why did you summon me? And did you order us lunch?"

"I've been talking to men from the mines, not too many, but maybe just enough. I think I may have something … or someone."

"The long and the short?"

"He didn't do it. Well … he did and he didn't."

"There's more," said Laforet.

"I need to tell you."

"What?"

"I let Burke go, telling him it was because I already had someone in custody."

"You lied to him."

"I suppose I did," said Campbell.

"Why?"

"Is it still lying if it's to someone I know is not in their right mind?"

"You're playing games with truth," said Laforet. "Is this to someone else's advantage? Or to yours?" The doctor scraped the floor with the feet of a chair and sat himself down. "Campbell, what have you done?"

The detective was trying to remain cool. "He and the victim were prisoners of war, forced into labour, in one of the salt mines —" he flipped back through his notepad "— a place called Soltau, north of Hanover."

"*Salt river.*"

"German too? You're always full of surprises."

"I remain a mystery. Go on," said Laforet.

"Yes, fitting. Apparently Fitzsimmons — if that was even his name — earned himself a certain position amongst the other prisoners. He was made something like a foreman. Fitzsimmons was taking orders from German officers, and then giving orders to his countrymen, his brothers in arms. When they were down in the mines, they didn't know which way was up."

"And what happened in our mines?"

"I'm not sure. Right now my only theory is that when they were down below the river, alone together, they were in Soltau."

Laforet was twisting his chair, trying to find a comfortable position. "Was Burke somehow putting things right?"

"Putting himself, or both him and Fitzsimmons, out of their collective misery? He gave me a story about it being an accident. Telling me the story, the look on his face, the look in his eyes … I believe that *he* believed what he was telling me."

"Honestly, do you think that he is a danger to anyone?"

Campbell poked his teeth with a thumbnail. "A danger to no one, except maybe himself. Damn it, how am I going to get inside his head?"

"Try meeting him in the mines."

Chapter 32

SPATS AND QUARRELS

McCloskey had never had a fuller or more varied plate in front of him than he did right now. It was a smorgasbord of trouble.

He was in his apartment, sinking in his thinking chair. It normally granted him a view of the top of the Dime building over in Detroit; however, Vera Maude — heated and with her hands on her hips — was blocking it, staring him down. It was late morning but it had already been a day. He leaned his head back, with one arm across his chest, holding old wounds, himself together. The leather was soft and smooth. He pressed his cheek against the cool and let his other hand dangle, unable to find that tumbler of rye that existed only in his dreams. Vera Maude was making the room vibrate, making it hot. He wasn't prepared for this, whatever it was. Not right now.

What day is this? What time is it?

Even with his eyes closed he could still see her.

"All right, what's going on between you and Pearl?" she asked.

He opened his eyes and lifted his head. "What?"

"I've been getting the distinct feeling for a while now that something's going on between you two."

He shook his head. "She and me are in business together, remember?"

"Yeah, well, just what kind of business?"

"Maudie, Jesus, there's nothing going on between me and Pearl outside the club." He paused and shook his head again. "Damn it … where's this coming from?"

"I don't know if I believe you."

"Maudie, why's it bother you so much? It isn't like me and you are married or anything."

"Oh, so there is something going on! Hey — what do mean *or anything*? I thought by now I would have ranked a little higher than *or anything*."

He sat up. "Maudie, I think this wedding's making you crazy."

"Don't change the subject." She turned, faced the window, and stared blankly down at the intersection while McCloskey studied her behind. She did an abrupt about-face and threw at him, "I know I can't be the only woman in your life."

McCloskey was genuinely confused. "Is that a question?" he asked. He was used to pulling crowbars and guns, and generally pushing other people's buttons when the situation called for it. He was still getting accustomed to using his words, though people often told him he had the gift. He'd say it was purely accidental.

"A guy once told me," he said, "only ask the questions that you already know the answer to."

That was an unintended curve. "What's that even mean?" she asked.

"I'm still working on it."

She leaned in and pushed her hands against his shoulders and he folded back into the chair. "So you're her benefactor or something, right?" she said.

"Her what?"

"Patron … you sign the cheques?"

"No," he said, "we only deal in cash." Bad time to get smart, but it was often a reflex of his. He was rarely so smart of his own accord.

"For what?"

"She earns it." That was bad too, but he couldn't seem to help himself.

"How?"

"You wanna play like this?" He straightened up. "What about you and Bernie?"

"What about me and Bernie?"

"What's going on between you two?"

"Nothing."

"I'm hearing his name a lot — Bernie this and Bernie that; stuff like, 'Oh, I can't, Jack. I'm meeting Bernie for coffee.' Is that all you're meeting him for?"

"Yeah, that's all I'm meeting him for," she said, mimicking him. "We like to discuss our writing and other stuff."

She stepped back and did a short pace about the room, barely enough to scuff her shoes.

"I just remembered I gotta go meet somebody," said McCloskey.

"Who?"

"I have to meet with Quan." McCloskey thought maybe he could try to end this on a high note. "We can talk some more about this later — if you want."

She looked down at him. "Okay."

He thought he saw her pout. *Uncharacteristic of her if she is*, he thought. Nevertheless he still had to fight off the urge to bite her lower lip.

The two walked down the stairs to the street in silence.

"Can I give you a ride anywhere?"

"No, thanks. I think I'd like to walk," she said.

He watched her move down towards the river, and when he lost sight of her decided it was probably time to head over to the club.

McCloskey pulled Quan into the pantry adjacent to the kitchen for a private conversation. It was about the size of a walk-in closet, lined with cans and small boxes of foodstuffs, with a bare bulb hanging close to the ceiling.

"Quan, tell me, you must tell me, when you came from Toronto, were you carrying anything?"

"Carrying?"

"Did you have any drugs, any opium on you?"

He was wiping his hands on his apron.

"I did."

"You had nothing when you came out of the river."

"No, nothing."

"What did you do with it?"

"I gave it to the smugglers. When we were at the boat, time to go, they ask for more money. We had nothing; we gave opium."

That sounded about right: Get them all the way to the finish line and then tell them they don't get to cross it unless they give up the rest of their valuables.

"While here, in the Border Cities, have you ever been in possession of any drugs or opium?"

Quan shook his head. "No, Jack, no."

"Have you used it? Look at me."

"No."

"I believe you." McCloskey gave him a little breathing room and then asked Quan if he had been talking to any known drug smugglers or users.

Quan shrugged and looked away. He said, "Yes." His tone made it all sound as if it were inevitable, perhaps even unavoidable for him.

McCloskey put his hands on Quan's shoulders. "Do you need help with anyone? I can take care of it for you; do you understand?"

Quan turned away again and didn't look McCloskey in the eyes as he said, "No, Jack, I do not need help."

McCloskey wasn't sure if he believed that. "Okay," he said. "Get back to work then. We'll talk again later."

Quan headed into the kitchen and McCloskey paused for a moment in the pantry, his palm pressing his forehead, his other hand on his hip. He needed to find out what the hell was going on. He was feeling a little out of his league with this drug-smuggling stuff. It was coming at a bad time, what with the club and the Wrecking and Salvage pulling him in two different directions.

"Is this all right?" he said, in the voice of a lover unhinged.

She smiled a smile that pulled the corners of her mouth into a curl. "Yes," she said between kisses, making him sure, "yes … I want this." Hot rye breath and the sticky tang of ginger on his lips.

It was in an alley off Mercer, on a town car on blocks, low with no wheels and a fractured carriage. Someone else's destruction-in-progress. He helped her up so that she could straddle the hood. She rested her polished heels inside the bent fenders. He stepped back for a look. Her hair was tousled and her blouse was casually making a departure around her shoulders. He was at a sudden loss for words.

"If he already thinks I'm messing around," she said, "well then, I guess I might as well."

"So I'm a *might as well*?" Not that he cared a smudge at this juncture.

She leaned back across the length of the hood, her arms framing the top of her head, that mane of hair let loose. "Lest it mean as much as you want so long as it means nothing."

One dim, bare bulb hung over a nearby delivery door. Her eyes and cheeks glowed and made the cold light warm. He gently worked her skirt further over her hips.

"What he doesn't know won't hurt him," she told herself, her eyes closed.

"But what he finds out could get me killed," said Bernie.

"He trusts me," she moaned.

"Oh —"

Her finger found his lips. "Don't say my name … I want this." She threw her head back one more time.

"Just this once," he said.

"Was that a question? Or some kind of answer? Once … wants … once …" She pulled him closer and closed his mouth with hers.

He pulled away. "Only once."

"Only wants," she said. "Let the needs take care of themselves."

"I'm living in the moment."

So long as the moment's mine to be had.

"Stop talking."

Chapter 33

REFORMATORY BLUES

LEE HING IS FREED

Laundryman Spends Two Weeks in Jail, Then Pays $200 Fine

Lee Hing, 19 years old, laundryman remanded two weeks ago by Judge W.E. Gundy for violation of the "dope" act and sentenced to six months imprisonment to the reformatory at Guelph, was released from the county jail yesterday when he agreed to pay a fine.

Hing had been held at the jail awaiting transportation to the reformatory. Yesterday he told W.A. Wanless, jailer, that he would pay the fine. He paid $200 and costs.

Morrison folded the *Star* and slapped it on his desk like he was swatting a fly. Having real police matters to attend to, he had missed yesterday's court proceedings. He rested his elbow on the arm of his desk and pressed his fist against one soft, pink cheek.

"Freed," he mumbled to himself, "but marked."

Six months lost in the reformatory, or an outcast on the streets of the Border Cities — either way, Morrison was losing another one. But there were always more, and that's what he kept telling himself.

Quan Lee would be taking on a little more responsibility, picking up the slack. Morrison decided he'd accidentally run into him when the boy was finished his shift at McCloskey's place, Shady's, and give him the good news then.

He should be pleased, thought Morrison.

There was a Lucky Tiger Tonic bottle full of whisky in the bottom drawer of his desk. He grabbed it, unscrewed the cap, and topped up his coffee. It touched the lip of his mug.

"After Shave and Face Tonic," he read out loud between sips, "To Smooth and Refresh."

He replaced the bottle, stood, and shed his hat and rumpled coat. He was decorating the rack in the corner when there was a knock and a shadow appeared at the door.

"Morrison?"

"What?"

"Message."

"Fancy." Morrison took it. "What? You looking for a tip?"

The constable disappeared and the detective opened the envelope. There was a card inside.

"*Répondez s'il vous plaît.*"

He tossed the card onto his desk and set his gaze towards the window overlooking Goyeau, already humid and shedding light on some old finger streaks.

Damn.

— *Chapter 34* —

UNDERCOVER

It was sometime mid-afternoon and after his fourth coffee of the day when Campbell had decided to work Morrison into tonight's perambulations. He just had to figure out how to go about it.

He knew his first problem was going to be the way Morrison kept his movements to himself — unless it was an actual case, and then he made his activities well-known. Campbell didn't want to have to resort to making up some bogus reason for needing to know where to find him. He thought he'd try something else. He walked out of the building to the street, turned around, and then walked back in, straight to the duty sergeant's desk. Their brief conversation had gone something like this:

"Next time you see Morrison, you should tell him it looks like someone kissed his front bumper a little too hard, unless he already knows. I just passed his vehicle and the thing is hanging by a single screw."

"Couldn't have been his car; he's in Walkerville meeting with their chief constable. Their weekly information exchange. He's due back around four thirty to bring the chief up to speed."

"Ah."

"Leaving again?"

"I only came back to mention that bit about Morrison's car. I'm actually off to the library to do a bit of research before heading home."

The desk sergeant, only vaguely interested, returned to his logbook or whatever detective fiction he was reading.

That's when Campbell had gotten the idea. He would go home, grab the street clothes he had acquired from Laforet, those found on the homeless dead and meant for incineration. The doctor always let Campbell sift through them, helping him come up with costumes that would occasionally render him unrecognizable for his nightly walks. He would go straight to his apartment at half past four, change into his get-up, don his overcoat, drive back to a discreet spot near headquarters, and wait for Morrison to exit after his meeting.

It was after 5:30 now, and sitting in the Essex in this heat all he could smell were the nights the unfortunate owners of the clothes had spent in doorways, parks, or huddled under a bridge; that and the smell of death. His overcoat saved the interior of the Essex from those indestructible odours, but not his nose.

Morrison finally emerged from police headquarters, alone, and walked right past his own car. That was good, thought Campbell. Careful not to lose sight of him, Campbell got out of his vehicle, removed his overcoat, threw it into the trunk of the car, and found his grubby hat.

In his frayed and tattered garb, he stayed on Morrison's trail. Campbell's biggest risk was being picked up for vagrancy. He double-checked that he had his badge with him.

Morrison headed east on Park Street, and then along the south side of City Hall Square, taking his time. He then continued north up the east side of the square, cutting over to McDougall, heading north, just past Assumption. With hardly a break in his step, Morrison entered Walker's Quick Lunch.

Almost directly across the street were a machine shop and a vacant building separated by a narrow laneway — narrow meaning the width of two sets of shoulders. Campbell tucked himself in there and kept an eye on the restaurant. Morrison came out again not a minute later, looked up and down the street, checked his watch, and then re-entered the establishment.

It was called Walker's Lunch but was actually open all day, catering most of the time to City Hall employees and the police department. The officers often came here after a shift.

Campbell waited and watched passersby. The streets were quieter now, what with people home from work and having their dinner, and most of the shops were closed.

6:10 p.m.

Coming from the north and moving at a fast clip was a man who looked to be constable Hawkeswood, in plain clothes. His dress and the direction from which he came suggested that he wasn't coming from the police station. He entered Walker's, and Campbell wondered if he was meeting with Morrison.

It was just before 7:00 when the two of them emerged and headed in the direction from which Hawkeswood had come.

Campbell waited until the two were a little farther up the block before stepping out of the laneway. He kept them in view. It wasn't difficult; there was hardly anyone else on the street. The downside was that it also made him quite visible. He pulled his greasy old hat down a little farther.

When his two subjects stopped at Chatham Street, Campbell had to quickly find cover. Not easy since all there was along this stretch were homes with front gardens. He ducked between two parked cars and hoped he didn't miss anyone sitting out on their verandah. Luckily Morrison and Hawkeswood shared only a few words before separating, Hawkeswood heading west towards the Avenue and Morrison continuing towards the river.

The market was shuttered. Empty carts pushed up against the side of the building and vendors' stalls were closed. Quite a difference from your average Saturday morning, when the place was a beehive of activity.

Morrison stopped at Pitt Street. Campbell shuffled over to one of the stalls, where he still had a good view of Morrison. For the first time since he left the diner, he looked over his shoulder, not once, but twice. Satisfied, it seemed, he crossed Pitt where he took a turn towards the Avenue. The streets were tight here and Campbell was losing opportunities for cover. He hung back a little.

Morrison stopped at Windsor Avenue, looked over his shoulder once again, and then hung a right toward the river. Campbell sprinted ahead, almost on tiptoe, hugged the building at the corner and carefully peaked around it. Morrison was on the other side of the street, walking more swiftly now. Without pausing, Morrison took one last look over his shoulder and entered the alleyway that separated Pitt and Riverside Drive.

Campbell moved quickly. He pressed himself against the building at the mouth of the alleyway and observed Morrison, who stopped about halfway down the block and knocked on the back door of a building on the right-hand side. A few seconds passed, the door opened and Morrison entered.

This was a bad spot for someone dressed like him to be standing around. He'd get picked up for sure. He knew he had his badge on him, but for some reason he was feeling that could end up blowing his cover. What he needed to do was find a safe place somewhere in the alleyway. The problem there was that he had no idea what direction Morrison would be heading once he emerged. Campbell decided to take a chance.

He moved slowly down the alleyway with his hands in his pockets and his head down — there was a possibility that Morrison would be making his exit just as Campbell was walking by — looking left and right for any opportunity for some kind of cover. There appeared to be nothing on this side of the door that he believed Morrison had entered. Tense, he paused and made mental notes about the door. It was lime-green with what looked to be a slot at eye level. A yellow dragon climbed the left side and across the top, ferociously gazing down at callers.

It suddenly dawned on him: *Chung Hong's … the Thursday night poker game McCloskey was talking about.*

He continued down the alleyway. Not far along, there was a recess, just large enough for a vehicle. It was probably a loading area. On the Chung Hong–side of the recess was a set of metal stairs. Campbell parked himself on the third step, keeping out of sight but at a good angle for leaning out and occasionally peaking around the corner.

While he sat, he occupied his mind with thoughts of Morrison. He searched his mind for any odd piece of information, any observation that at the time might have seemed irrelevant and he just filed away.

Perhaps there are one or two missing pieces in there somewhere.

His thoughts were interrupted when a man entered the alley from the opposite end. Campbell watched and listened as the man lifted ashcan lids and sifted through the packing in crates and boxes. He was getting closer.

The sight of Campbell startled him. The figure paused for a moment. He had a young face and his clothes looked not unlike those that made up the detective's disguise. He nodded without smiling and continued about his business down the alley.

It made Campbell think about the man, whoever he had been, who died wearing these clothes. They weren't an old man's clothes. Maybe they were worn by a man this transient had even known. Perhaps he thought for a moment he was seeing a ghost. *He's the age of many veterans*, thought Campbell.

He turned to watch the young man exit the alley, cross the street, and continue on his way. When he was out of sight, Campbell turned his mind back to Morrison.

At about 8:40 he heard a door slam, taking him out of his thoughts. He peeked around the corner. It was Morrison. He pulled his head back and listened. The big man's footsteps echoed slightly between the buildings, making it difficult at first to tell in which direction he was heading. Campbell waited. The footsteps were approaching.

Campbell eased himself up carefully, but the rusty steps still creaked. He rounded them, tucked himself underneath the stairs, sat down with his back against the wall and his knees up, his face pressed against them. Morrison must have heard and had possibly seen every movement.

The footsteps stopped at the stairs. A few seconds passed. Morrison was lighting a cigarette. The footsteps continued. Campbell waited until the sound of them stopped echoing between the buildings and then he unfolded himself and quickly moved to the end of the alleyway.

Once he got out in the open there were more city and street sounds, not to mention the distant noise of the train station and even the ferry dock.

Which direction?

Campbell took a chance and went back up to Pitt Street. There were more people moving about too. His instinct told him to head towards the Avenue. He spotted Morrison up ahead.

Campbell's luck quickly ran out: he lost sight of Morrison. He flipped a coin in his head to determine his next move. Heads he would take a right, tails a left. It was heads.

Damn. He's definitely not making for the British-American.

Surmising that Morrison went in the other direction, he doubled back in a hurry.

There … there he is.

Campbell could see Morrison, slowly galumphing his way up the Avenue. He seemed unconcerned about being seen as he crossed London and then Chatham. Between the doorways, the pedestrians, and the streetcars there was no shortage of cover for Campbell along here. He watched Morrison turn into the Allen Theatre.

Going to the movies, Morrison?

Campbell kept walking. He considered turning into the alcove of the theatre but decided against it at the last second. That was a good thing because leaning against the inside of it, just inside, was Morrison trying to light up another cigarette. Fortunately his head was down, but Campbell's heart skipped a beat. He paused several yards away and glanced over to see if Morrison was still there. He was, enjoying his cigarette and eyeing a building across the street. Campbell followed his line of vision.

The Auditorium Building.

Campbell looked around for a place to position himself. Steve Paris Shoes was on the other side of the theatre. They'd be closed for the day and he could tuck himself in their doorway — he was sure Mr. Paris wouldn't mind.

It was after 9:00 now. Morrison hadn't moved and apart from the moviegoers and those out for an evening stroll, the streets had thinned. The only thing about the Auditorium Building that might be of any interest to Morrison, concluded Campbell, was Jack McCloskey's club.

But what about it?

Campbell was now more curious about this than anything else. People who looked like they could be McCloskey's staff started trickling out of the building. Campbell looked over at Morrison, who straightened up, pulled his cigarette out of his mouth, and rubbed it into the pavement under his toe. It was as if he had been looking for someone in particular.

— Chapter 35 —

HEAVEN HELP ME

Saturday, August 18

They were putting the finishing touches on the place. Claude had the sweepers rearrange the tables and chairs for the third time in as many days, the pieces ending up right back in their original position. The new linens, freshly laundered, were then draped over the tables, straightened, and smoothed with careful hands in white cotton gloves. Claude had his boys polish the silver — again — while the waitresses folded napkins into the shape of diamonds and set them on side plates. The tables were finished by the time the flowers arrived. The florist and his wife came in holding crystal vases overflowing with bold arrangements of purple hyacinths.

In the kitchen Eddie, Quan, and their assistant, Vern, had completed their inspection of the produce and were now sharpening their steel weapons, muttering their final prayers, and readying for battle. They had developed a rhythm in the kitchen, which was essential in the small space. Long and narrow, much like a trench, the cooks always seemed to be dancing around each other in it. Their young assistant, still slightly offbeat, was occasionally body-checked into the counters and appliances. He'd pick it up soon enough.

McCloskey managed to stay out of the way while all of this was going on. He knew he had a good team; it was just a matter of learning to leave them alone and let them do their jobs. In order to look more the part, he had bought himself a tuxedo from Camden's in Walkerville, his first, and Vera Maude had bought a new dress at Smith's, a long, navy-coloured canton with a satin face. Apart from the stage costume that people had already seen in rehearsals, Pearl was keeping her other outfit — her mingling wear — a surprise.

Vera Maude was given the okay to invite Uncle Fred and Mrs. Cattanach, which she did, and they politely declined. That was expected. Uncle Fred may be up for a trip to Shady's for a boys' night, but Mrs. Cattanach, the church volunteer, was a different story. Of course Shorty would come, but McCloskey wanted to limit the gang's attendance to just him. He didn't want the seats filled with friends and family; he wanted to see some fresh faces in the crowd, people who would help get the word out.

The doors opened at seven. McCloskey noticed guests gravitated towards the bar right away. There were rows of champagne flutes and bottles chilling on ice. He thought he could hear a few groans. He knew some would disapprove of the evening's non-alcoholic signature drink, Ginger's Tease — sparkling white grape juice with a splash of ginger ale. McCloskey spotted a guest whispering into the bartender's ear, no doubt asking if there was *anything wetter behind the bar*. The bartender shook his head and continued pouring glasses.

After spending some time greeting people at the door, McCloskey started making his way around the room, shaking more hands, helping them find seats, and smiling at everyone. His face was starting to hurt. He promised them good food and a great show. He had felt more relaxed negotiating his way out of a bad rum-running deal on a government dock at gunpoint. He was of two minds: If this worked, he'd either keep rolling it out for the people of the Border Cities, or cash in his chips and hang a FOR LEASE sign on the door Monday morning.

It was time to check in with the talent in the dressing room.

"Make yourself decent, Pearl. You're on in two minutes."

"Are my seams straight?"

"Jesus, Pearl, I got councilmen waiting for me out there. I got other flesh to press. Now get the girls in line."

"Wish us luck."

"You know what I always say to that," said McCloskey.

"Yeah, that luck's got nothing to do with it."

McCloskey turned, a fist in his pocket and the other hand rubbing his chin, wondering away with that same old feeling. Without turning back, staring at the playbills the girls had posted on the wall for inspiration, he said, "Just light the room for me, Pearl."

She finished fussing with her stockings, stood, and kissed the back of his neck. "Just watch me."

Pearl led out the Windsor Follies, who came out first in the same costume — white sailor's suits, but with above-the-knee skirts instead of trousers. The idea was to have them set the tone of the evening. They seemed to do just that with two song and dance numbers: a rendition of Paul Whiteman's "Hot Lips," followed by Gershwin's "Do It Again." There wasn't a lot of room on the stage so they were limited as to what they could do, though no one in the audience seemed to mind. All the men in the room sat up a little straighter — out of respect for the uniform, they'd later tell their wives and girlfriends.

When Pearl and the Follies were done they filed off the stage, swinging their arms slightly at their sides, giving the impression of a march. They wove between the tables, saluting the guests. A few of them got a pat on the rear. They were used to that. They eventually made it back to the stage, much to the disappointment of the men. Without missing a step or looking back, they passed through the curtain.

While the applause was going, the waiters came around with the menus. The break in the entertainment gave the talent a chance to catch their breath and the guests a chance to examine their dinner options. There was much discussion over it. McCloskey hoped it was because there were too many solid choices. He quizzed his table about what they thought looked good to them. They were all feeling adventurous, except for Shorty.

Bernie's time had been trimmed, his spotlight slightly dimmed. He had imagined a larger role for himself, some deciding power on the entertainment side of things. He was none too happy, but when he saw the big picture was relieved that he had been kept on board. He had been beginning to worry that he would be cut altogether. The audience responded favourably, and he took a little something away from it. McCloskey had Pearl smooth it out — it really wasn't his territory — and it was now hers to run with.

When it was time for the dessert course, Pearl came out from behind the curtain in a floor-length sequined gown the colour of seafoam. She was beaming. She was turning it all on. There were a few gasps from the tables seated closest to the stage. She gave a short bow and then blew McCloskey a kiss. He looked over at Vera Maude, who squinted and wagged her finger at him, as if she had caught him up to no good. He shrugged.

"Thank you, thank you for being here for this very special night. I'd like to sing you an original number called "Heaven Help Me."

She looked over at Patch, her piano accompanist who would also pitch in on the vocal, and gave him a nod.

> *I got the wares, but no one's buyin' — no sale*
> *I got troubles, but no one's troublin' — troublin'*
> *I got reasons, but ain't no one list'nin' — deaf ears*
> *I got the blues while sisters ARE ROSY*
> *Heaven help me, 'cause I can't help myself.*
> *Oh, heaven help me, I just can't help myself.*
>
> *He's got the looks, and I keep lookin'*
> *He's got the moves, and I ain't dodgin'*
> *He's got the car, and it's not stallin'*
> *He's got the goods that I want so bad*
> *Heaven help me, 'cause I can't help myself.*
> *Oh, heaven help me, I just can't help myself.*
>
> *River's wide, tide is low, spirits high*
> *River's wide, tide is low, spirits high*
> *River's wide, tide is low, spirits high*
>
> *We got some bills, but they're not payin'*
> *We got our ills, and no one's healin'*
> *We got each oth'r, we're not complainin'*
> *We got our sins and the preacher's cashin' in*

Heaven help us, 'cause we can't help ourselves.
Oh, heaven help us, we just can't help ourselves.

Patch closed it up as the applause started. Pearl took a bow. It didn't seem like her smile could have gotten any wider, but it did. She gave the audience a wave. McCloskey briefly considered going onstage to thank her and take her hand while she took another bow, but this was her moment. The audience was looking for an encore. And she had one, of a sort.

"Thank you, thank you all. Would you like another?"

The wave of applause crested.

"Okay," she mouthed something to Patch in an exaggerated way and then turned and smiled at the crowd. He was reluctant, but she coaxed the tune out of him.

"Patch has been tinkering with this one for a while, that's why he was being a bit shy about it. I love it. He's going to perform it for us, and I'll just hum along. Ladies and gentlemen, 'You Were Made to Break My Heart.'"

Patch dropped himself slowly into the rhythm, and then it came, fingers hitting keys, hammers hitting strings. He closed his eyes, tilted his head back, and let the words come.

There's nothing I can do, I'm powerless
Can't stop your emotion once in motion
I've got a funny feeling
A not so funny feeling

You come home tremorin' like you got shook
And I know someone else did the shakin'
You cast a shadow on my heart
A shadow on my heart

Please don't come home now, she said
Don't come home
Not right now

Heartbreak don't come cheap; I pay a premium
They see the scars but I'm the one's untouched
Thought I knew her, guess I did
Guess I always knew her did
Flesh is weak but it cuts to the quick
Smiling while she shares her wiles and I while
myself away
She was made to break my heart
Break it up and down

If you could come home now, I said
Come home now
And find me time

A fool to friends, but I can still bend a smile
Her wants begets a vacancy in me
I find myself stagg'ring sober
And shouldering empty arms

Love's a terrible thing, especially when
Passion plays its trump and everyone loses.
That band of gold's bad for your circulation
Keep me somewhere close while you wander

If I could only forget your every yesterday
And meet you over and over again

You were made to break my heart
Made to break it.

Patch's hands slowed and brought it down, then touched the keys one last time, holding the chord. For a moment the audience was silent. It was Pearl who started the applause. She knew talent when she heard it. She rushed over to Patch, gave him a kiss on the cheek and wiggled through the curtain to the dressing room. She had to prepare for the next act. Maybe she could throw the audience a curve.

The plates on the tables looked split between two-thirds Quan's Chinese menu and one-third roadhouse fare. McCloskey was relieved to see that and thought Quan should be proud.

The older folks started making their way to the door around ten. The stragglers hung on until shortly after eleven. McCloskey wasn't rushing anyone out the door. He continued working the room.

Vera Maude was thinking how much she liked seeing him in a tux. It suited him.

"Well, Jack, I think it was a success. You might have to consider doing this full-time." She was only half joking.

He had a big, dumb grin on his face. "Thanks, Maudie. Did I tell you how nice you look tonight?"

"No. But I know you've had other things on your mind. I bet you're exhausted."

"Actually I'm a little wound up. I sure could use a drink."

"I bet you know a place," she said, smiling.

"You know, I should let you in on a little secret: this place isn't all that dry."

"I'm shocked, Jack McCloskey, shocked!" she said. "So, where do you keep it? And why didn't you think you'd get raided tonight?"

"Actually, I thought I would. I'm a little disappointed, it would have been a great addition to the show."

"I don't think Pearl would have liked that too much."

"No, no, she wouldn't have." He paused. "So are you two okay?"

She put her serious face on, looked past him at nothing in particular, let him dangle for a moment, and then finally said, "Yeah, I think so."

"Pearl's all right, you know."

"I know, now. Let's get back to that drink. Where're you hiding it?"

"Where I hide everything: in plain sight."

She looked around the room. "So am I supposed to guess? Is that how I get my drink?"

"So long as you guess correctly."

She looked at one of the vases holding the hyacinths. "Are the flowers soaking in it?"

"They'd be wilted over by now."

She got up from her chair. "Plain sight, eh?" She walked about the room, stopping at the aquarium. It was as many gallons as four feet could hold, on a heavy wrought iron stand, lit from the top, and besides the fish pulled from the lake, it contained the usual props: some pretty rocks, a pirate's treasure chest, a cannon barrel, and a bottle wedged in the gravel. With her finger pressed against the glass, she said, "Jack ...?"

"You like brandy?" McCloskey stood up, removed his jacket, and rolled up his sleeve while making his way over to the tank. "I'm a smuggler, Maudie, remember?" He reached in ...

"Ooh, Jack, do they bite?"

... and pulled out the bottle.

"Let's have a splash." He had a waiter's corkscrew ready in his pocket. They sat down and he poured.

"Let's have a toast," he said.

"Yes," said Vera Maude. "Let's."

— *Chapter 36* —

AMONG THE BULRUSHES

"Campbell?"

It was late. McCloskey had been in a dead sleep. He stumbled out of bed and into the front room, smacking his shoulder on the doorframe. He had no idea how many times the phone had rang before he finally picked it up.

"On my way."

He set down the earpiece, hustled back to his bedroom, and pulled on the clothes he had tossed across the chair only a couple of hours before.

The roadster was parked right outside the terrace. He climbed in, shot down Dougall, and turned left onto the Drive, trying to rub the sleep out of his eyes.

The streetlights became fewer and farther between once he passed the ferry terminal and the salt mine. There were a few porch lights throwing their glow around like loose change as he passed through Sandwich, and then darkness again as he came out the other end. It was a starless night and he could smell the rain in the breeze coming from the north.

Hanging lanterns — a new touch — criss-crossing the parking lots at Chappell's, Oriental House, and the Westwood gradually brought things back into perspective. He hung a sharp right at Prospect Avenue and came to an abrupt halt a couple yards away from Janisse's ambulance. It looked like the driver didn't want to chance getting stuck in the mire. When McCloskey got out of the roadster he could see flashlight beams poking around the tall grass near the shore. A young couple were standing nearby, the guy holding his gal close. She was trembling and boo-hooing her way up to a full bawl while he looked a bit wobbly, probably drunk. It was difficult to say who was holding up whom. A uniform was positioned between them and the owners of the flashlight beams, hands on his hips. He turned when he heard McCloskey approach and seemed to think he could hold him back, but that was before McCloskey grabbed the man's wrist and used it to push him away.

"Hey, mister, you can't —"

"And yet I do," said McCloskey. He was working on what a clever newsboy once referred to as his own "critical lingo."

The keepers of the flashlight beams heard the tangle and immediately pivoted their shine in the direction of the bootlegger.

"Watch your step." Campbell's tone was somber.

Laforet had been crouching around the perimeter of the body. He straightened up and nodded at McCloskey.

The bootlegger took his cue and knelt down. It looked like Quan's clothes. There was some mud smeareed here and there on the hands and face. Then he noticed the fresh scar over the brow.

"Yeah," said McCloskey, "that's Quan."

"I'm sorry," said Campbell. "When was the last time you saw him?"

"This evening, at the club."

"Did he say or do anything that struck you at the time as unusual? What was his mood like?"

"He seemed agitated," said McCloskey. "I asked him if everything was all right ... he just put it down to overwork. He had picked up some hours at Hong's laundry. Who found him?"

"Those two," said Campbell. "My guess is they were looking for a soft spot in the tall grass. When they came across the body they ran back into the Westwood and begged for the manager to call the constabulary. Fitzgerald arrived about ten minutes later."

"Laforet? Your thoughts?"

The doctor was still getting used to these allowances being made to McCloskey. He went along with it for Campbell and the victim's sake. "Well, as you can tell by the impression in the weeds, we turned him over. What you are missing is the blow to the back of the head. If he didn't die from the blow, he could have also drowned, even in this shallow water. I didn't see any bullet wounds or possible points of entry in his clothing."

"And no one in the roadhouse heard anything unusual," said Campbell, back to thinking out loud. "Though it's possible he was moved to this location."

"You know that no one in the Westwood is going to say anything, right?" said McCloskey.

"Because none of them are supposed to be there," said Campbell. "Was Quan in any kind of trouble?"

"We were doing everything we could; you can ask Hong, Pearl … anyone at the club."

Fitzgerald approached. "Detective, will you be needing these two for anything else?"

"No," said Campbell. "Show them home."

"Sir?"

"Thank you."

Demoted to chaperone, Fitzgerald sulked away with the lately besotted, now traumatized, couple. In the morning they would have a unique, very unexpected reason for wishing never to call on each other again.

When the constable was out of earshot, the detective moved in on McCloskey. "Jack, tell me, did you ever see Morrison talking to Quan?"

Laforet looked away but his ears were perked.

McCloskey's eyes went wide. "No, why?"

"Just wondering."

"You're a detective; you're never just wondering," said McCloskey. "Have you?"

"Have I what?"

"Seen Morrison talking to Quan."

Campbell wished he could see the river over the bulrushes. The river grounded him. "No," he said.

"That bothers you."

Laforet wished he could step in.

"You missed something," continued McCloskey, "and that bothers you."

"Gentlemen," the doctor said, growing impatient, "there are more important matters to which we should attend."

The detective and the bootlegger collected themselves as best they could while the lines were blurring.

"I'll contact you later tomorrow," said Campbell, "when Laforet has something for us."

"This has to be right now," said McCloskey.

Laforet looked at Campbell.

"Jack," said Campbell, "this has to wait."

"No, it can't wait — I'm not going to take a number and wait."

Campbell turned again to Laforet, and Laforet nodded.

"All right, Jack. Help with the stretcher."

"Forget the stretcher." McCloskey steadied his footing and then bent down, taking Quan's body in his arms. He carried him through the mud to the ambulance and was once more reminded of all the bodies he had picked up off battlefields in France, including his injured brother.

"Should someone be contacting the next of kin?" asked Laforet.

"That would be his father in Vancouver," said McCloskey. "I have no idea how we would go about getting hold of him."

"Letters with a return address maybe," said Campbell. "I could look into that. Where did he room?"

"Over Allies, the diner near the Walkerville Theatre."

"Okay. And don't share this with anyone, McCloskey." Campbell was glad there was no Sunday edition of the *Star*. He could just imagine the kind of picture they would want to paint of the scene. Better to get as many facts together before they had a chance to go to press with anything.

"Gotcha."

ACT FIVE

Chapter 37

AUTOPSY

Sunday, August 19

The detective pushed open one of the swinging doors with his elbow and entered the lab, pausing to set his homburg down in the only space on the doctor's desk not currently occupied by papers, books, or clipboards: the explanations, illustrations, and measures of things.

Laforet was at the other end of the room, the white tile cool and antiseptic, standing over a sink and scrubbing his hands up to his elbows. He didn't turn to look — he recognized Campbell's footsteps. The detective was, as usual, right on time.

Light stands circled the table where Quan Lee was laid out. Campbell circled the table once and then a second time, giving the body a cursory examination. All these weeks and months on the job, and Campbell still struggled to find words other than "remains" or "corpse," which to him seemed somehow disrespectful, not to mention a little unsavoury. He figured as long as they had a name he would use it. If they had not yet been identified, then Jane or John Doe would suffice. The best he could do for now was "body," but in the back of his mind he knew he might eventually come around to using more unsavoury language.

How many bodies would it take? Mortal coil … vessel …

Laforet had just finished stitching the torso back together: a neat, long *Y* done with skills that would be the envy of any seamstress or tailor in the city.

"Give me the details."

"He didn't drown." Laforet reached for a towel and moved to the other side of the table, opposite Campbell. "There was no water in his lungs."

"How did he die?"

"It was an overdose of morphine."

Campbell looked up. "Impossible."

"Believe me, I know a morphine overdose when I see one. The organs, the blood, the needle marks … they tell the whole story. He stopped breathing before he hit the water."

Campbell pulled his glass from his pocket and unfolded it from its leather sleeve. "Any signs of struggle?" he asked, squinting through the lens at one of Quan's hands.

"I know what you're thinking, and it's possible violence wasn't necessary."

"What do you mean?"

"There was also alcohol in his blood — a significant amount. Right now I'm guessing it was a homemade rice wine."

"They got him drunk first." Campbell started circling the table again.

"You're having trouble adding this all up."

"If someone merely wanted Quan dead, there could have been easier ways to go about it. And why drop his body in the bulrushes like that? Why not just throw him in the river?"

The two mulled that over for a moment before Campbell spoke.

"There was a panic."

"Death by misadventure?"

"Died somewhere he wasn't supposed to be."

"Now dead somewhere he never was," said Laforet. "Done by an amateur?"

"Supposedly."

"I never liked that word."

"Or someone who likes to think they know how to confuse a police detective." Campbell stopped circling the table. "So much of what we like to think ... so much comes from luck, coincidence, and misadventure."

"Do you think he acted alone?"

"No," said Campbell, "no I don't. The disposal of the body, and ..."

"And what?"

"Not only not acting alone, but also answering to someone. Amateurs, as you suggested, who made a mess of things." Campbell studied Quan's face again, but it held no clues. It held a kind of disturbance. "Who do I tell first?"

"What do you mean?" said Laforet. "Half the city must know by now."

"McCloskey won't have talked."

"Are you purposely forgetting Constable Fitzgerald, the ambulance driver, the young couple, and the staff of the Westwood?"

"Not to mention the Westwood's patrons," said Campbell, his hands digging into his trouser pockets.

"You said they wouldn't talk for fear of exposing themselves."

"People love to talk, blather on about things they really know nothing about; it's an addiction for some, an escape. Quan's landlord must be phoning around looking for him. He's probably already contacted Woo Hong, Li-Ling's father. And if he has, then Woo has most likely contacted his brother."

"Start with the landlord," said Laforet, "and then go to Woo Hong's — and take McCloskey with you. I'll be here if you need me."

"Thanks." Campbell turned to leave but stopped. "One more thing: Let's keep this morphine stuff between us for now."

"That might be wise."

Chapter 38

HOW LONG YOU BEEN REHEARSING THAT LINE?

"So is he in the habit of visiting this place on Sunday nights?"

McCloskey was leaning across the counter that ran almost the length of the Cadillac Café, quizzing Ping about the potential whereabouts of a certain detective on the Windsor force. His elbows were getting a workout.

"A smuggler looking for a cop who doesn't want to be found. Now there's a twist." The restaurateur thought this very amusing. It had been a long and uneventful day.

"No joke."

Word of Quan's death obviously hadn't reached every corner of the city quite yet. It was a good thing, for some, that the *Star* didn't publish on the Lord's Day. Ping looked around; there was no one in the joint except for the two of them and the cook, who was distractedly reading a foreign paper that had been wrapped around a stack of bamboo steamers.

"All right, Jack. On nights like this the one we are talking about drinks at Gretchen's Lunch."

"Isn't that the one …?"

"South side, after Montreuil, closer to Albert."

"You think he'll be there now?"

"Want me to give them a call?"

"And say what?" said McCloskey. "I'm not advertising, remember?"

Ping shrugged. "It's your show."

"Okay, wait … ask them, 'Have any rye left, or are you letting your fat friend with the badge drink you dry?' Can you do something like that?"

"Sure."

"Hold on — what's your connection with Gretchen?"

Ping smiled. "There is no Gretchen, Jack. It's my cousin Kiu's. He barters his rice wine — good stuff. That's the connection." Ping picked up the phone and got the operator's attention.

Click, click, click.

He started speaking in his native tongue. McCloskey wasn't sure why he was listening so intently. Ping nodded a few times at the voice on the other end of the line and then hung the earpiece.

"He's there."

"Thanks, I owe you one."

"Yeah, yeah, go."

McCloskey took the Drive as fast as he could without attracting the worst kind of attention. He parked on the opposite side of the street, near one of the gates at Ford. He got out of his vehicle and looked around for Morrison's. There had been a light but steady rain in the afternoon and the combination of heavy humidity and greasy pavement worked to hold the rainbow-streaked puddles in place.

He spotted Morrison's wheels on the same side of the street as the diner and took up a position in the doorway of a grocer on the corner. The entire front of the shop including the recessed entrance was glass, so he had a good view while remaining in distorted shadows.

He didn't have to wait too long. He saw Morrison waddling away from the diner and stepped back further but left the detective's car in clear sight. As soon as Morrison reached for the driver's door, McCloskey stepped out of the doorway and onto the sidewalk.

"Leaving already, detective? The night's only beginning."

Morrison flinched, looked towards the voice. "McCloskey?"

"Yeah."

"How did you —"

"Morrison, I've got more feet on the ground in the Border Cities than you'll ever. I thought you would have known that by now."

The detective glanced over at Gretchen's just as someone was walking out. The figure headed in the other direction.

"All right, what's this about?"

"It's about a kid named Quan Lee."

"Your missing rice boiler? I heard his people sent him on a slow boat back to China for importing more trouble to an already troubled community."

"How long you been rehearsing that line, Morrison? I don't buy it. I think you had something to do with Quan's death."

"Why would I want anything to do with that kid?"

"I think you were looking to make good use of him, but he got caught in your gears. Maybe you learned he had a conscience and could become a liability. Best to nip that one in the bud."

Morrison sized up McCloskey, wondering how much this bootlegger knew, wondering if he was going to get physical, if he was carrying, if he would give him his worst. He had heard McCloskey could get a bit wild.

"You *think*? McCloskey, you don't know what to think anymore, you shell-shocked rum-head. I figured out a way to make sense of this street game … a game that, thanks in part to the newspapers, makes no sense at all to your average Border citizen. You could have done the same for yourself, but you keep hesitating. You won't pull that trigger."

"I'm going to get to the bottom of this, Morrison, and then I'll decide what I want out of you. Right now I'm just telling you that I'm not going to let it go. I'm not going to let it go until it all sits right with me. So don't get too wise."

"Is that some kind of threat, McCloskey?"

"I don't waste my breath with threats. Now go home or wherever it is you planned on flopping tonight." McCloskey turned and left Morrison standing with his thoughts in the drizzle.

Campbell was in one of the phone booths at the Prince Edward Hotel, needing some privacy and not wanting to make the call from home. Yesterday he had found out that local switchboard operators were using old party lines to allow certain numbers to tap into certain conversations. He wondered if there wasn't some way he could wire his home telephone directly to the switchboard here at the Prince Edward. He would have to add that to his to-do list.

"Morrison?"

"Campbell? … How did you get this number?"

"From your realtor buddies."

There was pause long enough to go to the kitchen and make a sandwich.

"Morrison? You still there?"

"Okay, what do you want?" Morrison sounded wary.

Campbell had his back to the window of the booth. "I think either you killed Quan Lee, or you've got someone else doing your dirty work for you."

Another pause.

"I don't know what you're talking about."

"You know what else I got from your realtor buddies?"

"So you're going to try to blackmail me into confessing to a crime I didn't commit and know nothing about?"

"Something like that. But no one's going to get off scot-free, not even the realtors." Campbell paused. "He was just a kid, Morrison, a good kid, and someone Jack McCloskey had taken under his wing."

"Jack McCloskey, now there's an upstanding citizen if there ever was one. Maybe you should be talking to him. I hear he had Quan running drugs through his club. Maybe Quan was becoming a liability."

Campbell paused and looked over his shoulder. "And giving you a run for your money, right, Morrison? Is that how you saw it?"

"I can make it so the realtors can't tie me to anything. It'll just look like you stumbled across their little operation and followed a possible trail to me, but it turned out to be a dead end."

"It's not just the realtors I can pin on you, Morrison. I've had a file on you for years and it's grown to the thickness of the city directory."

Morrison's wheezy chuckle came through, and then, "Oh, so this isn't just about Quan. This is just you wanting to take me down, and you're going to use this poor, innocent, dead kid to do it. You know all they're going to see is one detective trying to take down another detective, sully his good reputation. You know, the force kind of frowns upon that sort of thing. This isn't like you, Campbell. Regardless, you're in over your head and there's no looking back. So, we got anything else to talk about?"

There was a pause.

"I'm convinced you're somehow responsible for the death of Quan Lee," said Campbell, "and one way or another you will pay for that."

"So I guess we really don't have anything else to talk about."

"I'm not finished with you yet."

"Maybe not, Campbell, but I'm finished with you."

Campbell sat in the booth for a moment and tried to gather his thoughts. Morrison was right: this wasn't like him and maybe he *was* in over his head. He was also right about the police department. Campbell remembered how they had turned on Detective Henry Fields.

He opened the door to the booth, thought about getting some food, and then decided one of his walks would be the best thing.

Morrison hung the earpiece and set the phone back on the table. He had been pacing the room with it the whole time. "You didn't hear any of that."

There was a girl sitting in a wingback chair wearing a blue silk robe with lilies and chrysanthemums on it. She was also wearing what looked like stage makeup. She could have been one of Pearl Shipley's Windsor Follies for all he knew.

"I never hear anything," she said.

"I think you should leave now."

"Drive me home?"

"No, I got work to do. I'll give you cab fare. Let me call them."
She stood up and gathered her robe. "Thanks for a swell night."

"Yeah."

At the door to the bathroom she said, "Will I see you again?"

Morrison had to think about that. "I don't know." He was standing there, scratching his chin and staring blankly at her. "Go and get dressed."

Chapter 39

TELL ME IT'S ALL JUST TALK

Monday, August 20

Jefferson and Linc were packing a shipment in the basement of the shop: three crates full of headlights mingled with a couple dozen bottles of strong beer. They were also discussing the rumours flying around about Quan Lee's death.

It was Jefferson who was first to comment on how McCloskey was clearly having a hard time getting over it, that it seemed to keep revisiting him — and in unexpected ways. They had never

seen him like this. It had been a couple days of moods, silence
broken by some levity, and then flashes of the McCloskey temper,
where he would storm out of the shop, not saying where he was
going or when they might expect him back.

"Yeah," said Linc. "What's all that about?"

"I don't know … maybe he's trying to walk it off."

"Or maybe he's doing some investigating of his own." Linc
was also trying to manoeuvre around the ashcans overflowing with
automobile scraps. Things were piling up. "We got any more straw?"

"Over there." Jefferson nodded toward a burlap sack slumped
against a post under the workbench, his hands full.

"That's the end of it?"

"Yep."

"One of us'll have to drop by the creamery," hinted Linc.

"I'll go."

A familiar knock startled the two, and the trap door opened.
Shorty descended the stairs, holding his hat in place. Someone
upstairs and upstanding dropped the door back in place, waiting
for the next signal.

"Hey, yous."

"Hey."

"Anybody seen Jack?"

"He was here a little while ago," said Jefferson.

"He paced around for a few," added Linc. "Muttered
something and lit."

No comment from Shorty. He faked some business poking
through the crates. "How's it going here?"

"We're almost done."

They stood quiet for a moment, each of them with more
than a little on their minds. It was Linc who broke the silence.

"You hearing anything on the street?"

It was the first they had seen Shorty all day.

"Hearing anything like what?" he asked.

"Like maybe Jack's been talking to people, asking questions," said Jefferson, "trying to find Quan's killer and not having much luck."

"I wouldn't know anything about that."

"How about this: Was Quan really dealing opium?" asked Linc.

"No," said Shorty. "He wasn't into any of that."

"Well then, if he wasn't into any of that," said Jefferson, "then why? He was a good kid, right? I mean, that's what we all kept hearing."

"I don't know," said Shorty. "He must have got mixed up in something else."

"Wrong place at the wrong time," said Linc.

"And what about the police investigation?" said Jefferson.

"Snail's pace," said Shorty.

"You know why?" asked Linc.

"Yeah," said Shorty, "I think I know why."

"Then again, maybe it's more complicated than that," said Linc.

"How do you mean?"

"Maybe the cops don't want Quan's murder solved. I know people that been down that road."

"Why wouldn't they want his murder solved?" said Shorty.

"The cops ... they have their own reasons for everything. Trust me."

There was that familiar knock and the trap door opened again. They turned toward the stairs, only half hoping it might be McCloskey — in a better mood. It turned out to be Gorski.

"Jesus, look at the long faces. Why don't you just break out the armbands and get to hanging the black crepe on the windows?" he said. "We still got work to do, you know."

Some of the crew was getting annoyed with all the "we" talk. Linc and Jefferson started closing the crates.

"Before you ask," said Shorty, "I don't know where Jack is at."

"Maybe he's interviewing fry cooks," said Gorski.

"Somehow I doubt it."

"Shouldn't be hard," said Gorski. "Jack just tells his buddy Hong, or whatever his name is, that he'll take the next kid who steps off the boat."

"I don't think it's going to be that easy for Jack."

"Euh." Gorski waved that off and stepped away from the workbench. "I'm going to get some food."

Linc and Jefferson noticed that Shorty didn't share Gorski's appetite.

"That calendar is six goddamn years old." Shorty pointed at it, hanging over the narrow bench positioned against the long wall. "1917."

Link and Jefferson looked at each other. "I know," said Linc, "but the dates are the same this year."

"And we like the cars in it."

"What do you mean the dates are the same?" said Shorty.

"See," said Jefferson, "Monday, August twentieth."

A Dodge Brothers touring car had been featured that month.

"Huh, yeah, same days."

"Same days," said Linc.

Shorty did another lap around the big workbench. "All right, get these crates out … I have to meet a guy who's got a line on some carburetors."

"Anything else tonight?"

Shorty stopped, already halfway up the stairs. He gave the knock and then with one hand on the underside of the door and the other on the draw chain, he turned around and said, "No, nothing … and when you're finished with these, take the night off."

He completed his ascent and the two waited for the door to shut good and tight.

"Is the bar open?" asked Linc.

"I hear you, but what if Jack makes another appearance?"

"I have a feeling we won't be hearing anything from him for the rest of the day. Tell me he doesn't got bigger fish to fry."

They were about to start labeling the crates when Jefferson put another pause in the action.

"Didn't Shorty seem a little off?"

"More than usual?" asked Linc. He nailed the last crate shut.

Jefferson pulled a bottle off a shelf and set it down on the crate nearest him. There were clean shot glasses in a cookie tin on the same shelf. He poured the first round and made a toast.

"To Quan Lee."

Clink.

Linc poured the next and made another toast.

"To Border Cities Wrecking and Salvage."

"We're here to pick up the pieces," said Jefferson.

"Did you just make that up?"

"You like it?"

"Yeah," said Linc, gripping the bottle. "One more?"

"One more go 'round."

Chapter 40

DID HE HAVE ENEMIES?

The constable followed the approaching flashlight beam with his eyes while the Salt Works night watchman and the Canadian Pacific security guard argued territorial rights over a body found halfway down the hill dividing the factory and the tracks.

"Fitzgerald, is it?" asked Laforet. "Do you always draw the short straw?"

The constable nodded.

"And where's Campbell?"

"We couldn't locate him, sir."

"Not at his apartment?"

"They went knocking."

"Nor at his usual haunts?"

"The ones we are aware of?" The constable shook his head.

"I see. Maybe on one of his walks. No other detectives answering?"

"No, sir," said the constable. "That's why we contacted you."

"All right then," said Laforet, gathering himself. "Shall we?"

They carefully made their way down the slope of dewy grass and found Morrison on his back, gazing up at the stars with dead eyes. Laforet shined his flashlight up and down the body.

"Bullet wounds ... exit wounds. No one heard anything?" he asked the night watchmen.

"No," said one.

"Not with the noise from the plant and the trains," said the other.

"It's a wonder anyone gets any sleep around here," Laforet remarked.

"Fell backwards after the shots, you think?" asked Fitzgerald.

"I'd say his assailant was looking to roll the body down the slope and onto the path of the next oncoming train, hoping to make things just a little more complicated for us. I noticed up at the top, at the crest, that there were deep ruts — angled perpendicular to the slope — ending where the grass started, and the grass was flattened, as if Morrison had collapsed. Then his assailant attempted to push the body, leveraging himself by digging his heels into the dirt and gravel." Laforet was using his hands to describe this, as if directing actors in a dramatic scene. "The body didn't make it all the way down, and the perpetrator fled, not wanting to linger."

"What do you figure he weighs?" asked Fitzgerald, considering the expired detective as if fitting him for his funeral garb.

"Three hundred, give or take an ounce ... Damn it," said Laforet, looking up the hill, "where the devil is Campbell?"

"The constables are keeping an eye out for him, sir, combing the streets as it were. Sir, I'm wondering."

"What?"

"How are we going to get the body out of here? A winch?"

"No," said Laforet, ignoring the remark. "We finish the job and roll him carefully down toward the tracks."

The pause was left hanging until the constable picked it up.

"And then what?" he said.

"Which one of you is with the railway?" asked Laforet. "Forget it," he said, pointing to one of the night watchmen. "You, send for a handcar or pump trolley or whatever those contraptions are called. We'll load him onto one of those."

"And take him where?"

"Tell me, is this Campbell's usual hell? Or has he been saving this up just for me?"

"Sir?"

"Where are the tracks on the same grade as the street? Somewhere south of Wyandotte? You'll take him there. I'll contact Janisse and have him meet us with his ambulance — at Elliott?"

"East of the tracks."

They glanced at the railway man, who had obviously gleaned his instructions, as he left the scene without any further provocation, hobbling along the shoulder of the tracks to retrieve the handcar. Laforet now turned his attention to the security guard from the Salt Works.

"There was a murder on your property. You and your superiors will be called upon in the morning, after I've examined the body. Make yourself available no later than nine," said Laforet. "Now go away."

The security guard scrambled up the slope and continued his rounds. Laforet and the constable watched, grinning.

"I suspect it's the most excitement he's seen in quite some time. Now, Fitzgerald, is there anything you can further offer the investigation? I've heard all the usual questions. For instance, did Detective Morrison have any enemies?"

Fitzgerald straightened up a little.

"Detective Morrison collected enemies like some guys collect baseball cards. Wait ... doctor, what are you suggesting?"

"I know I'm no detective, but don't you think this to be a little unusual?"

"How do you figure, sir?"

"What could Morrison have been doing here? If it was something to do with the salt company, he would have first taken it up with them, don't you think?"

"I suppose so," said the constable.

"And there is evidence, as I have pointed out, that after Morrison was shot, someone tried to dispose of his body. So why was he here?" asked Laforet.

"I'm sure I have no idea, sir."

After the body was removed to Laforet's lab, the doctor went looking for Campbell. His first stop was police headquarters, where there was no word from the detective or any of the constables who had been told to keep an eye out for him. He then walked from police headquarters to Campbell's apartment over on Arthur. From the outside, the place looked dark.

Doubtful he's asleep, thought Laforet, *given his sleep habits. Then again ...*

Laforet entered the building and ascended the stairs. There was no answer at Campbell's door. A neighbour, awakened by the knocking, popped her head into the short hallway.

"No," she said, answering the doctor's question. "I haven't seen or heard from him since this morning."

Laforet walked back to the station, got in his car, and drove towards McCloskey's apartment at Chatham and Dougall. He waited until he got there before deciding whether or not he would actually go knocking on the bootlegger's door. He sat in his car for a moment, staring up at the lit window before climbing out and crossing the street to the door of the terrace.

The conversation was a little awkward. McCloskey had no idea where Campbell might be, and hadn't seen him all day. Laforet was out of his element here. He wanted to question McCloskey the way a law enforcer would, but he really couldn't. He had to resort to simply choosing his words carefully. McCloskey reluctantly invited him in.

"I'm sorry," said Laforet, "I wasn't aware you were entertaining." He touched the brim of his hat, acknowledging the girl seated on the chesterfield. "Good evening, miss."

"Good evening, doctor. I'm Vera Maude," she said as she stood and extended her hand.

From Copeland's, thought Laforet.

He approached her. "Nice to meet you. I was just looking for a colleague of mine, a detective by the name of Campbell. I thought Mr. McCloskey might have crossed paths with him sometime today, or this evening."

McCloskey took the opportunity to slip into the bedroom to make a phone call. Laforet could hear the cord slither under the closed door, but nothing else.

"This evening? No," she said. "We've been out. Dinner and a movie."

"Sounds nice. So you and Mr. McCloskey were occupied all evening?"

"Yes."

"And —"

McCloskey reappeared from the bedroom, telephone in hand, tense, red-faced.

"I'll take you home, Maudie."

"I guess I'll be leaving now."

Laforet went first out the door and down the stairs, followed by Vera Maude and then McCloskey. They were silent.

Chapter 41

THROUGH THE MOTIONS

Tuesday, August 21

Morrison's death punched holes through the fabric of the Border Cities and now everyone on either side was taking their turn looking through them. No one could have fathomed how it might unravel things, but unravel them it did. While it was time for some to seek shelter, for certain others it made more sense to just plain disappear.

McCloskey suspended all activity at the salvage yard, even the legitimate stuff. They were closed for renovations. Inside the shop, a second workbench was positioned over the trap door and the floor was mopped with a fresh layer of engine grease that was then scuffed with a few pairs of old trench boots. The latch on the back fence was dismantled and its shadow painted over so that no one would know otherwise.

Police had been phoning at random hours. McCloskey invited any and all of them to drop by, and to bring along any photographer from the *Star* they wished. He'd let them comb the yard, even toss the place if they felt they needed to. The ones that took him up on the offer, which was most of them, he could easily divide into two camps: those constables who Morrison had in his pocket, and those who were crusaders for the cause of Prohibition and welcomed the opportunity to sift through this well-known bootlegger's alleged hub of operation. Both these groups knew there was no love lost between McCloskey and Morrison, and both groups had their own reasons for regarding McCloskey with suspicion. Then there were constables who were really not doing much of anything, the rookies still trying to figure out their place and anxious not to find themselves in the wrong camp. Lastly there were the constables who were clearly just going through the motions, the ones with whom McCloskey had an understanding, a sort of *don't ask, don't tell* kind of understanding, similar to the one he had with Campbell. They were the ones who were walking a fine line.

"Can they do this?" Shorty had asked.

"I want them to," McCloskey responded.

During each visit, McCloskey would sit tight and wait patiently. He knew they'd be back sometime, anytime, soon, maybe with a fresh crew. Sure enough they arrived three days later and repeated the exercise, throwing in a few twists.

"Business light this time of year, Mr. McCloskey?" asked one of the constables.

"I hear they're making a better automobile."

"So you might be out of business soon?"

"Not likely."

Of course they never found anything, and looked slightly disappointed at this outcome.

"How's the investigation going?" he asked one of the crusaders.

"It's going."

McCloskey knew this one didn't care if he did indeed off Morrison. He figured crusaders like this were of the belief that *they only kill their own*, and that McCloskey would, rightfully, be next.

The investigation was being led by a young detective from Toronto, Terence Bashford, with a provincial police officer tied to his hip. Apparently the department was saving the best for last.

"You have an office on Riverside Drive."

"I do," said McCloskey. "It's not much but it has a nice view."

"We will need to see it."

"The office or the view?"

"The office, Mr. McCloskey."

"My office?"

"Yes, Mr. McCloskey, your office."

McCloskey always thought that the best way to set up someone determined to find something where there was nothing was to sound as suspicious as possible. It could be a game, and he could drag it out.

"Certainly. My car is parked outside; you could follow me down the Drive."

While all of this was a bit of a challenge, he wondered what Campbell was going through.

"Were you and Morrison close?" asked Bashford.

"Close?" said Campbell.

"Did you share knowledge of cases? Did you ever consult with each other?"

Campbell didn't hesitate. "No, there was never anything like that."

"That strikes me as a little unusual."

Campbell wasn't sure what to say. He had never been called on like this before.

"We didn't work that way."

"How did you work?"

"He had his cases, and I had mine."

"He never came to you?"

"No."

"You never went to him?"

Campbell paused. "No."

Bashford waved Harcourt, the Ontario Police officer, over and whispered something in his ear.

"We'll follow you to your office," said Bashford.

There was another detail at Chung Hong's, turning all kinds of goods and foodstuffs over. McCloskey didn't have to give him a call — Hong was always prepared and he co-operated fully. In return, the badges left the place looking like a train wreck.

"Are you going to clean this?" Hong asked.

"Clean what?"

They slammed the door behind them. Hong knew very well that they wouldn't pick up after themselves, but he had to say something, even if they weren't taking notes.

But someone is always taking notes, thought Hong.

Or carrying a knife. The man wasn't wearing a badge or a uniform. This was something else. Everyone stopped talking and the man holding the blade positioned the tip under Hong's chin and used it to steer him toward the back room.

"Hong, Hong … Hong."

Hong couldn't swallow with his Adam's apple bobbing under the blade. The knife-wielder lingered a moment and then stepped back, holding his grin. This was his scene, such as it was. At that moment a suit entered. The man looked young and he carried a badge.

"I'm Detective Bashford, and I don't give a fuck about anything you knew two minutes ago. This is the way it is now."

Campbell didn't like what Morrison's death was doing to his ability to reason. He now had McCloskey on his list of suspects. Campbell had read the reports about the bloodshed at that house on Riverside Drive last summer; he knew what McCloskey was capable of. He had also heard talk of his war record. He thought he knew the man, but perhaps he didn't, not really.

Why would he do it? Simply to take out a loose cannon? Was Morrison threatening to upset the order of things in McCloskey's world? Did he have something on McCloskey, something serious enough for McCloskey to want him dead?

McCloskey meanwhile was going through similar things in his mind about Campbell. What did he really know about this man other than that he was a good detective, detested violence, and left McCloskey alone so long as he kept his Webley in its holster? Campbell was very private, but he knew the detective had problems with certain elements in the department, certain elements such as Morrison, who had been becoming more and more of a threat to the integrity of law enforcement in the Border Cities.

And what did Campbell really think about him? Could he be on the detective's personal list of suspects?

Why not? thought McCloskey.

While all the stones were pretty much left unturned in the investigation into Quan Lee's death, none were left to lie in Morrison's. Everyone was feeling the heat. McCloskey and his crew were feeling some tension between themselves and their Border Cities clients. Many of them automatically suspected him, and when the law came knocking on their door with questions, their first reaction was "What the hell did McCloskey do to bring this on?" Yes, the balance had been upset. Maybe in their interests, Morrison was better alive than dead. Without meeting to talk about it, the gang went on a sort of hiatus and McCloskey avoided the club, leaving Pearl to run things.

"Can you handle it?" he had said in a phone conversation.

"Yeah, sure, Jack." She hesitated and asked if there was anything she needed to know.

"The less you know, the better. I'm guessing the police have been through once or twice."

"They know the menu off by heart." Another pause. "Stay safe, Jack."

"Yeah."

Click.

His next conversation was with Vera Maude. Friday morning he phoned the bookstore asking if she was working today, saying that she was handling a special order for him.

"I'm sorry — she's with a customer right now."

"That's all right. I'm stuck in my office most of the day today. When is her shift done?"

"Five," said the voice on the other end of the line. It wasn't Copeland. It sounded like Lew. "Can I take a messa—"

Click.

McCloskey waited on the street for Vera Maude to leave the store. She walked out with Lew at about a quarter after, they said their goodbyes, and she made for the London streetcar. He maintained a distance.

This gave him a chance to improve his public transit etiquette. He didn't want his car seen in front of Uncle Fred's place. And no one would expect Jack McCloskey to be taking a streetcar across town. Just to make sure he didn't get picked out in the crowd, he was sporting a rumpled trench coat, straw hat, and sunglasses.

As they rolled along London Street, McCloskey took in another one of what Vera Maude called "street views": a view of the city from the perspective of someone like her. He looked at Vera Maude — he was keeping her in his line of vision — the people sitting around her, and the people emptying out of the offices and buildings along the way. What did they know about the detective that was gunned down behind the salt mines? Did they care? They probably just wanted to get home to their families, their dinner, and the evening paper in their reading chair.

The law will take care of it. McCloskey suspected that was what they were thinking. *And sometimes they do take care of their own.*

The downtown quickly broke up and became neighbourhoods with churches, schools, and little gardens. People started gradually trickling out of the streetcar. When they got to McEwan, Vera Maude exited from the front while McCloskey, along with a few other passengers, exited out the side. He followed her up the street and quickly lost any cover he had. He caught up with Vera Maude before she reached her building.

"Excuse me, miss, I think you dropped something."

She turned and he removed his sunglasses and folded his collar back down.

"Jack …? Jack!"

"Shh."

"Where have you —"

"You been reading about that detective that got himself killed?" asked McCloskey.

She approached with caution. "Yeah."

"We shouldn't talk until this blows over."

"What's going on?"

McCloskey had to tell her something without really telling her anything. "Either the investigation really wants answers or they want it to look that way. I don't know. None of my usual guys are talking right now. We're just lying low and co-operating, waiting for the day when it's business as usual."

"But what if they don't find the guy who did it?"

"They will." He wanted to kiss her. "I have to go. I'll stay in touch. Avoid my place for now."

Chapter 42

THE WRONG MAN

Saturday, August 25

"Jack, I need to talk to you," said Shorty.

This was refreshing to hear after a few days of an uncharacteristic silence. McCloskey was behind his desk in his office on the Drive. He put his pen down, glad for the break in the paperwork sent from the accountant, but wondered what new trouble might be on the horizon. Shorty's tone and demeanor suggested it couldn't be good. But then maybe, thought McCloskey, Shorty was also looking for a break from all of this.

"Sure, sit down."

Shorty had just beaten the hard rain but had still walked here through a drizzle. Now the wet was sheeting the almost floor-to-ceiling semi-circle window behind McCloskey, and the buildings across the street were a grey-green blur. Without removing it, Shorty gave his coat a shake, tipped off his hat, sat down, and set his chapeau on his knee. He took a moment to gather himself and McCloskey took the time to shuffle some paper around, making it ready for tomorrow's meeting.

"It's about Morrison."

Everything's about Morrison right now, thought McCloskey. *Can't someone bring me just a little something that isn't about Morrison?*

"Yeah?" said McCloskey. "What is it?"

Shorty took a deep breath and started playing with his hat again, avoiding McCloskey's gaze. Tilting his head slightly to one side, he said, "I didn't think it would get this hot. I really didn't think it would …" He trailed off, waving a free hand in the air at nothing.

McCloskey waited and, when nothing seemed to be forthcoming, leaned forward, no longer quite so distracted with ledgers and letterhead, and said, "What are you trying to tell me, Shorty?"

Shorty was biting his lip now, glancing up at the ceiling. He looked for something on which to focus, the moulding, a detail in the plasterwork perhaps, anything but his boss's face.

McCloskey's mind was leaping around. "Shorty … no."

"Jack …" He was looking right at McCloskey now, coming to terms.

"No."

"Yeah, Jack … I did Morrison."

For a good minute the only sound in the office was of the rain on the window and a deep sigh out of McCloskey. He turned in his chair to watch the water run down the glaze. "Why?" he asked.

He gave Shorty time to put some words together, words he already knew wouldn't explain, couldn't justify.

"I thought it would be good for everybody. I thought, nobody'll miss him. I mean Morrison, shit, Jack …"

McCloskey turned back around. "Are you also telling me you weren't in any kind of confrontation with him, and this wasn't any kind of fight?"

Shorty paused. "Yeah, I guess I'm telling you that."

"You called him out to kill him."

Another pause. "Yeah, I guess I did."

"That's murder, Shorty." McCloskey could barely fathom it. "How could you do that?" The question wasn't meant to be rhetorical. "You know we never, ever —"

"Jack, it wasn't like you never." Shorty's back was up a little.

McCloskey stood up to face the window, his hands on his hips. He looked below and could make out dark figures trying to cross the street, dodging cars, heads down in the rain.

Would you rather get wet or get run over?

"Jack … Jack, I'm sorry. Like I said, I never guessed it would get this hot."

That's not what McCloskey was thinking about right now. He was thinking, *I thought I knew this guy.* He dropped his arms and turned. "I don't care how dirty he was, or how much of a thorn he was in our sides, he was still a goddamn cop. You took down a Windsor police detective. What the hell? You know this could ruin us."

"You think the police are on to you?"

"They're on to me as much as they want to be right now. They can use this, Shorty. Think about the cards they have in their hand right now. They could find a way to pin it on me and …"

"I'm sorry, Jack."

Footsteps could be heard in the stairwell and the two turned their heads and hushed to listen. The footsteps stopped, then faded as the body entered the office on the floor below. They relaxed. McCloskey sat on the edge of his desk and Shorty's shoulders dropped farther.

"Jack, I can fix this."

"You know you can't."

The rain stopped but the sky got heavier, tipping the balance between the natural and artificial light in the room. Small vessels caught off-guard, bobbing up and down the Detroit River, were looking for safe harbour. Something worse was probably coming.

"You know there's only one way we can fix this."

Chapter 43

RETREAT

Sunday, August 26

McCloskey was still trying to make sense of things. Thoughts and memories continued to ricochet, mingle inside his head. He felt the need to forget everything and everyone. But if he did that, he wondered, what would hold him together?

His sister-in-law, Clara, was gone; she had had enough of him, his problems, and the Border Cities. She skipped and didn't leave a forwarding address. He flipped through his mental notebook, trying to remember their conversations, the ones that helped. It didn't work. He then thought a physical rather than mental workout might once again do the trick, like it did when he came back from the war. He returned to the gym and punched the bag off its chains. He sparred a few rounds in the square circle and knocked his partners flat. A trainer told him that maybe he should just run it off at the Jockey Club track.

He had to find a new way, a new place.

Or an old one, he thought.

Ever since his adventure downriver with Quan and Li-Ling, thoughts of the old homestead had been lurking in the back of McCloskey's mind.

Maybe now's the time.

He hadn't been out there since last autumn. Clara saw to make it a part of his convalescence after someone tried to off him with a cheap shot at Michigan Central station. She had tried to help him remember who his would-be assailant might have been and why he was at the train station in the first place. The investigator's only evidence was the bullet they pulled out of McCloskey's chest. The bullet was replaced with a scar, along with residual anger, confusion, frustration ... emotions that were his but to which he was still trying to connect.

Clara would use words like *unresolved*, and *unfinished*.

It was a little over a year ago when he and Clara had made their first trip out to Ojibway. He remembered the sun was high and the shallow waters were warm. They came for the quiet, the fresh air, and a little therapy. Whenever Clara found the right moment, she would carefully manoeuvre him into his past, his family history, and the war. She was his sapper, trying to defuse his psychological minefield. He knew what she was up to, so he found that small part of him that still listened to what other people had to say and decided to go along for the ride. It got a little rough at times. She always seemed ready for it though; he gave her that. He had also known that it was only the beginning, and she wouldn't let go until he was in a better place. There would be more to come. She had given him so much and never asked for anything in return.

They usually arrived with a full basket from the farmer's market or a roadside stand along the way: fresh fruit and vegetables, baked goods, a couple of steaks and a roaster. Clara would busy herself in the kitchen while he'd give the property a work-over. He'd trim the shrubs, prune the fruit trees, and push the lawn mower back and forth across the patches of grass.

McCloskey remembered that on one of their earliest visits, he had looked up from his work and noticed Clara watching him from the kitchen window. She held a dish in one hand and a tea towel in the other, wiping it dry. He had turned back and rested his chin on the handle of the thatching rake, staring down at the charred remains of the fishing cabin where his father and brother had met their end, now overgrown with weeds. He imagined her putting the dish down and picking up another while watching him methodically go at it, breaking up the cinders and pulling up the weeds and saplings. He worked it until he had a loose stack and then he returned to the kitchen with a focused and determined look on his face. Clara stayed out of his way. He rummaged around a bit and found what he was looking for on the sideboard: a small can of lighter fluid. He marched back out. She watched him squeeze the little rusty can until it puckered in his grip, wheezing out the last bit of fluid it had left in it. He took a match to the dry heap, crouched down — arms bent on his knees, cheeks cupped in his hands — and watched it burn. It was like he was re-enacting something. It was like a ritual. When the leaves and scrub finished burning, he picked up the rake again and mingled the ashes with the sand and dirt so as to let nature take its course. McCloskey had stood and took a deep breath, turned, and saw Clara sitting on the little wooden steps that led down from the kitchen door and into the yard. She got up and brushed herself off.

That blue floral sundress ... cornflowers they were.

At the end of that day and the fine days that followed they would sit silently on the rickety picnic table between the house and the shore that McCloskey had built with his father, stare out at the river, and watch the sun set.

It was on their last trip out, late last November, that he boarded up the doors and windows, it being the end of the season — long beyond, in fact. He remembered feeling that he might never return to Ojibway, that he no longer had reason to and would abandon the homestead.

But now he felt this was something he wanted to share with Vera Maude. She could help him reinvent the place, make it mean something entirely different to him, maybe something more. He looked over at his passenger, wondering what Vera Maude might be thinking. She was still a bit of a mystery to him.

He had to take it easy up the path from the road; everything was overgrown again. He glanced over at Vera Maude, whose eyes had gotten wide. The city girl was taking it all in.

He stopped the roadster at the end of the gravel drive. He came around to help her out and then grabbed the crowbar off the floor behind her seat. He got right away to pulling the boards off the ground floor windows but kept one eye on Vera Maude as she walked to the shore. He thought she must be glad she decided to wear her rain boots but was probably regretting the white frock.

In a short while McCloskey finished prying boards and pulling nails and leaned the wood against the back of the house. He needed to cool off, so he walked down toward the shore where he found Vera Maude trying unsuccessfully to skip stones across a mile of river. The ripples on the water were glittering with sun.

She had unpinned her hair and those chestnut waves were now teasing her shoulders in the breeze.

He thought he was being stealthy, but she must have heard him coming. Still facing the water, she said, "I've never been out this way before — years ago we used to make trips to Essex by train to visit my older siblings for birthdays, certain holidays, and get-togethers, but never along the shore. Funny, when I think about the country I don't think about the river, I just think about endless corn and tobacco fields."

McCloskey was noticing her already sun-kissed cheeks. He smiled and asked her if she would like a tour now.

"Would that be the nickel tour?"

"For you, two bits."

They made their way back to the house and he opened the screen door for her.

"Wait," she said.

"What?"

"I think I've got a pebble in my boot."

"How'd you get a pebble in your boot?"

"Gee, I don't know." She put one hand on his shoulder and removed her galosh with the other, turning it upside down. "There," she said, tucking her bare foot back in the boot.

"Ready now?"

"Ready," she said.

"Keep in mind I haven't had much of a chance to tidy it up."

Vera Maude and her smirk entered the kitchen. McCloskey followed.

"I guess I should start by airing the place out," he said.

It was damp, and not a little musty. It occurred to McCloskey that as they made their way through the place he should discreetly make sure there weren't any four-legged squatters. So far he wasn't hearing any evidence as he took a broom to the sticky cobwebs.

"So this is where you grew up?"

"This is where I was born."

She looked at him and then around the kitchen in disbelief.

"I tested the pump," he said, pointing at the sink. "It still works. Shoot, that reminds me — I should have brought something for us to eat. Sorry, I guess I wasn't thinking. The general store is up the road a bit. We could have a clam bake on the beach."

"With real clams?"

"Actually, more like wieners and beans in this cauldron. We can go see what they got."

"You sure about that?"

"I was kidding about the wieners and beans. In the city, I don't know how to cook. Out here, I can cook."

"I'd be fine with wieners and beans," said Vera Maude.

"Really?"

"Really. But why don't you show me around first."

"Well," said McCloskey with outstretched arms, "this is the kitchen. I remember eating most of my meals at this table or standing over the sink … or at that picnic table." He walked over to the window. "Or sitting cross-legged on the beach, snacking on a roast chicken leg or some kind of fried sandwich."

"Your mom did the cooking?"

"At first," he said, "when we were really young."

"And later?"

"Later, well, I guess we just fended for ourselves and ate when we were hungry."

"I've never seen a stove like that before," said Vera Maude.

"My ma could bake," said McCloskey. "Pies, pies with meat and pies with fruit. I remember in the cold months, she'd finish cooking up something, and she'd leave the oven door propped open. Me and my brother would warm our hands over it." He smiled again. "Didn't warm our feet though. C'mon, I'll show you the front parlour."

McCloskey entered first. He was surprised at the state of things, that and the smell.

"Okay," he said, "so the furniture has to go."

It looked like it had been either retrieved from the dump or pulled out of the river, the chesterfield especially.

"Oh I don't know, maybe a couple pillows, a nice throw. And is this the dining room?" Vera Maude broke away from the tour.

"We didn't do much dining here. Usually only on Sundays and special occasions."

The table looked as old as the house. There was no cover on it, and one of the chairs was missing a leg.

"When it had seen a few too many spills, my pa would sand it down. C'mon, let's go upstairs."

"You lead."

"Use the banister."

The bathroom was right at the top.

"I don't think you want to go in there," he said.

"But what if I …?"

"At least not yet."

"And this was your room."

"You can tell? Not my brother's or my father's?"

"No, yours." She was looking around. "Your shirts … your brand of rye … you're longer than the bed."

McCloskey pointed down the hall at the other two rooms. "My pa's room, and my brother's."

"You got the view of the river."

"I watched the river and my pa watched the road." McCloskey was back to reflecting. "For a while at least, I guess we were quite the team. C'mon, let's get some fresh air."

The kitchen reminded McCloskey of something. "Now, back to the subject of dinner," he said. "Would you prefer fish or chicken?"

"What happened to our clam bake?"

"The clams took a vote."

"Okay, I like — you're not going to tell me that I have to catch my own fish, are you?"

"No."

"Do I have to strangle my chicken?"

McCloskey rolled his eyes. "No."

"You gonna pull a rabbit out of a hat?"

"I can do rabbit," he said.

"I don't like rabbit."

"Me neither. All that fur."

"All those feathers."

"Then perch it is. I'll just —"

"Wait, don't tell me — *I know a guy.*"

"Is that how I talk?"

"What? You don't like my Jack McCloskey impression?"

"Okay, let's forget about the hooks and worms. I know a place —"

"*I know a place.*"

"Again with that?"

"Sorry. I can't help it."

"I was gonna say, where the perch will jump right into your net."

"No, no, I'm not —"

"C'mon, Maudie. I know it might not be like one of those moonlight cruises upriver, but this is the way we do things downriver."

"I'm not dressed for it."

"The way I see it, you're not dressed for much else other than skipping stones on the beach."

"All right. What do I have to do?"

"You have to stop being so serious, Maudie. I'm only kidding. C'mon, let me show you the general store."

"Another tour?"

"This one has candy."

"Where's my hat?"

They headed out the door and back into the roadster. The sun was getting high already. Driving down Front Road got McCloskey's mind wandering again.

Yeah, he started thinking, picking up a thread he had left dangling earlier, *I could make this our retreat, a place where we can get away from things.*

Chapter 44

PROSPECT AVENUE

Wednesday, August 29

Mud went knocking at Shorty's door just after dawn. He had to make sure he caught Shorty before he slipped out anywhere, never to be heard from again. There'd be time and a place for that, but not now.

Shorty knew by the hour and the look on Mud's face what this might be about. He invited Mud in anyway.

"I hope I didn't wake you."

"I was already up. Did you want some coffee?" The truth was Shorty had hardly slept at all these last few days.

"No, thanks. I can't stay long."

They were standing in the middle of Shorty's front room. Mud looked around. He had been to Shorty's place before and it was usually neat as a pin. It looked like it hadn't been tidied up in a while. He noticed the phone was off the hook.

"Shorty, I just came to tell you … everything's been arranged."

Shorty's face remained expressionless. His sunken eyes looked dead. "Everything," he said.

"You're to meet a guy at the Westwood at midnight. He's going to take you across. Bring whatever you need, but my advice would be to travel light."

Shorty knew what he meant by that. "How will I know him?"

"Don't worry; he'll know you," said Mud. "Oh, and Jack wanted me to give you this." Mud pulled a thick envelope out of his inside pocket and handed it to Shorty. Shorty knew what it was.

"Tell Jack thanks."

There was a pause in the conversation that left them staring at the floor. Mud broke the silence with, "Jack put a tail on you."

McCloskey had taken to occasionally using operatives to check on his own people. They didn't come from an agency but rather from somewhere among the players in the auto industry, somewhere deep. It had all started in the spring when Mud got tangled with a couple of them and McCloskey had to come to his rescue. He had been caught watching through binoculars the comings and goings at the loading docks at the Studebaker factory. For these activities he would don his garage gear and carry around a toolbox. He'd position himself behind the boxcars parked on the Pere Marquette tracks that ran alongside the main building and take notes. He was working on a scheme to divert parts deliveries to the salvage yard. On what would turn out to be his last reconnaissance, a man in a plain dark suit and overcoat suddenly appeared up close in his lenses, looking right at him. Turning he found another man dressed similarly standing behind him.

He was brought to an empty room not within the walls of Studebaker but rather in a vacant building over on Walker between American Auto Trimming and Buhl Stamping. When they refused to identify themselves or engage in any conversation, Mud got a little nervous and decided to play his one card: the Border Cities Wrecking and Salvage card with McCloskey's name on it. They examined it and then left the room, presumably to make a few phone calls. About a half hour later he heard a couple doors open and close and a conversation starting up in the hallway. The voices were low so he couldn't make anything out. Some time lapsed before the men re-entered, this time with McCloskey in tow. *Let's go*, was all McCloskey had said and led him silently out to his car.

In the weeks following, Mud had started noticing some strange coincidences — mostly to do with McCloskey all of a sudden being a couple steps ahead of everyone in the gang and calling out some of the boys on questionable deals. Mud was starting to think his boss had eyes in the back of his head and his ear to every wall. Then he connected the dots. McCloskey had enlisted the aid of those men.

Mud never brought any of this up with his boss and never shared it with anyone in the gang, not even Shorty. He managed to put the operatives out of his mind. That is until yesterday's conversation with McCloskey. McCloskey didn't mention any names or go into any great detail. It was just *this is what's going to happen.*

"I know. He wasn't very good," said Shorty.

"Jack was hoping you'd notice him."

There were actually two of them, but Mud didn't share that part. Being too distracted by the first and most obvious, the second tail is the one no one ever notices.

"Is he still outside?" asked Shorty, resisting the temptation to peak through the curtain.

"Yeah."

"Is he taking me to the Westwood?"

"No."

"But he'll be following me out there."

"Yeah."

They stopped talking again for a moment before Shorty said, "Tell Jack I'm sorry."

"Okay." Mud didn't really know what else to say, except, "Good luck, Shorty," before making for the door. Outside he paused on the sidewalk and straightened his tie. It was his signal to the operative, wherever he was.

It's a go.

The cabbie turned up Prospect Avenue and took his fare right up to the door of the Westwood. Shorty paid the man, picked up the small grip he had with him that carried a few essentials, and headed inside.

Being a Monday, the joint wasn't exactly jumping. Shorty did a walk around, trying to see if he could pick out the face of a man in the business of smuggling people across the border. And then he heard a voice behind him.

"Going somewhere?"

Shorty turned. He hadn't seen the man when he was surveying the room. He had the height and general dimensions of McCloskey. In fact, in the dim light and the shadows, he thought it might be his former boss and for a fleeting moment felt a sense of relief.

"I've got a table reserved for us."

He led Shorty over to a two-seater in a dark corner. "You look like you could use a drink."

When they passed the bar, the man gave the bartender a signal that apparently meant *bring us a couple ryes*.

Shorty studied the man's face in the candlelight. He had bright, squinty eyes, thin lips, and sharp cheekbones. With his fair hair and ruddy cheeks, Shorty thought he could have been a sailor at one time.

A waitress set the tumblers down and returned to the bar.

"Have you done this sort of thing before?" asked Shorty.

"Maybe once or twice," said the man, and they each took a sip from their tumblers. Shorty's sip was a little larger than the smuggler's.

"How long will it take to cross?"

"Not long," said the man, looking up at the wall clock that hung above the door. "We should go."

They finished their drinks. Shorty reached for his grip and then followed the man through the kitchen. He could feel everyone's eyes on him. They went out the back door and found the path that led through the tall grass to the shore.

It was a small, open vessel with a disproportionately-sized outboard motor. At full speed it probably skipped along the water like a flat stone.

Shorty touched the man's shoulder. "Tell me, please, am I going to make it? I mean, why make the trip if you don't have to?"

"I got my orders."

The man manoeuvred the vessel so that Shorty could climb in without incident. Shorty threw his grip in first, grabbed the edge of the boat with one hand, and balanced himself with the other until he found a place to put his foot. He sat down.

"Is this okay here?"

"Just fine." The man wiggled the vessel over the narrow band of sand and rocks until he was up to his knees in river and the outboard blades were submerged. He climbed in without even rocking the boat.

"Where exactly are we going?" asked Shorty. "Can you at least tell me that?"

"You see that bright light up there on the left?"

"Yeah," said Shorty.

"You see that amber light up there on the right?"

"Yeah."

"That dark stretch in between."

The man got the engine going. It purred at first, but once they got a little further out, it roared.

In the middle of the Detroit River, Shorty looked up and for the first time in his life noticed how different the stars looked out on the water. They looked brighter.

Chapter 45

TONG

CELESTIAL HAS 19 DECKS OF OPIUM HIDDEN

Mounted Police Officer Makes Arrest; Yip Wing Remanded When Arraigned on Charge in Police Court

Noticing a Chinaman acting in a suspicious manner on Sandwich Street East last night,

Sergeant Birtwhistle, RCMP detachment, placed him under arrest. He gave his name as Yip Wing, 19 Sandwich Street East, and when searched, 19 decks of opium were found in his possession.

The accused carried the opium in a little tin box, and federal police believe that he was peddling the drug to his fellow countrymen. Wing declined to make a statement as to how he came by the drug, and a search of his rooms failed to reveal the presence of a pipe or apparatus of the opium smoker.

When arraigned in police court today, Wing did not plead, and on the request of his lawyer, W.H. Furlong, he was remanded for three days. Bail was fixed at $300.

"The arrest of Wing is one of a series of arrests made by the Mounted Police on Chinese in this district, and is in accord with a countrywide drive by the Mounted Police officers against the drug traffic in Canada. Several Chinese, possessing narcotics, have been arrested since the first of the year on the border, and the police are making every effort to stamp out the traffic.

Mounted Police departments all along the border between Canada and the United States have been working with American federal officers to check the traffic, and a large number of convictions on both sides of the line has been the result.

Hong had called the meeting. He said it had to take place somewhere outside of the downtown, and at a place none of them normally frequented. McCloskey suggested a service station, Overidge's, on Giles a few blocks east of the Avenue. He knew he could trust the mechanic because his boys had made Overidge a link in Border Cities Wrecking and Salvage's supply chain. The only information McCloskey gave Overidge was that he needed to have a private conversation with a couple of friends, and that they would be arriving separately at ten-minute intervals.

McCloskey got there first and pretended to be checking out Overidge's modest used car selection while keeping an eye out for Campbell. The detective was right on time. He parked his Essex in one of the spots on the other side of the gas pumps — the doctor's waiting room. He didn't approach McCloskey. He followed McCloskey's suit and started kicking some tires. He drifted closer towards McCloskey and without looking right at him said, just loud enough for him to hear, "You have any idea what this is about?"

"No idea."

They made like they were having a conversation about the price of gas.

"You talked to him," said Campbell. "What was his tone like?"

"Same as always. Hong doesn't give up much. That's one of the things I like about him."

Actually, thought McCloskey, *he sounded a little nervous.*

"I'm guessing it's something serious."

"Yeah, I have a feeling it is."

McCloskey was keeping one eye on the street now. Then he saw Hong's car slow down in front of the station, probably making sure he had the right place. McCloskey's first impulse was to wave him over to where he and Campbell had parked, but he smothered it and instead hoped he would just figure it out. He did.

Hong got out of his car, walked right past McCloskey and Campbell without making eye contact, and went inside to the service desk, where Overidge was seated.

"Okay … he's talking to Overidge … probably giving him some instructions … Overidge just gave him a big nod … he's leading Hong back out, so keep talking."

"I'm done," said Campbell. "What's going on?"

"Start over … and make some gestures … with your hands … more enthusiasm."

"With my hands? More enthusiasm? Have you considered stage direction as a sideline?"

"You might laugh but … hold on … Overidge is pointing out a car to Hong, probably explaining its features … Overidge is going back inside … he's sitting at his desk now. Stay put, Campbell … I'm telling you about gear ratios now."

"What ratios?" Campbell asked.

Hong slowly wove his way in and around the cars, examining each closely until he got to the one next to which the other two were standing.

"Excuse me," he said.

"Oh, pardon me," said Campbell.

As Hong moved around them, McCloskey said, "We're going inside; wait a minute and then join us."

The detective and the bootlegger stepped into the reception area where Overidge gestured them toward the only available service bay.

The smell and the grease everywhere reminded McCloskey of his salvage operation's garage. The main difference being this was where cars got a new lease on life and not where they were sent to the afterlife. They didn't say anything; there would be no words until Hong arrived. He finally entered and Overidge closed the door behind him.

"Gentlemen," said Hong.

While he remained poised and appeared calm, Hong seemed to be having trouble getting it out.

"Gentlemen, have you ever heard of Tong?"

Campbell and McCloskey looked at each other, and then at Hong.

"You men, you people have your societies, orders, lodges, and … gangs. So do we. In order to survive, thrive, be safe, we had to organize. At first it was all very simple. But then, like everything else, it became complicated. Needs changed, attitudes changed. Some elements believed not enough was being done. Some of them needed financial help, so they looked for ways to make money. They looked for opportunities, and they found them. Communities grew and some prospered under their control. This of course led to certain … disquietude in the larger community. These elements became greedy and began to extend their reach. And then the violence. I thought we were safe from all of that here, in the Border Cities, but I was naive. Jack, I know your business. Every day you and your people, without really knowing it or understanding it, open the door a little wider. Tong are here, and they have left their mark."

"The three arms," said Campbell.

"You knew," said McCloskey.

"Yes, I knew," said Hong. "I knew but I didn't want to know. 'Three Arms' is the name of this particular group."

"What about the victims?" asked Campbell. "Could they still be alive?"

"Likely not. And you will not find their bodies. The only way you would find them would be if the Tong wanted you to find them."

"So what happens now?" asked McCloskey.

"We go about our business," said Hong.

"I don't know if I like that," said McCloskey. "How is that even possible now?"

"My advice to you, Jack, is to make sure you limit your interests to whisky. And my advice to you, detective, is to broaden your interests — sorry, Jack."

"Okay," said Campbell, "you seem to already know quite a

bit about Tong, and this group in particular. Is there anything else you should be sharing with me about them?"

"As in did this Tong murder Quan?" added McCloskey.

"No," said Hong, "not Tong. Someone in Morrison's world."

"But —"

"Good day, gentlemen."

"McCloskey …"

The bootlegger and the detective paused their conversation as they found a quiet corner among the headstones in Windsor Grove.

"What is it, Campbell?"

"The three arms, they form a triangle."

"So?"

"A triangle that can't be broken."

"I understand those arms are not too connected anymore."

"No, no … they're alive."

McCloskey glanced up and down the rows of marble.

"The arms?"

"No — the three men, each with one arm. They won't be broken. It just occurred to me. I have a feeling."

"I have a feeling you're not finished," said McCloskey, "and neither is this … Tong."

"What do I do now?"

"Wait for something to happen."

"You know, McCloskey, I'm the one that is supposed to prevent that next thing from happening."

McCloskey knelt and started wiping the engraving on one of the headstones. The names and dates and sentiments had become shallow, almost illegible over time.

Campbell continued. "I have very little to go on."

McCloskey straightened up. "You … we could come up with a way to smoke them out. Did you take their fingerprints, from the arms I mean?"

"I did."

Chapter 46

WILT THOU TAKE THIS WOMAN?

Saturday, September 1

Much to Vera Maude's surprise, all of her siblings showed up and then some, including Aunt Gertie — Uncle Fred's sister — and Gertie's daughters, Hazel and Lillian. There must have been a baker's dozen of Maguires, all in their finest. The scene was making her head spin.

Too much Maguire, she thought.

The matron of honour was Mrs. Cattanach's best friend, Flossie. Her real name was Florence but Mrs. Cattanach had known her as Flossie since pinafores were *de riguer*. Like Mrs. Cattanach, Flossie also did work for the church and was a widow, and she couldn't be happier for her friend.

The best man was A.B. "Abe" Drum. He and Uncle Fred had met at Windsor Gas Company, in the accounting department, and retired the same year.

McCloskey was there at the insistence of Uncle Fred, as was Glenn Furlough, Uncle Fred's barber.

Vera Maude finally stopped twitching when the pianist started with the *Lohengrin* wedding march. She looked over at Lew, who was mouthing the words, and then she caught McCloskey stifling a yawn and pinched his arm.

"Hey," he whispered.

"And there's more where that came from," she said.

"These vows are sacred, in flesh as well as spirit. They speak of love, respect, and trust. It is a bond. You make a public declaration of your love, uttering these vows to each other in front of friends and family, and before God. The vows come first, perhaps simply, but you are made and determined by your deeds. Make your bond a statement to faith and faithfulness."

When McCloskey was finished checking on her and Lew, Vera Maude noticed him scoping alternate exits and entrances. It was becoming a force of habit.

"Frederick Stuart Maguire, wilt thou have this woman to be thy wife, and wilt thou pledge thy faith to her, in all love and honour, in all duty and service, in all faith and tenderness, to live with her, and cherish her, according to the ordinance of God, in the holy bond of marriage?"

Vera Maude straightened her dress and accidently brushed her hand against McCloskey's. She looked up at him but his mind was elsewhere.

"I will," said Uncle Fred.

"Julia Faith Cattanach, wilt thou have this man to be thy husband, and wilt thou pledge thy faith to him, in all love and honour, in all duty and service, in all faith and tenderness, to live with him, and cherish him, according to the ordinance of God, in the holy bond of marriage?"

"I will," said Mrs. Cattanach.

There was gentle applause and some quiet sobs. Vera Maude noticed she was squeezing McCloskey's hand. He faked a *makes me no nevermind* attitude, keeping his eyes fixed on the bride and groom.

"Oh dear, the rains have started," said the custodian, in his louder-than-usual voice.

Aunt Julia, formerly Mrs. Cattanach, looked at her husband.

"Well we'll just move inside," said Uncle Fred.

"We can't," said the custodian.

"What do you mean we can't?"

"We thought we'd fixed the roof in the hall, but it's taken to leaking again. We have buckets on the floor and we've had to turn the hydro off."

Vera Maude heard McCloskey mutter, "They can't have this."

"Is all the food ready, and everything else?" he asked, louder.

"Of course," said the custodian.

"I have a place we can go."

Vera Maude looked up at him. "Jack, you can't be serious. Uncle Fred and Aunt Julia, the wedding party ... and Reverend Paulin at Shady's? Will Pearl's Follies be waiting tables?"

"You got a better idea? We have no time, the food is ready and everyone wants to sit down, relax, and toast the newlyweds. I'll take care of moving everything over. I'll call for Betsy —"

"Oh, and now who's Betsy?"

"She's the truck we use at the wreck yard."

"Jack!"

The wedding party and the guests were looking a little lost. Aunt Julia was looking like she might burst into tears at any moment.

"Maudie, please, for Fred and Julia." He turned to the custodian. "Take me to a phone. Maudie, hang back and try and keep everyone calm." He smoothly took Lew aside. "Lew, I need you to —"

"Say no more, Mr. McCloskey."

The custodian led McCloskey to his office, which was more like a broom closet.

"Who's this? Linc? … I need Betsy here at St. Andrew's right this minute. Is she in the yard? … No, tell him it's going to have to wait … Yeah, it's raining, I know … where? … Hang on, for grease sake." He turned to the custodian. "What's your name?"

"Reddick."

"Reddick, where can we pull up a truck closest to an entrance?"

"They can pull up close to the rear doors if they come in off Victoria."

"Did you get that, Linc? Enter the church grounds off Victoria. I'll have someone flag you down. And bring an extra umbrella if you have one." McCloskey hung up the phone. "Reddick, you're going to go out there and make sure Linc pulls up at the right place, then I want you to come back and help with the food. Got it?"

"How will I know the vehicle?"

"It's really ugly and marked 'Border Cities Wrecking and Salvage.'"

"Right — big ugly truck."

"Can't miss it. Hey — mind if I make another call?"

"It's all yours, mister."

McCloskey got the operator's attention again and she connected him with the club. "Claude? Jack ... Yeah, fine ... Listen, the house is empty right? ... Keep it that way; I have a party coming in ... Around forty ... It's a wedding party ... No, no, no ... Well, we might have to reheat some things so make sure the kitchen is fired up ... I'll need people under cover from the rain, escorted to the door, you know ... Great ... Okay ... See you in about fifteen minutes."

McCloskey headed back into the church. He went right to Maudie, who was standing with the newlyweds. Fred was comforting his bride.

"I've got a vehicle on the way right now that can transport all the food and everything else to my club. Everything's going to be fine; we're going to have a good time."

Linc arrived minutes later with Betsy. Vera Maude's brothers helped load the food into the back of the truck. Linc made sure the canvas was strung and taught across the stakes in the flatbed.

Vera Maude's siblings from the county had arrived by motorcar. Austin and his wife were commissioned to drive the bridegroom and the best man to the church, and Dorothy and her husband were commissioned with doing the same for the bride and the matron of honour. They followed the same route to the club.

"I saw you fight once," said the gentleman. Apparently he was a friend of the bride's family. "After the war ... here."

"Yeah?" McCloskey was feeling a bit exposed. Nice people, but not *his* people.

"You took him in the first round, as I recall," the gentleman said, smiling.

The memory was slowly coming to surface. *More fights than I can remember*, thought McCloskey.

"Summer," said the gentleman with his pointed finger, "now I recall. It was behind a garage and a pile of lost pieces."

"Lost pieces?" repeated McCloskey.

"What do you mean *lost pieces*?"

"Nothing," said McCloskey. He thought the gentleman might be slightly touched.

"Are you still in the fights?"

"No, no I'm not."

"Not even for a prize?"

"I'm sorry, I don't think I caught your name."

"Fortescue," said the gentleman, extending his hand, "John Fortescue."

"Well, Mr. Fortescue, it's been a pleasure, but I really should look in on the kitchen."

"Certainly, my good man."

After the meal and the toasts and the embarrassing, impromptu speeches, the newlyweds made off and the party dispersed to parts unknown. McCloskey had assigned a few crew members from Wrecking and Salvage to put Shady's back in order. He and Vera Maude retreated to his apartment, where they spent a relaxing late-summer afternoon.

"Jack, it's for you."

"Maudie, I told you about answering my phone." He had just come back from fetching them some dinner and a copy of today's paper.

"The ring sounded important."

"Give it to me."

She was still holding the earpiece.

Click.

"So who was it?"

"I asked him and he said, 'McCloskey's assassin.'"

"My what?"

"Do you know anyone named Charlie Baxter?"

"Couldn't be," he said, going over to the window overlooking the intersection.

"Jack?"

"Did he say anything else?"

"Yeah, he asked me if I had read any good books lately."

"Jesus, Maudie."

"Wait ... why do I know that name?"

If he could, McCloskey would be pacing right now, but he couldn't take his eyes off the window. "The guy who tried to kill me last summer."

"Jack, when you say things like, *the guy who tried to kill me*, my first thought is always going to be, *you'll have to be more specific.*"

"How'd he sound?"

She finally hung the earpiece after letting it dangle for a moment. "Come to think of it ... he sounded a little disappointed."

"You gave me away."

"All I did was answer the phone. It sounded like it might be important. I can always tell by the ring."

He turned from the window. "By the ring?" He turned his focus back on the intersection. "I guess he's got my number now ... and yours." He paused; wheels were turning. "I'll have to tell Pearl."

"Tell her what?"

"That her boyfriend's back in town."

"You mean this Charlie and Pearl, they were ...?"

"Yeah, they were. I'm going to need help getting you home. I can't do it myself, not now."

"Wait, what are you talking about, Jack? Who ..."

"I don't know their names, and you can't ask them."

"Why not?"

"It's best that way."

"You're sending me away in a car with some men and you don't even know their names, or —"

"Yeah."

"What if I don't want to?"

"It's just a precaution."

"Jack, if you're trying to frighten me ..."

"I'm succeeding?"

"How do you find the ... them?"

"They come to me."

"How?"

"A signal." McCloskey was already moving a narrow chest of drawers to the left of the window. He removed a mostly red folded piece of cloth and gently shook it open.

"A flag?"

"The colours of the 99th Battalion."

"You got a flagpole on the roof?"

McCloskey hung it, sideways, from two hooks in the window frame. He then moved the side table over, positioned it behind the flag and removed the shade from the lamp.

"Couldn't you just call them?"

"Their number is unlisted, and for good reason. The gang doesn't even know about them. It's better that way."

"Who are they?"

"My operatives."